lie or die

A SHELBY NICHOLS ADVENTURE

Colleen Helme

Book Cover Art by Damonza.com Copyright © 2013 by Colleen Helme
Book Layout ©2013 BookDesignTemplates.com

Lie or Die/ Colleen Helme. -- 1st ed.
ISBN 1478277467
ISNB-13: 978-1478277460

Dedication

To my Grandpa
William LaVon Chappell
Thanks for taking me prospecting – we didn't find any gold,
but we had a great time together!

ACKNOWLEDGMENTS

I want to thank my fantastic family for your support and enthusiasm. I couldn't do it without you. Thanks to Tom, Erin, and Melissa for being my first readers and for your great input. Thanks to Melissa for being an amazing sounding board for plot direction, and for your skillful help with my website design. Thanks to my great editor, Kristin Monson, for your proof-reading and editing skills. Thanks to Damon for the fantastic cover art. Last but not least, thanks to all of my fans who love reading about Shelby Nichols and her crazy adventures!

Shelby Nichols Adventures

Contents

Chapter 1

Hunting for lost treasure runs in my family.

As a youngster, I went prospecting with my Grandpa up into the mountains to look for gold. He had plenty of ideas about where the gold was, and we always found lots of pretty rocks, but never any gold. Just the same, I've always thought it would be cool to find some buried treasure.

Now I was actually looking for a lost treasure, although technically speaking, it was stolen money, and it wasn't really lost. The bank robber who stole it knew where it was, and he had been willing to kill his partner to keep it all to himself. Lucky for me, I had a clue as to where it might be. Even better, the bank from which it was stolen was willing to pay me to find it.

The bank manager, Blaine Smith, had discovered that I worked for the police as a paid consultant and hired me on the spot. He didn't even blink too hard to learn that I had 'premonitions,' and that's how I helped the police.

Since I didn't want anyone to know I could read minds, saying I had 'premonitions' seemed like a safer way to go. Especially after what had happened with Uncle Joey, the local crime boss. His 'niece' Kate had been after my husband, and with my talent, I found out about Uncle Joey. I threatened to expose her if she didn't leave my husband alone. Uncle Joey's hit-man, Ramos, had orders to take me to the big boss, and I had to tell Uncle Joey I could read minds to keep him from killing me.

After that, he used my special ability for his own purposes, until I had enough leverage to bargain my way out. We now had a precarious alliance. I still had to work for Uncle Joey, but now it was on my terms. So far, so good, but it put a terrible strain on me, knowing how easy it would be for him to change his mind.

Besides Uncle Joey, my husband Chris, was the only other person who knew the truth about me. Unless I counted Ramos. Even though he thought he knew the truth, I had never confirmed his suspicions, and I intended to keep it that way. The less people that knew I could read their minds, the better.

It was hard enough to work things out with Chris. Knowing I could hear his thoughts was rough on him. He was mostly resigned to his fate, but there were times it really got on his nerves. Like now... he was thinking that I was crazy to take on the job of finding the stolen money, especially based on the only clue I had.

"But when you pair the word 'underwear' with a box or crate, that could mean something." I said defensively.

"Yeah, like the money is hidden inside a box of underwear," he shot back. "What kind of a clue is that? What underwear box? Where is it? In a store? In a closet? It could mean anything! See... you really don't have much to go on."

I sighed. He was probably right, but with my new consulting agency on the line, I had to give it a shot. Maybe I just needed more information. "I still have to try. I already told the bank manager I would. I just wish I had a better clue."

Chris shook his head. He was thinking that my tendency to get in over my head was nothing new. He just wished I would learn when to stop. There was a point where most people knew when to back off, but not me. What would it take? Even nearly getting killed wouldn't stop me. Why was I so different? What was it in my make-up that made me so darn stubborn?

He glanced at me, realizing I had probably heard everything he was thinking. Again. Which made having this conversation that much more difficult for both of us, but mostly him.

"I don't think it's more difficult," I said, needing to squelch his frustration with me. "I mean, it might be okay if you actually said what you were thinking, but since you don't, I think it's helpful for me to know. Now that I know you think I'm stubborn, I can try to be more open to what you say."

"Right," he huffed. "So, are you going to back off? Because really, I don't think you have much to go on."

Now it was my turn to squirm. "Probably not," I said. Chris' eyes gleamed in triumph, so I rushed on to explain. "I want to look into it, and if I don't find anything, then I'll admit defeat."

"Okay, fine." He was thinking 'whatever' but I'm glad he didn't say that. It would have hurt my feelings. "So what are you going to do?"

"I'm going to talk to the bank manager tomorrow and go from there." I had a few ideas up my sleeve, but decided not to let Chris in on it. Since he thought I was crazy to take this job, I didn't feel like explaining myself. I'd wait until I got some more leads before I did that.

Since I already had an appointment with the bank manager for the next morning, I spent most of the evening on the Internet reading up on bank heists and money laundering. I found the best information on howstuffworks.com. Their podcasts were great. I went to bed feeling hopeful that I had some good questions to ask, plus I wouldn't make a fool of myself.

Chris came to bed feeling a bit sheepish for being so hard on me, so I cut him some slack. "Hey, remember how Uncle Joey wants to send us to Seattle? Maybe we should start thinking about when would be a good time to go."

"Yeah," he said. "Although I don't know how fun it will be if we're looking for Kate and Hodges."

"True," I agreed. I had special feelings for Kate. Feelings of revenge and intense dislike, that is. She had been after my husband, even though he was a happily married man, so she wasn't on my list of people I wanted to run into. She was also the person responsible for all of my troubles with Uncle Joey.

He was actually Kate's Uncle Joey, even though he wasn't really her uncle. It was because he didn't like being called Uncle Joey that I called him that. Now it was a habit I couldn't break. Especially since I knew it bothered him.

Kate had found out that Uncle Joey was the man responsible for her father's death. She was trying to put him away for good when her accomplice, Walter, got in the way. To avoid Uncle Joey's wrath, Kate escaped with Hodges, taking a few million dollars' worth of jewels and money Hodges had stolen from Uncle Joey. Now Uncle Joey wanted it back, and he was willing to send me and my husband to find them... all paid for by him, of course.

I was hoping for more of a second honeymoon than a working trip. If Uncle Joey knew where Kate and Hodges were, it wouldn't be too hard to get close enough to hear their thoughts and let Uncle Joey know what they'd done with the money.

But did I really want to get involved with Kate again? Not so much. Maybe Chris was right, and I was in over my head and not thinking things through. But I wasn't a 'normal' person anymore, and I was trying to embrace that. I really wanted to do some good with my mind-reading skills. If only it didn't have to involve Uncle Joey. But I didn't have a choice. I had to make some concessions with Uncle Joey, or he'd take away what little control I had.

"You're awfully quiet," Chris said. "What's going on?"

"You're right about me," I admitted. "I am in over my head. Especially with Uncle Joey. What am I going to do?"

Chris gathered me in his arms. "We're going to take care of this together," he said. "Don't worry about everything at once. Just worry about the bank for now. We'll figure it out as we go."

"What would I do without you?" I asked, snuggling against him. He was thinking that I'd probably be in worse trouble, and hoping I had learned my lesson about trying to take care of everything on my own. Plus, I should listen to him more. But he couldn't ask for a miracle.

I knew I wasn't supposed to 'hear' any of this, so I had to act like it didn't bother me. I tightened my hold on him and sighed, wishing it was easier to shield my mind from his thoughts. He was probably right about everything he'd thought, including the fact that I didn't like to use my shields around him. I had to face it. I wanted to know what he was thinking more than I wanted to block his thoughts, even if it wasn't always what I wanted to hear. How crazy was that?

I leaned up and kissed Chris smack on the lips. Right now, all I wanted to think about was how much I loved him. It surprised him, and he was thinking how glad he was that

I hadn't heard his thoughts just now. Especially about the miracle part. I chuckled, and soon all thoughts of our disagreements went out the window. Which was just what I had hoped for. After that, sleep came easily.

The next morning I was on my way to the bank to visit with the bank manager. I pulled into the parking lot and noticed the car behind me pulling in as well. As I got out, a familiar figure did the same, and my heart sank. What was Rob Felt doing at the bank, and why was he following me?

He was the private eye the bank had hired to find the money in the first place, but when he couldn't come up with anything, they hired me to replace him. I wasn't sure he knew he was fired, and I didn't want to be the one to tell him.

I quickly shut my car door and hurried into the bank before he could stop me. It would have worked if I could have gone right in to see Mr. Smith, but of course I had to wait, and Rob Felt caught up with me in the lobby.

"What are you doing here?" he asked, turning the tables on me, since that was my question for him. He didn't trust me, and worse, thought I had killed a man. That made me mad.

"If I thought it was any of your business, I'd tell you," I shot back.

He pursed his lips and squinted at me, thinking I would regret that remark when he got through telling Blaine Smith that he saw me with the assassin Mercer, the day Mercer was killed. If his suspicions were right, it was me who'd killed him. He was not about to let me take over his investigation without a fight.

I couldn't let him get that far. He was the only person who could place me with Mercer that day, and although Ramos killed Mercer to keep him from killing me, it was something I had to keep a secret. I realized antagonizing Felt was not the way to handle this, and changed tactics. "If you must know, Mr. Smith hired me to find the stolen money. Didn't he tell you?"

"Yes, but..."

"So why are you here?" I asked, pointedly. "I don't think he'll be happy to see you unless you found the money."

"I might know something he'd be interested in," he said, thinking of Mercer and me.

"Well, you're wrong," I countered. "Smith knows all about my brush with Mercer, and why he was after me. I don't know who killed Mercer that day, but they did us all a favor. So if Mercer was your only lead to the bank robber, Mr. Smith already knows that."

Rob fidgeted. How did I know he was going to tell Smith about that? "He wasn't my only lead," he lied. "And why would he hire you? What do you know about any of this?"

"I've got a clue," I said.

Not wanting him to know anything about my 'premonitions,' or who'd killed Mercer, I thought maybe offering him a portion of the money would keep him quiet. "Since you have other leads, why don't we share information, and I'll give you a cut of the finder's fee." That was a pretty dumb thing for me to say, since I knew he was lying about having a lead, but I was desperate. My stomach tightened, and I realized I was starting to sound like Uncle Joey.

His brows rose in surprise. This was looking more promising. Too bad he didn't have any other leads. But he could always make something up, and I'd never figure it out. He didn't think I was that smart... more like the women in the ditzy blond jokes. He smiled, and my stomach settled. Maybe sounding like Uncle Joey wasn't so bad.

"Mrs. Nichols?"

"Yes?" I turned toward the receptionist.

"Mr. Smith will see you now." I quickly followed behind her, leaving Felt mumbling under his breath. A few seconds passed before he caught up with me.

"You can't get rid of me that fast," he said. "We have a deal, don't we?"

"As long as your information proves valuable." I slowed my step. "Give me your card and I'll call you."

"I think it would be better to sit in on your meeting, just to make sure you don't forget me."

He was a real pain in the butt. Is that how a person had to act if they were a private investigator? Still, I didn't want him blabbing anything about Mercer and me. "Fine," I agreed.

The secretary opened the office door, and Mr. Smith stood to greet me. "Hello Shelby. Thanks for coming. I'm eager to get... Mr. Felt? What are you doing here?"

"He followed me here today," I said quickly. "He wants to help, and I thought it wouldn't hurt to find out what he knows before I proceed with the investigation."

Smith looked from me to Felt and back. He was thinking he'd missed something, and wondered what was going on. Most likely, it was Felt making a pain of himself. He was sorry for me though, and wished he'd never hired the man. "All right," he said. "Take a seat." He motioned to the chairs in front of his desk.

Felt was a bit flustered under Smith's scrutiny. He'd told him everything he knew last week, and had nothing to add. Unless he told him about seeing Mercer and me sitting together on the bench the day Mercer was killed.

Not wanting to go there, I quickly took control of the conversation. "Before I take the case, I have a few questions."

This surprised them both.

"Um... sure," Smith said, settling back in his chair. "What would you like to know?"

I sighed with relief, and continued. "How long ago was the money stolen?"

"A little over a year," Smith answered.

"How do you know it's still hidden? I mean, if it's been that long, why hasn't the robber laundered it yet? Do you have a way to track the bills, and they haven't shown up, or what?"

Smith was nodding his head. "Yes, we do. All of the bills that were stolen were brand new, and we have a record of their numbers. None of them have shown up in circulation anywhere in the country."

"What about out of the country? Could they have bought goods in Mexico with the money, and sold them here for clean bills?" I wanted him to know I had done my homework on money laundering.

"We've thought of that," Smith said. "But by now, they would have shown up somewhere. And it's like they disappeared off the face of the earth. That gives us hope that the money is hidden, and the robbers don't want to move it for a while. They could be willing to let it sit for years, thinking the more time that passes, the better chance they'll have to start spending it."

I nodded, realizing that if one of them hired Mercer, he would have used the money for that. So why didn't it show up? Of course I knew Mercer had an offshore account somewhere, but to make the wire transfer, the money would have to be in a bank. Something didn't add up.

"Okay," I said, thinking out loud. "We know the robber paid Mercer to kill his partner, Keith Bishop, so he must have used the stolen money to pay him."

"Not necessarily," Felt said. "If he wanted to keep the money out of circulation, he could have taken out a loan or something, figuring he would pay it off later once the money was available."

"Yes," Smith agreed. "If he would have used the money to pay Mercer, we would have known about it by now."

"All right," I said. "That leads us to believe that the money is hidden somewhere."

"Yes," Smith said. He was thinking that was what he said in the first place, but decided not to get frustrated with me. "I'm hoping with your premonitions, you can help where other methods have failed." He glanced at Felt. "So, do you have anything new to add since we last talked?"

Felt's gaze jerked to mine in astonishment. He could hardly believe that I had duped Smith, and taken over his investigation on the crazy idea that I had premonitions. "You've hired her over me because she has premonitions? Are you mad?"

"Under the circumstances," Smith glared at Felt, "with your investigation going nowhere, it is a risk I am willing to take. Now if you have nothing new to add, you may leave."

Felt's face turned red with anger. "I'm not giving up. If I find the money, I still want to be paid the finder's fee. All of it." He stood, and with a derisive shake of his head at me, left the room.

"Sorry about that," Smith said. "He's a rather unpleasant fellow, but he did come highly recommended. That's still no excuse for his behavior."

"It's all right," I said. "Most people don't believe in premonitions, so I'm used to it."

"But you'll still take the case?" he asked. Losing that much cash had put a strain on the bank, and the board of directors, as well as the owner, wanted it back. It was insured, but for some reason that wasn't enough. Someone up the ladder wanted it found.

Hmm... that seemed interesting. I smiled. "Yes, I'll do what I can, but I can't guarantee anything."

"Great," he said. "Anything I can do to help, just ask."

"There is something," I said. "Do you have the copy of the police report and what they know about the robbers? I might need to interview some of the people involved. It could help with my premonitions."

"Not here," he said. "But I've talked to the prosecuting attorney. He has everything you'll need for the investigation and is willing to share what he has with you. His name is Don Gamble. I'll give him a call and let him know you're coming."

"All right. One more thing," I said, before he picked up the phone. "I know you were only paying Felt if he found the money, but I don't work that way. I take an hourly wage of fifty dollars an hour. If I haven't made sufficient progress within twenty hours, you can decide whether to keep paying me or hire someone else. Because of my method of payment, you won't owe me any finder's fee if I do find the money."

He narrowed his eyes. I was a lot more shrewd than he gave me credit for, but it was a good deal, especially if I was successful. Plus, fifty dollars an hour was considerably less than most private investigators charged. In fact, it was too good to pass up. "Agreed," he said. "Keep track of your hours, and we'll meet again once you've hit twenty."

We shook on it, and he put in a call to Don, letting him know I was investigating the robbery for the bank and needed access to any of the information he had on Keith Bishop.

With Don's address in my hand, I drove to his office with a smile on my face. It worked! I had a plan to talk to as many friends of Keith Bishop as I could, hoping something would turn up in their thoughts. If his partner was a friend or relative, I might even end up talking to him. I would know he was the accomplice from his thoughts. Wouldn't that be something? It could also be dangerous. Talking to the man who stole all the money, and hired Mercer to kill his partner, gave me the creeps. I'd have to work on my poker face, so I didn't give anything away.

I started singing 'carry my, carry my...p-p-poker face' until I pulled into a parking place and turned off the car. Don's office wasn't too far from Chris. With any luck, I could stop by and pay Chris a visit when I got done. Maybe we could even go to lunch.

Don seemed young to be a prosecuting attorney, but he was nice and helpful. "I was just about to archive these when Blaine called, so they're all boxed up." He pointed to five boxes stacked against the wall. "You're welcome to make copies of whatever you need, but I can't let you take the files. I hope that's okay."

"Oh, sure," I said. Wow... five boxes of stuff was a lot of information. If I had to look through all of those boxes, I could be here all day, and probably tomorrow as well. Even though it meant more billable hours, I'd rather not spend them this way. "Um... I only need what you've got on his family and friends, not the actual case information. Does that make sense? I just want to talk to anyone who knew him, like his employers. That sort of thing."

"That sounds like the police investigation," he said. "I think that stuff is in this box here." He picked the box up like it weighed hardly anything, and carried it out to a room with a copy machine and table. "You can look through it in here, and make whatever copies you need."

"Great. Thanks so much."

"No problem. I hope you find something." He was thinking how disappointed he was to never finish the case. Keith Bishop was killed before the trial barely got started, and all his hard work went down the drain. Of course, it had saved everyone a lot of money now that he was dead. The alleged assassin that killed him... what was his name? Ah, Mercer... was dead too. It seemed like a lot of people had died over this money, and the man responsible was still out there. Anyone who got close to the money was dead. I seemed like a nice lady... he hoped it wouldn't kill me too.

"Thanks," I said with a bright smile, mostly because he thought I was nice. As he left the room, I opened the box and shuffled through the files. There were several that had what I needed, and I made lots of copies. By the time I was done, I had a pretty big stack.

I talked to Don, and he helped me put all my copies in a box. Like a true gentleman, he even carried it to my car. Who said lawyers were bad? Of course, since I was married to one, I was a little biased. Still, I didn't like all those nasty lawyer jokes, or come to think of it, the dumb blond jokes either.

That reminded me of Felt, and I wondered if he had done all of this, too. He was at the courthouse, dressed as a woman, the day Bishop was killed. Why was he there that day? He couldn't have known that Mercer was hired to kill Bishop until later, and that's why he started following him. But why was he there in the first place? I could probably ask, but I doubted that he'd tell me the truth. Of course, what did that matter? I could read his mind. I smiled with satisfaction. This was the right business for me.

I started up the car and glanced at the clock. Making all those copies had taken me longer than I thought. It was close to two in the afternoon, probably too late to go out to lunch with Chris. So I went home instead. I staggered under the weight of the box, but managed to carry it all the way into Chris' study. I figured since he wasn't home during the day, I could use his study as my office.

I found the time card app on my iPhone and set it to keep my hours straight, including the time I'd spent already at the prosecuting attorney's office. I settled in at the desk and went to work, writing up a list of people, their addresses, and their relationships to Keith Bishop. By the time the kids got home from school, I had the list ready to go and my work cut out for the next day.

I was especially excited to visit the first place on my list. It was a shop owned by Keith's aunt, Dottie Weir. He'd worked there occasionally, and it was called "Novelty Creations" and subtitled, "for all your lingerie needs." This could be it! The break I was looking for!

I could hardly wait to show Chris. Then he'd have to take back everything he'd said about my stupid clue. Not that I wanted to shove it in his face or anything, but still, I was pretty happy. It gave me credibility and made Shelby Nichols Consulting official. Of course, I hadn't found the money yet, but I had possibilities now.

My cell phone rang, and my elation plunged. The caller ID said it was Thrasher Development. From the way my heart pounded, I knew my blood pressure had gone sky high. Uncle Joey had that effect on me, and I hadn't even talked to him yet.

"Hello?" I asked.

"Hi, Shelby," Uncle Joey said. "I'm afraid I have some bad news."

He paused, and I couldn't stand the suspense. "Bad for me, or bad for you?" I blurted.

"What's bad for me is bad for you," he replied, coldly.

I didn't want to argue, so I kept my mouth shut.

"I won't be sending you to Seattle after all. I just found out that Hodges is dead. His body washed up on Puget Sound sometime yesterday with a bullet in his head. The authorities think he was killed about two weeks ago."

"Two weeks ago?" That surprised me. "So is Kate still there? Do you think she did it?"

"I don't know," he said. "But I'm sending Ramos to check it out. In the meantime, I'll need your services tomorrow. I'm promoting two of my men to take the place of Walter and Johnny. I need to know what everyone's thinking when I admit them to my board of directors. It should only take about an hour."

I hesitated before answering. Did I really have to go? "Okay," I agreed, knowing I didn't have a choice. "What time?"

"Ten o'clock. See you then." He disconnected.

I held the phone to my ear for a little longer than necessary, then despondently put it away. Being summoned to Uncle Joey's felt like going to my execution. I tried to shake it off. It wasn't life threatening, so that was a plus. I could handle working for him for an hour, especially since he was going to pay me. I'd be done by eleven, and could go right to the lingerie store after that. It could work. As a bonus, there might even be some cute underwear at the store I could buy.

Then it hit me. Where was Kate if Hodges was dead? What happened to all the money and jewels they took? Could Kate be dead too? A little thrill of hope went through me, and I felt bad. It wasn't nice of me to hope she was dead. Besides, if Hodges was dead, I wouldn't put it past

Kate to be the one who killed him. She probably wanted all the money for herself. I hoped Ramos found out what happened. I would rest easier knowing she was far away from here.

Chris came home, and I couldn't wait to tell him about the lingerie store. "I have some good news and some bad news," I said. "Which do you want first?"

He was thinking that the bad news probably had something to do with Uncle Joey. How did he always know? "The good news, of course."

Dang, I thought for sure he'd go with the bad. "I found a lead for the stolen money." I explained about the lingerie store and waited for him to congratulate me. "Dottie Weir? Hmm... that's an interesting name." He was thinking it was probably just a fluke, but it wouldn't hurt to check it out. "But that's great you have more of a lead," he added.

How could he think it was a fluke? He just didn't want to admit he was wrong. "I'm going to check it out tomorrow, so hopefully I'll know if there's more to it."

"So, what's the bad news?" he asked.

I was a little disappointed that he dropped it so fast, and I didn't want to tell him I'd been summoned to Thrasher Development, so I went with the other part. "We're not going to Seattle after all. I don't know about you, but I'm pretty disappointed about that."

"Why? Did Manetto change his mind?"

"Nope. Hodges is dead," I said. "Apparently he was killed a couple of weeks ago, but his body just washed up somewhere on Puget Sound."

"What about Kate? Is she all right?"

Was that real concern I detected? I didn't think he liked Kate that much. "Uncle Joey doesn't know. He sent Ramos to see what he could find out."

"That's nuts. I wonder what happened." He didn't think Kate would actually kill someone. She was too smart to do something stupid like that.

"Not that smart," I said. "Did you forget Kate was ready to kill me?"

His eyes narrowed, and I could hear him growling in his mind. Wow, he'd never done that before. "Um... sorry," I apologized. "But I wouldn't rule her out if I were you. Besides, why do you care?"

"I don't know," he said defensively. "I just hate to see anyone I know in trouble. I don't think she really would have killed you. Some people are all bluff. They make threats they would never carry out."

"So her pointing a loaded gun at me was just a threat?" I fumed.

He huffed in frustration. "Okay, you probably have a point, and it doesn't do any good to argue about it. But since we are arguing, could you please stop listening to my thoughts?"

His voice was pretty loud by then, and it surprised me. "Did you have a bad day?"

"Not really," he said, but he thought, *not until I got home.*

"Until you got home?" I said, outraged. I didn't want him to hide behind those unspoken words. "It's okay. I get it. I'll just go get dinner ready."

"Shelby, it's not..."

"No, I get it." I interrupted him, and rushed into the kitchen. He didn't follow me to smooth things over, and a little part of me wilted. I knew that something had to change. Either I had to put up my shields around Chris, or he had to stop getting mad every time I listened to his thoughts. This was the situation we were in, and it wasn't going to change. How we handled it was what would make us or break us.

It hit me that I was the one who was stupid. If I didn't get my shields up around him, the simplest thing to do was not respond to his thoughts. Why did I always do that anyway? It was like I was purposely trying to make him mad. That was just dumb. From now on, I would keep my mouth shut and only respond to his spoken words.

I relaxed my shoulders and sagged in relief, knowing I had a plan. It might be hard, but it was something I could do, especially since I couldn't expect Chris to just accept that I could read his mind all the time. That probably wasn't fair, even if deep down I wished he'd just get used to it. No, it was up to me. I could do it.

The rest of the evening went better. I put up my shields and Chris began to relax. Later, I realized how much of a strain we'd both been under, and I was more determined than ever to be as normal as possible.

To do that, I decided it was best not to tell Chris about my visit to see Uncle Joey tomorrow. When it came to Uncle Joey, there were times it was better Chris didn't know. Replacing two of Uncle Joey's dead people wasn't that big of a deal, and certainly not something I had to worry Chris with. I could handle Uncle Joey on my own. I hoped.

Chapter 2

I left for Thrasher Development a little early. Not that I didn't want to be late, but it didn't take me that long to get ready. Mostly because I didn't have to put on the wig and glasses I'd worn when I first started working for Uncle Joey. Since everyone knew who I was, it didn't matter anymore, although I still felt vulnerable. But at least I wasn't wearing black. My white denim jacket, layered over a pink cami and paired with a short ruffled skirt, went perfectly with my new boots.

On the drive there, I noticed a car following close behind. I was nearly to the office when it dawned on me who it was. Felt? What was he doing? Was he purposely making my life difficult? It was too late to shake him off, so I turned into the parking garage. At least without an electronic sticker on his car, the door wouldn't open, and he couldn't get in.

He sped past, but I knew he'd find out what I was doing there, and I pursed my lips in frustration. I didn't need him to pry into my relationship with Uncle Joey. I needed to figure out a way to lose Felt, but besides telling Uncle Joey to get rid of him, I wasn't sure that would happen. Still, there had to be something I could get on Felt that would make him back off. I sighed, knowing it was just one more thing to worry about.

I stepped into Uncle Joey's office, and all thoughts of Felt fled my mind. I was early, and Jackie wasn't at her desk. I could hear her talking to someone down the hall near the office where all the security equipment was kept. Since Ramos had gone to Seattle, it must be someone I didn't know.

Just then, Jackie stepped out of the office, and noticed me standing by her desk. "Shelby!" she said. I smiled and waved. "There's someone you need to meet." She turned back to the office, and soon a man followed her down the hall. His body filled up the hall, and I realized he was huge. About six feet six inches tall, and built like a soldier or bodyguard.

Jackie made the introductions. "Shelby, this is Douglas, our new security advisor."

"Nice to meet you," I said.

"Likewise," he answered, extending his hand. His hand was so big, mine seemed to disappear inside, but thankfully he didn't squeeze too hard or he might have broken a bone or something. *So this is Shelby.* That thought came through clearly, surprising me. I smiled brightly, and pulled my hand out of his grasp. How did he know about me?

"What about Ramos?" I blurted. "Isn't that his job?"

Jackie chuckled indulgently, hoping I hadn't offended Douglas. "Yes, but Ramos had to go to Seattle for a while. While he's gone, we needed someone with his expertise to fill in. Douglas came highly recommended, and we are very lucky to have him."

"Thank you Jackie," he said, inclining his head. "And please, call me Doug." He was thinking that his mother was the only one who called him Douglas, and it always made him feel like a little boy. Mostly because that was the name she used when he was in trouble.

My neck was getting a crick in it from looking up at him, so it was a relief when Jackie motioned me down the hall toward Uncle Joey's office. Doug headed back to the security office, and I leaned toward Jackie to ask what was going on. "If Ramos is only gone for a week or two, why are you hiring someone else? Ramos will think you don't want him anymore."

She glanced at me with her brows drawn together, like I was an idiot. "Joey doesn't want to take any chances now that Miguel is here. Besides, Mexico taught him that he could use a little more security."

"Oh," I said. "Okay. So you're going to keep him around when Ramos gets back?"

"Yes," she answered. She was thinking that it wasn't any of my business, but she could understand since it concerned Ramos. He had saved my life a time or two, so naturally I would be looking out for him. "Joey wanted to see you in his office before the meeting," she said.

I followed her to his office, where she knocked before opening the door. "Shelby's here." She ushered me inside, and firmly closed the door behind me.

"Have a seat," Uncle Joey said, without glancing up. He finished writing, and threw down his pen. "There, that should do it." He glanced up at me and frowned. Why wasn't I sitting down like he asked?

Good grief! I casually strolled to the chair in front of his desk and sat down. Glancing up, I caught him smiling at me, pleased that I'd obeyed his unspoken request.

"Who's Doug?" I asked.

He frowned, taken off guard by my question. "My new security man. Did you meet him?"

"Yeah, but he made me uncomfortable."

"Why? What was he thinking?"

"Oh, nothing really," I said. "He just seemed to know who I was already. Did you tell him about me? I mean, nobody knows what I do, right?"

"No, of course not. But Jackie might have said something about you coming in today. That's probably it." He was wondering if he'd hired him too fast, and decided to do a more thorough background check on him.

"That's probably a good idea," I agreed. "You can't be too careful, even if he came highly recommended."

Uncle Joey studied me. "Yes, well, if you get anything from him, be sure and let me know. In the meantime, I have my hands full with this promotion. There are a few things going on with my organization that have me concerned, so it's important to know what everyone's thinking in the meeting today."

"Yeah, I get it," I said.

He was thinking it was the big trial that worried him. He knew most of the evidence was circumstantial, but if there was a leak in his organization... he caught me staring at him and frowned. He almost said something, but a sudden thought occurred to him, and his eyes lit up.

"We'd probably better get into the meeting," I blurted, not liking where his thoughts were going.

"You'd know," he said. "If you were at the trial, you'd know if someone was lying."

"What trial? What are you talking about?"

He smiled like the Cheshire cat, and I got a sick feeling in the pit of my stomach. "We'll talk about it later. Everyone should be here by now. We'd better go in." He stood, and motioned me toward the door. "After you."

I huffed, knowing he had me over a barrel, and there was nothing I could do about it. Disgruntled, I made my way to the conference room. As I entered, Ricky stood and smiled.

He was glad to see me, and wondered if I still had my stun flashlight. He'd bought one just like it for his girlfriend. I almost reached into my purse to show him I had it, but resisted the impulse, just smiling back instead.

Victor and Marc weren't as enthusiastic to see me, but they nodded politely. I glanced around the room, surprised that the others weren't there. Uncle Joey took his seat, and we took that as our cue to sit down.

"As you know," Uncle Joey began. "I have appreciated all you've done to take on the extra load left by Johnny and Walter. Now it's time to replace them with people we can trust. As you've probably guessed, I've chosen Johnny's nephew, Jimmy, to take his place. As for Walter, I thought it best to choose someone familiar with the books in that part of the neighborhood, so I asked Nick Berardini to take his place."

It was hard to catch all of their thoughts at once. They all seemed good with Jimmy, but Nick was another matter. I waited for them to voice their opinions, but they all just nodded instead. Frustrated with their silence, I spoke up, asking the question that was on all of their minds. "Why not Nick's father?"

Uncle Joey's brows rose in surprise, and everyone stared at me. Ricky was thinking I had a lot of guts to question Manetto. It just wasn't done. When the boss made a big decision like this, nobody questioned him, even if they had questions.

Uncle Joey was wondering how I knew about David. He was sure he'd never mentioned him before.

I held his gaze, and tilted my head toward the men, lifting my brows. His eyes lit with understanding, and he took a deep breath. He got it, but his lips thinned. He wasn't sure he liked how I put him on the spot. How did that make him look in front of his men?

I pursed my own lips, holding in my exasperation by sheer will. Wasn't this why he wanted me here? Fine. I was not going to say another word.

"I was hoping to keep this quiet a little longer," Uncle Joey finally responded. "But now I see that this is something we need to talk about. What I tell you stays in this room. That goes for all of you." He pinned his gaze on me, and I found myself nodding just as eagerly as the rest of them.

"David is doing a special job for me that requires a certain amount of discretion. As most of you know, a complaint has been filed against Adam Webb, the head of Webb Enterprises. In fact, the trial is starting next week. I have a business arrangement with Adam that needs to stay private. David is doing what he can to keep it that way."

He leaned back in his chair. "While this trial is going on we will have to watch ourselves extra carefully. Don't trust anyone outside of our business associates. If someone starts asking questions, I want to know about it immediately."

He waited for a moment to let that sink in. "Good. There's also the matter of Kate and Hodges. I just found out yesterday that Hodges is dead, and Kate has disappeared. I've sent Ramos to Seattle to find out what he can, and hopefully find the money they stole. In the meantime, I've hired Doug Carter to help with security."

Marc was thinking that if things were a little dicey, right now might not be the best time to hire someone new. I thought he had a good point. I glanced at Uncle Joey and inhaled to speak, but he narrowed his eyes at me with a warning in his head to keep my mouth shut. It stopped me cold.

"Doug came highly recommended by someone who owes me, and I feel confident in his abilities." Uncle Joey stopped, realizing he was explaining himself. He never explained himself. He was the boss. He knew how to take care of business, and his men trusted him to do that. Didn't they? Were they always questioning him in their minds? Or was it just me? That sort of thinking had to stop. He didn't get where he was by making mistakes. He had friends in places most people didn't even know about. That was what made him the man he was today. He deserved their respect, not a bunch of questions.

Uh-oh. This was bad. Ricky and Marc straightened in their chairs. They could tell Uncle Joey was upset, but none of them knew what to say. Vic picked up on the tension and glanced at Uncle Joey nervously, then looked at me, thinking that whatever was going on, it was probably my fault.

I inhaled sharply. Why was he blaming me? Of course, thinking about it objectively, it probably was my fault. Uncle Joey confirmed it when he spoke his next words. "I need to speak with Shelby for a moment." He stood and left the room with the command, *come with me*, echoing in his thoughts.

With great reluctance, I followed him to his office. Now what? Why was he so touchy anyway? I was only doing my job. Still, my stomach clenched with apprehension.

He opened the door, allowing me to enter before him, and closed it tight. Taking his seat behind his desk, he waited for me to sit down, his fingers tapping on the desktop. "I think we need to set some things straight," he began. "First of all, you are not to speak during our meetings. I don't want your opinion, or that of my people, until after the meeting is over when we can talk privately. Is that clear?"

"Sure," I said. I thought about explaining myself, but decided against it. Uncle Joey did not want to hear it. He was angry, but lucky for me, not all of his anger was directed my way. There were other things he was worried about, and it didn't take much to set him off.

He took a deep breath, and got his anger under control. "Good. There are many things about my organization that you don't know, and I think it would be better for you if we kept it that way." His point made, he switched back to the matter at hand. "Now... I take it the only objection they had was about Nick's father?"

"Yes," I quickly agreed. "They seemed fine with everything else."

"Good," he said. He was thinking that maybe my abilities would be of better use to him in other ways than these meetings, where I wouldn't hear something that could make me more of a liability than an asset. We had an agreement, but he knew I worked with the police, and he wouldn't put it past me to stab him in the back if I got a chance.

Surprise ran over me. Why was he letting me hear all this? He knew I was listening.

"Would you do it, Shelby?" he asked.

"Stab you in the back?" I blurted, caught off guard. "No... I wouldn't do that. We have an agreement." I hoped that was the right thing to say. Sometimes it was better to lie, especially when the alternative could be death.

"I'm glad to know that. Just keep in mind that while you work for me, you are under my protection, which for you seems to be a good thing." Uncle Joey was thinking that although Ramos had saved my life, it was because of him that he'd done it. "Plus I'm paying you."

"Exactly," I agreed. "I can see I spoke out of turn in the meeting, but I was just trying to do my job. Now that I know you don't want me to do that, I won't... unless you specifically ask."

He nodded, his lips curving into a slight smile. "I'm glad we understand one another. I have a lot on my plate, and I don't want to have to worry about you." There was a certain amount of loyalty in his organization and, although he'd grown fond of me, he wasn't sure I'd ever feel that way toward him. He couldn't let his feelings get in the way of business. It was probably due to having his son, Miguel, along with Jackie, in his life. It was making him soft, and he couldn't afford that. Not now, not ever.

He came back to himself, realizing I'd just heard his thoughts. It didn't bother him at all. "Well," he said pleasantly. "I guess we'd better get back in there. Jimmy and Nick should be here by now."

"But I thought... oh never mind." He confused me, and I couldn't help shaking my head.

Uncle Joey noticed. "What?" he asked, stopping me in my tracks. "What's the headshake for?"

"Nothing," I said. He raised his brows expectantly, not letting it go. I gave in. "All right. If you must know, I was just thinking that you're really good at this... at what you do."

His face brightened. "Ah... so you admire me. That's nice."

This time I kept a pleasant expression on my face, even though it was hard not to roll my eyes. He chuckled, not fooled by my expression for a minute.

We left his office and found two men waiting by Jackie's desk. Uncle Joey greeted them enthusiastically and showed them into the conference room.

Jimmy seemed pretty young for the job, but he was in awe of Uncle Joey, and I knew he'd be loyal, especially after both his Uncle Johnny, and his Cousin Jerry's murder. He appreciated the way Uncle Joey took care of Walter, the man who'd killed them.

Nick was about my age and harder to read. He was on the short side, had dark wavy hair, and a five o'clock shadow, even this early in the morning. For some reason he put me on edge.

We took our seats, and Uncle Joey gave a nice speech about Jimmy and Nick, which I tried to tune out while I listened to everyone's thoughts. The only thing that came through was that Nick was certain his position was payback for all his dad's hard work. It was about time, and he was willing to use the position for whatever power it would give him. He hoped to expand his father's business and use Manetto's clout to make new friends and, if possible, get rid of a few enemies... permanently.

Hmm... that sounded pretty cold-hearted. Just the kind of person Uncle Joey would like. I decided to steer clear of him, especially when he caught me studying him. I jerked my gaze away, but not before he started thinking about me and wondering what I did for Uncle Joey. He figured it was something important, and decided that was the first thing he was going to find out.

Oh great, now I had to worry about him too.

The meeting ended, and Nick didn't waste any time. He turned on the charm and headed straight for me. "I've heard about you... Shelby, right?" He continued without giving me a chance to answer. "Now that I think about it, haven't we met somewhere before? You seem familiar to me." He was lying through his teeth.

"I don't think so," I responded. I glanced toward Uncle Joey, hoping he'd see me and come to my rescue.

"Hmm... well in that case, I hope we can get to know each other better." He smiled with a lop-sided grin, making him more approachable and handsome. He was quite the charmer. "It will be nice to come to the office if you're here."

"Well... I don't work here full time, just occasionally when Uncle Joey needs me."

Nick's eyes widened. "So you're his niece? Now it makes sense. That's probably why I've heard of you." He was thinking that it didn't make any sense at all, since the niece he'd heard of had red hair. Hadn't something bad happened to her? She couldn't be me, but he'd only heard of Manetto having one niece. What a puzzle this was turning out to be.

Uncle Joey came to my side, just in time to hear Nick's comment about me being his niece. He glanced at me with narrowed eyes before turning his gaze on Nick. "So I see you've met Shelby."

"Yes," Nick said with enthusiasm. "I can even see a family resemblance." He was totally sucking up, and it was hard to keep a straight face.

"Really," Uncle Joey answered, pleased. Nick using that angle made his job a lot easier. Maybe he should let everyone think I was his niece. It would work since I insisted on calling him 'Uncle Joey' all the time anyway. "Good, then you'll also be glad to know that she's off limits." He said this with a smile, but there was a threat behind his words.

Nick stepped back in surprise. "Oh... sure. I didn't realize..."

"Of course you didn't," Uncle Joey said, giving him a pat on the back. He narrowed his eyes and smiled thinly, just to make sure Nick understood.

Nick was now more interested in me than ever, but he took his cue and excused himself. Before walking out the door, he turned back with a smile. "Oh... and I'll take care of that matter we discussed earlier," he said. At Uncle Joey's nod, he left the room.

By then everyone else had already left, leaving Uncle Joey and me alone. "Well?" Uncle Joey didn't waste any time.

"Um... Jimmy will be great. He's totally loyal to you."

"What about Nick?"

"He's got a lot of ambition," I said.

Uncle Joey laughed. "Tell me something I don't know."

"He wants to expand his father's business, and hopes to use your clout to do that. He's also not opposed to eliminating anyone who gets in his way. With your resources, of course."

"He wants me to do his dirty work, huh?" Uncle Joey said. "Well, we'll see about that. Anything else?"

"Yeah, he's also pretty interested in me, and what I do for you."

"I figured that much," Uncle Joey said. "Especially after you called me Uncle." He was sure I knew he didn't like it, but that hadn't stopped me yet.

"Is that why you let him think it for real?" I asked.

"Partly," he answered. "But it just occurred to me that it might offer you some protection from anyone who knows me. If they think you're my niece, they'd probably leave you alone."

"Oh... I see," I said. Was he serious? Or was he just getting back at me? It seemed like it was a little of both.

"Is that it?" he asked.

"Yeah," I said.

"Then I think that's all for today," he said. "Thanks for coming in."

"Sure," I said, eager to leave. I hurried to the hall, and caught a glimpse of someone as he ducked out of sight around the corner. Was that Doug or Nick? Uncle Joey almost ran into me.

"What is it?" he asked.

"I'm not sure, but I think someone might have been eavesdropping on our conversation." I pointed down the hall. "They went that way."

Uncle Joey hustled faster than I would have thought possible. I quickly followed. We rounded the corner to a door that opened out into another hall. This was where the restrooms and exit to the staircase were located.

Uncle Joey pushed open the staircase door and leaned over the railing, with me trailing behind. Footsteps echoed from below, but stopped with the swinging of another door a few stories down.

"It won't do any good to follow now," Uncle Joey said, thinking the person running down the stairs could have been anyone in the building, and not necessarily the person eavesdropping on us. But then where did that person go?

"We should see if Doug is in his office," I said.

"Good idea," he agreed. We hurried from the staircase, back into the hall, and the door to the men's room opened. Doug came out, and he glanced at us with surprise, but I thought I caught a glimpse of relief from his thoughts. Did that mean it was him?

"What's going on?" Doug asked, concentrating on Uncle Joey.

"Nothing," I quickly said.

Doug was confused at my answer. Why was I lying? "Mr. Manetto?" he asked.

Uncle Joey was trying to figure out what I was doing. He shook his head and gave up. "Do we have surveillance cameras out here in this hall?"

"No sir. Would you like me to set some up?"

"Yes, but right now, I want to see the footage from just a few moments ago in the office hall."

"Sure," he said.

We followed Doug into the security room, and waited for him to rewind the footage of the hallway. He backed it up, and we saw everyone come out of the conference room, including Nick. The hall was empty, but a minute later, it looked like someone came in from the door to the restrooms. That was a blind corner, and the angle of the camera was tilted off just enough so that all we could see was his shoulder. He stood there until I came out of the conference room, and quickly pulled away. It was basically what I'd seen myself.

Uncle Joey sighed, trying to remember what I'd said to him, and if it was enough to give me away. "Will you please adjust that camera?" he growled, looking pointedly at Doug.

"Yes sir," he said, thinking it wouldn't really make any difference. That corner we were looking at was at an angle the camera couldn't penetrate, no matter how he adjusted the angle. It was perfect for listening in on any conversation that went on in the conference room. As long as the door was open. Then he thought he'd better do a good job for Manetto, or he'd get sacked, and he couldn't afford that right now. Not after all his hard work to get hired.

Hmm... if he was the one spying on us, wouldn't he be thinking he'd gotten away with it? He did seem to know an awful lot about it, though. Could it be him?

Doug left to get a ladder, and Uncle Joey motioned for me to follow him to his office. After he closed the door behind him, he sighed. "Remind me to never talk to you unless we are in my office, and the door's closed. Was it Doug?" he asked.

"I don't know," I said. "His thoughts are hard to read, but he wasn't thinking that he'd gotten away with it, so I guess not."

"Then that means it has to be Nick," Uncle Joey said.

"Not necessarily," I interjected. "It could have been any of them. They were all wearing dark suits."

"That's true," he conceded. "But out of them all, who would do it?"

"Nick," I said. "Because he was the most interested in what I do for you."

"I don't know if he heard enough to tell him what you do."

"Even if he did, how could he believe it? I mean, who reads minds for Pete's sake?" I shrugged. "Whoever it was may not have been close enough to hear that much anyway. We weren't talking that loud, and the corner isn't real close to the conference room."

"True," Uncle Joey said. "There's not much we can do except have you listen to their thoughts next time, and see if you hear anything then."

"Right," I agreed, already dreading my next visit. "I really miss Ramos. If he were here, this wouldn't have happened."

Uncle Joey took that hard. Maybe he shouldn't have sent Ramos off so quickly. He had friends in Seattle, but he didn't want them to know Kate had taken his money and gotten away with it. No, Ramos was his best choice, and until he got back, he'd just have to make do. "He'll be back soon, maybe this weekend if we're lucky." He was hoping Ramos would find Kate, and bring her back with him. That would make it all worth it.

"All right, well... I'll see you later." I stepped toward the closed door.

"If anyone in my organization talks to you, I want to know," Uncle Joey said. He was thinking it would be a sure sign of guilt.

"Okay," I answered. "Bye." I marched out the door with quick strides, eager to get away. I got to the elevator and punched the button, realizing it would be a huge mistake on my part to ever let my guard down around Uncle Joey. He had not only put me in my place earlier, but I realized he was all that stood between his men and me.

If they ever found out what I did for him... what? What would they do? Try to use me against him? That wouldn't work so well. Besides, they were all on the same team, right? They might want to use me for their own purposes, but Uncle Joey wouldn't let that happen. We had an agreement. It made me even more indebted to Uncle Joey, and it was definitely to my benefit that he stayed alive and well. So much for ever escaping him.

I found my car and decided that instead of wallowing in my misery, I needed to compartmentalize my life. Yes, I was involved with Uncle Joey, but that was just a small part of what I did. I had a job to do and lost money to find. It was time to concentrate on the success of Shelby Nichols Consulting Agency.

I pulled my car out of the parking garage and centered my thoughts back to the lost bank money. The lingerie shop wasn't far, and I was eager to see what it looked like. A few minutes later, I found it in a little strip mall off Main Street.

The "Novelty Creations" sign hung above the big windows where mannequins wearing sexy lingerie were prominently displayed. I opened the door, and a little bell rang, announcing my presence. A young woman came out from the back and greeted me, telling me to let her know if I needed any help.

At the moment, I was the only customer in the shop, so I took my time to browse through the tables of underwear. The first table had a nice assortment of styles and sizes, but the second table was not what I expected. Now I understood where the 'novelty' part came in. Embarrassed, I quickly put the underwear down, and decided to talk to the clerk.

"Did you find what you needed?" she asked.

"Actually, I was wondering if I could ask you a couple of questions," I said. "Are you Dottie Weir?"

"No," she answered. A blanket of suspicion covered her thoughts. "Why do you want to know?" Was I from the insurance company? She'd already filled out everything they wanted.

"I'm a private investigator, and I just wanted to ask her a few questions," I said, hoping to put her at ease.

"Well, that's going to be hard, since she's dead," she answered. "What's this about?"

"She's dead?" I asked, feeling my stomach drop. "When?"

"About a year ago."

"Oh."

"I inherited this shop," she said. "I'm her daughter, Emily. Maybe I can help you?"

If she was her daughter, did that mean Keith was her cousin? I'd have to be careful. "That would be great," I said. "I'm actually here about some lost money that I'm trying to find." I listened to her thoughts, but only detected mild curiosity. Might as well get it over with. "I understand Keith Bishop worked here for a while. Did you know him?"

Her mind closed up with anger. "Yeah, he was my cousin." She put it together. "So you're looking for the money he stole? Are you with the police?"

"No. I'm working for the bank he robbed. Do you have any ideas or thoughts about where the money might be?"

She was thinking that Keith was responsible for her mother's death, and that she'd always suspected he'd used the shop as a cover for something illegal. But after he went to jail there was nothing going on, so it couldn't have been true.

What did she mean by that? "What was Keith's relationship with your mother? Did he have anything to do with her death?"

"I've always thought so... although he didn't exactly kill her," she said, but the fact that I asked made her want to confide in me. "She died of a heart attack, but Keith was here the night she died, and they had a huge argument. At least that's what Uncle Dean told me. He's Keith's dad, and my mom's brother. Mom called Dean after Keith left, and that's when she had the heart attack. Dean called the paramedics, but she died at the hospital a few hours later.

"Dean was so mad at Keith, I thought he was going to kill him. But he never got the chance. Keith was arrested the next day. Since mom died, Dean's been trying to make it up to me. We've become partners in the business. He does all of the accounting, pays all of the bills for the store, and keeps track of the inventory. You know, all the background stuff. All I have to worry about is the sales end of the business. I don't know what I would do without him."

"I'll bet," I agreed. "It's great to have someone to lean on." Whoa, this was big. Could Dean be the partner? If he was, how could he have his own son murdered? "How did Dean feel when Keith was murdered?"

"It was bad," Emily said, her mouth curved into a frown. "It broke his heart. He was always hoping that it was a mistake, and that Keith had nothing to do with the bank robbery. I think deep down though, he knew the truth."

"The police think Keith's partner had him murdered. Do you have any idea who his partner might be?"

"No," she said. "Keith never brought anyone around here, and I'm glad he didn't." She was thinking that Uncle Dean had never been able to figure it out either, even though he'd spent a lot of time looking. They'd even checked out his old girlfriends.

"Could it have been a girlfriend?" I asked.

"No. He had lots of them, but I don't think any of them could have been his partner."

"Why not?"

"He never had a steady girlfriend," she shook her head. "They were just flings. He wasn't good at long-term relationships."

"That makes sense," I said. "Can you think of anything else?"

"No. But if he hid the money, he didn't hide it here. I've been through everything, and I would have found it by now." She'd looked everywhere, even tearing out the walls and floor in the back room looking for a false opening. It wasn't here.

"I see," I said, somewhat discouraged. "Well... I can't thank you enough for talking with me. I'd like to talk to your Uncle as well. Is there a good time to catch him?"

"He has a day job, so he's only here in the evenings," she said. "I'll give him your number if you like, and he can call you."

"That would be great. Here's my card. Feel free to call me if you remember anything else." After handing her my card, I held up a pink teddy. "Can I buy this?"

She smiled. "Sure."

As she was ringing up my purchase, the bell rang, announcing another customer, and I was grateful I'd gotten in my questions while no one was there. I thanked her, and turned to leave, nearly stumbling into Rob Felt.

"Will you stop following me?" I asked, jerking back a step.

"Nope," he answered. He was thinking that I'd been in here a long time, and figured it had something to do with the money. He'd ask the clerk as soon as I left.

I was tempted to tell her not to say anything, but she was thinking he was a jerk, so I didn't have to. I stepped around him to leave, and realized he was wearing a dark jacket. Just like the one I saw at Thrasher Development. Was he the person eavesdropping on Uncle Joey and me? If so, that meant he had to know of my connection with Uncle Joey. How could I ask him about that?

"You're just wasting your time," I said. "I'm working on another case, and it has nothing to do with the money."

"We'll see about that." He didn't think I had any other cases, so that was a bunch of crap. He glanced around, thinking the lingerie shop was probably a dead end, but he'd check it out anyway.

"Whatever," I said under my breath.

Stepping around him, I hurried out the door, and got in my car. Where next? If Felt was following me, now was my chance to lose him. I pulled into traffic and headed to the police station.

Chapter 3

Walking into the police station, I paused to straighten my new ID badge. Detective Harris, or Dimples, as I called him, had given it to me after I'd helped him solve a case. This was the first time I'd worn it and, as I made my way to Dimples' desk, I glanced around to see if anyone would object to my presence. I got a few looks, but most people just acted like it was normal to see me there. Upon reflection, it probably was, since I'd been to the station often enough in the last few weeks.

I caught sight of Dimples across the room, just as he was picking up the phone. I listened to his thoughts, and realized he was about to call me. Thinking it would be a funny joke, I hurried to his side and tapped his shoulder. Keeping a serious expression on my face I said, "I'm here. What do you need?"

"Sweet... mother!" he shouted. "I was just calling you. How did you...? Wait a minute. Whoa... that was just weird."

I couldn't help it. I burst out laughing. "Sorry," I said in-between giggles. "But you should have seen your face!" I finally got under control, especially when I noticed he didn't think it was so funny.

"So you're not here because of your premonitions?" he asked, embarrassed and slightly confused.

"Oh... yes, I am." I decided it was better to lie at this point, mostly so Dimples wouldn't be embarrassed. "I hope that's okay." When he just nodded his head, I continued. "Sorry about that, I didn't mean to make you feel bad. It was just... I couldn't help it, and it was kind of funny."

"Yeah," he smiled. "It probably was." He was thinking that living with me would be tough if I did that very often. It gave him a new respect for my husband.

"So... look at this." I lifted up my badge. "Looks good, huh?" It was time to move on. I didn't want him feeling sorry for Chris, since it made me feel bad.

"Hey. Looks great!" he said. "I knew it would come in handy, especially if you're going to sneak up on me."

"Exactly!" I agreed. "So you'd better watch out." He laughed good-naturedly, and we were back to normal. "So, what did you need me for?" I asked.

"Um... right," he said, switching gears. "I'm helping the FBI with some gang interrogations, and thought having you there might be helpful. I just finished talking to them about it, and they gave me the go-ahead to ask you. That's why I was calling."

"Oh," I said. "That would probably work for me. Do you know any more about the case?"

"Not a lot, just that there've been several murders lately and no one's talking."

"Gotcha," I said. "Are they doing the interrogation here?"

"No, at FBI headquarters. I was going to see if you could go over with me a little later, but since you're here we could go over now. Will that work?"

"Sure," I agreed. Since I'd come to ask him what he knew about the police investigation of Keith Bishop, I could pick his brain when we got back.

"Great. Have a seat, and I'll call to let them know we're on our way."

Fifteen minutes later we walked into the federal building. I'd never been inside before, and when they asked to see my badge, I got nervous since it wasn't exactly real. The worker scanned the barcode, and my picture must have popped up on his computer screen, because he was thinking I looked a ton better in person. What? My picture wasn't that bad was it? Maybe I'd better get a new one.

We took the elevator to the sixth floor, and I followed Dimples through a maze of desks until we came to an office that had the name Henry Gilmore on the outside. Dimples knocked, and Henry ushered us in, introducing himself as we sat down.

"Detective Harris told me about you," Henry said. "That you have premonitions about things." He smiled, but was thinking it was probably a waste of time. "What do you need to do? Hold an object like the murder weapon or something?" He was thinking that's how they did it in the movies.

"No," I said. "It doesn't work like that. At least not for me." I glanced at Dimples, and he nodded encouragingly. "I have to be in the same room with the person who's being questioned to get anything off them." I suddenly remembered the FBI agent who had been watching my house when the Mexicans were after me, and how he thought I was a good 'reader', so I went with that. "It's like I can read them... if they're lying... you know, or hiding something... stuff like that."

"Oh," Henry perked up. That was something he knew about. That made sense, but there were a lot of people who could do that, and it didn't help much since most of the gang members they were questioning wouldn't talk.

"That's when I usually get premonitions about them," I said. "When they're being questioned. Even when they don't say anything."

He took a big breath. That was just what he'd been thinking. Maybe there was something to me after all. He decided to take a chance. What could it hurt? "All right. Let's try it out. How do you need to do this?"

I explained that I needed to be in the same room, and asked for a pad of paper so I could write down my impressions. "I'd rather not speak to him myself or say anything," I explained. "I want to stay anonymous."

"Okay," Henry agreed.

Given my history, Dimples thought that was a great idea.

"I also might have a question for you to ask," I added. "But I can write that down, and hand it to you."

"Anything else?" he asked.

"Nope, that should do it." I turned to Dimples. "You're coming, right?"

"Sure," he said, happy that I wanted him there. It was like we were partners or something. He liked that.

I followed Henry down the hall into a room with a desk and video cameras set up to record the interview. This room had the two-way mirror into the interrogation room. With video feed and monitors, it was a lot more high-class than the police station. Two agents were manning the cameras, and after pushing a few buttons, nodded that they were ready to go.

Henry turned to me. "You ready?"

"Sure," I said.

He held the door open and ushered us toward the table. After we sat, Henry motioned for the agents to bring the gang member in. Two agents entered, holding the arms of a beefy young man whose hands were cuffed in front of him. His jaw was set in defiance, and his cold, dark gaze glared at

Henry, then shifted to include Dimples and me. They sat him down in a chair opposite of us, and fastened his cuffs to the table.

"Hey Derek," Henry said.

Derek sneered, thinking how much he hated being called that. Razor was his name now. He was wondering what new ploy Henry was going to try this time. Not that it would work. Switch was blood, and he'd wet up anybody who got in his way. He wasn't tellin' nothin'.

"Your crew's had a hard time of it lately," Henry began. "What's going on? You lost your shot caller, and now it looks like you're all tuned up."

"What?" Razor asked.

"Switch is dead," Henry confirmed. "Want to tell me about it?"

"No. He's not dead. I just saw him."

"He's down in the morgue right now. Who killed him? Bloodhound?"

"What? Are you messin' with me?" Razor answered. Shock spread over his face. He was thinking that if Switch was dead... it changed everything. Bloodhound was the only one who could ride on Switch, but he wouldn't have killed him. Someone was threatening his territory, and it wasn't anyone from around here, not with the truce. He had to find out who did this and make them pay. "You chargin' me with somethin'?"

"Obstruction of justice, if you don't tell us what's going on."

"Man, I don't know," Razor whined. "I keep telling you that. Whatever's going down's got nothing to do with my hood."

"Why'd you run?" Henry asked.

"You know me," Razor replied. "I always run. If they know I'm talking to you, I'm as good as dead."

"You really don't know who killed him?" Henry gave it one more try.

"Hell no. I didn't even know he was dead."

"Okay," Henry answered. "You can go. But we'll be watching you closely." He knew he couldn't keep him in custody any longer. He glanced at the agents. "Get him out of here."

Once he was out of the room, Henry stood. "One of our undercover agents is here. Do you mind if he comes in to hear what you have to say?"

"Um... okay," I agreed.

"Good." Henry waved toward the mirror, and a moment later a man joined us. His head was shaved, and he was sporting a few tattoos. Baggy pants and a muscle shirt completed his disguise, along with several piercings in his nose and eyebrows. Henry sat back down without introducing us. "So... did you get anything?"

I glanced at Dimples, a little nervous about how to respond. The undercover agent was thinking this was bound to be interesting, although he didn't believe I could help them. He kept a serious expression on his face to intimidate me, especially when he noticed me staring at his piercings and tattoos. It made him want to laugh, since they were the fake kind, and I didn't know it.

"Well," I said, trying to organize my thoughts. "I'm sure you could tell that your news upset him pretty badly. His next move will be to find out who killed his friend, and make them pay."

"Yeah, that's probably right," Henry agreed. "Anything else?" He wasn't too impressed, since that part was pretty obvious.

"Not really," I said. Maybe this was for the best. I didn't really like working with gangs. For one thing, it was hard to understand what they were talking about, and for another, they were scary dudes. That included the undercover agent.

Henry was disappointed in me, and thinking it was a waste of time to bring me in. The undercover agent held his hand over his mouth so I couldn't see his smile of derision. I didn't like that much, so I tried to think if there was anything else I could add. "The only other thing I picked up was that there must be somebody new in the mix, since he and Bloodhound have a truce."

"His gang has a truce with Bloodhound?" This was news to Henry. "How do you know that?"

"I don't exactly," I blurted. "It's just an impression I got, and it might not even be right. That's just how it works with me. Anyway... the kid's scared. Someone new is moving in on his territory. That's about it. Sorry I couldn't help you more."

"Oh, that's okay. You did help." Henry was thinking if there really was a truce, it put a new light on things. Someone new coming in on their territory would certainly explain a lot of what was going on. But who would take on both gangs at once? It must be someone with a lot of muscle and money to back them up. Interesting.

The undercover agent was staring at me. How did I pick all that up? He'd known Bloodhound and Switch were talking about a truce, but didn't know why. Only that a few of the gang members were being targeted on both sides. Why would that lead to a truce, unless someone else was to blame? He could probably find out more at the club. With a shrewd glance my way, he quietly left the room.

I stood, eager to leave. I did not want to get mixed up in that sort of thing, and decided then and there to stay away from the FBI. Henry had other ideas, and was about to ask if I could come back.

"I'm not sure I can come back," I said. "I've got a lot on my plate right now, what with starting my new business, and working with the police. I mean... if you get in a real bind, you can call, and I'll see what I can do, but other than that, I'm pretty busy."

Henry could tell I was stonewalling him, and it piqued his curiosity, especially since that was exactly what he was going to ask me. Why was I so nervous? I hadn't been in any danger, so that was out. Maybe I saw more than I let on, and that made me uncomfortable.

Why was he analyzing me? I thought I'd better give him something. "I've never met anyone in a gang before, so I'm not real comfortable with that."

"Huh," he said. "I was just wondering about that." How did I know? Talking to me changed his perception about psychics. He'd never met anyone like me. I had to be the real deal. "It's understandable that you're not comfortable, but I hope it won't keep you from helping us in the future."

"Let's just take it one day at a time," I said, giving him a bright smile.

"Sure," he grunted, narrowing his eyes. I hadn't answered his question, but what could he do? "Thanks for coming down."

I nodded, and shook his hand. After he shook Dimples' hand, we left him staring after us. It felt like a hole was being burned into my back. Once we got in the elevator, it was easier to relax. Dimples could tell I didn't like being there, and he could sympathize, but he didn't understand why a gang member rattled me so much, especially after I'd been involved with some of his cases.

Of course, after what had happened with Mercer, he could see why I might not want to get involved. Come to think of it, I was a like a magnet for trouble. Add a gang or two to the mix, and it would be a nightmare. It was probably better for me to stick to just helping him.

"I'm sorry I dragged you down here," he said. "I'm sure you have plenty to keep you busy without this too."

"Thanks," I said. "I appreciate that." It was kind of funny to me that he drew the line at my helping the police, but he was probably right. "Plus, you guys pay me. The FBI didn't even offer that."

Dimples' brows rose with surprise. "True." He would never get used to how I talked like I'd heard his thoughts. "So you should just stick with us."

"Exactly," I agreed.

We got back to the police station, and since Dimples was feeling bad about asking me to help the FBI, I decided now was a good time to ask him about the Keith Bishop case.

"I'd be glad to help," he said.

"I'm mostly interested in his activities prior to his arrest," I said. "I have all the police reports from the prosecuting attorney, but I was wondering if I could talk to the detectives who headed up the investigation. See if they remember anything they didn't put in their report, stuff like that."

"Sure," he agreed. "If I'm remembering right, it was Hansen and Williams who handled the case. In fact, you've met Detective Williams already. He was with me when we interviewed you about the bank robber at the grocery store the first time we met."

"Of course," I said. He was the one who didn't have a lot of patience. I hoped he didn't remember how crazy I acted back then.

It was my lucky day, because we found Detective Williams sitting at his desk. He was delighted to talk to me, especially after Dimples had kept me all to himself. He was a little jealous of our relationship, but mostly because he knew I'd helped Dimples solve a few cases. Of course, he didn't believe anyone could have premonitions, so my helping him had been a fluke, but it was still a sore spot between them.

"So what can you tell me about Keith Bishop?" I asked. "Did you ever check out his aunt's shop?"

"His aunt?" Williams couldn't remember her.

"Yeah, her name was Dottie Weir, and he worked at her lingerie shop, um... Novelty Creations?"

"Oh, yeah, now I remember. That was an interesting shop. Have you been there?" He was thinking he'd go back if he wasn't so embarrassed. Maybe he could send his wife? That would work, and she could get...

"I went this morning," I said, interrupting his wanton thoughts. "I found out that Dottie Weir died just before Keith was arrested. His cousin Emily owns the place now. She thought he might have been using the shop as a front for something else he was involved in. Did you know anything about that?"

He nodded. "We wondered about that too. There were some shipments he had going from the store. I remember we intercepted one of the shipments, but all we found in the crates were boxes of underwear. It was pretty disappointing. That's probably why we left it out of the report."

"Did you return them?" My spidey senses were tingling. Maybe this was it, and the police had missed something.

"Yeah," he said. "I remember how upset Dottie Weir's lawyer was about us confiscating her stock. We told her she could come right in and get them, which I'm sure she did."

"Was this before or after Keith's arrest?" My heart pounded with anticipation.

"After, since that was when we were looking for the money and trying to find his partner," he said. "Why?"

"Dottie Weir died before he was arrested. At least that was what her daughter told me."

"So, who picked up the stuff? The lawyer or the daughter?"

"I don't think the daughter knew anything about it," I answered.

"Well, it doesn't really matter," Williams said, dismissively. "I mean, all that was in there was a bunch of underwear."

"Yeah, true," I answered. But I didn't really believe it. Somehow, the money was tied up in that shipment. But that didn't make sense either. Otherwise, the police would have found the money. So what did it mean?

"Thanks for talking to me," I said. "I appreciate it."

"No problem," he answered. "Sorry it was a dead-end."

"That's okay. If you remember anything else, let me know."

"Sure thing," he said.

I tried not to let my disappointment get the best of me, and wandered over to Dimples' desk to say goodbye. He was on his cell phone, and when I approached, his face got kind of blotchy. Like he was blushing.

"I'll pick you up tonight then," he said, keeping his face averted. "Seven o'clock... yeah... me too. Bye."

Did Dimples have a girlfriend? "Got a hot date, huh?" I teased.

"Yeah," he said.

"Sweet!" I was delighted. I'd felt bad at the Museum Gala when he didn't have a girl on his arm. He'd explained that he didn't have time for a relationship. I guess things had changed. "How'd you meet?" If anything, his face got even redder. It was adorable on him.

He took a deep breath, and let it out slowly to compose himself. "I actually bumped into her, as in, almost knocked her down. I was at the bagel shop down on the corner getting coffee and didn't see her. Both our coffees spilled all over everything. It was horrible. I helped her clean up and bought her another one. We talked, and she seemed interested, so I got her number."

"So this is the first time you've called her?" I asked.

"Oh, no. We've gone out a few times over the last month or two. I've been taking it kind of slow." He smiled and shrugged, thinking he was going to invite her to his place after dinner if all went well.

"Ah," I said. No wonder he was blushing. "Well, that's great! I hope it goes well. Where are you going for dinner?"

"Um... I've got reservations for that new restaurant downtown. Tuscany's." He hadn't told me he was taking her to dinner, but of course it was me, so it made sense in a wacky way.

"Wow, impressive," I said. "Well, have a great time."

"Thanks." He smiled, and his dimples did that crazy dance that always made me chuckle.

I left with a lighter step, eager to get home to my husband. It had been a long day, starting with Uncle Joey, then the lingerie shop, the FBI, and ending with Williams. I could tell Chris about all of it, except maybe Uncle Joey. Of course, if I didn't tell him, it would probably backfire and make things worse. There had to be a way I could tell him that would make it okay that he didn't know ahead of time. I know... I could tell him Uncle Joey sprang it on me, and there wasn't time to let Chris know. That should work. It was all Uncle Joey's fault anyway, so why not?

Dinner was ready and on the table when Chris called. I cringed, knowing what his call meant before I even answered. "Hey," I said.

"Hey babe." His voice was low and sexy, sending shivers up my spine. "I'm sorry, but I'm going to be late tonight.

We've got this big trial starting Monday, and I'm helping to get it ready. I should be home around eight-thirty or nine."

"Does that mean you'll be working this weekend too?"

"Just tomorrow, not Sunday," he answered.

"Do you want me to save you some dinner?"

"No, we've got some take-out here. This is Gary's case, so he's taking good care of us. But it's a pretty big deal, and we want to make sure we're ready."

"Yeah, I'm sure it's important." Gary was the Pratt part of Chris' law firm, Cohen, Larsen, and Pratt. "Well, thanks for calling. I'll see you in a bit." Too bad he didn't call earlier, before I made all this food. But... on the bright side, we probably had enough dinner for tomorrow night too, and not having to figure out another meal was always a good thing.

I called the kids to the table, and we started to eat. Our kids, Josh and Savannah, were used to their dad staying late so it didn't faze them. While we ate, I realized how fast they were growing up. Josh was fourteen, and Savannah twelve. The school year was almost over, and soon it would be summer. That's when it hit me that we hadn't even talked about a summer vacation.

Josh had three years of school left before he went off to college, and that meant five for Savannah. Then they would be gone. Maybe we should plan something nice, so it would be memorable. "Hey, what do you want to do for summer vacation?"

Josh shrugged. "I don't know." He didn't really care. He was just glad to be out of school.

The first thing that popped into Savannah's mind was Paris. This surprised me, although she had been taking French this year, so in a way, it made sense. Then she quickly changed her mind and said, "Disney World... no wait, The Wizarding World of Harry Potter! Or maybe both. That would be a blast!"

I glanced at Josh and he shrugged, but he was thinking it would be boss. His friend, Parker, had gone over spring break, and it was all he could talk about. But it was probably pretty expensive.

I took a deep breath, wondering how expensive something like that would be. Probably a lot. Maybe I shouldn't have said anything. "Well, we'll have to think about that. And see if we can afford it."

Savannah slumped, thinking that we never got to do anything fun. Since dad was working so much, why didn't we have enough money? She would be willing to give up dance lessons for the summer, and maybe even other stuff too. She could do more babysitting if that would help.

I thought about my nearly eight thousand dollars in the bank account from Uncle Joey. I could certainly use some of that money. Although, for some reason, it was hard to think of that money as mine, and if I used it, did that make me more indebted to Uncle Joey? On the other hand, I'd nearly been killed a few times over his money. He owed me.

"I'll talk to Dad, and we'll see if we can do it," I said. "After I see how much it costs."

Savannah's eyes lit up with excitement. Was I serious? It would be so fun! But maybe she shouldn't get her hopes up. She'd better wait and see. But at least it was a possibility.

We finished dinner, and Savannah offered to help clean up without me asking. She was thinking about the vacation. "Come on, Josh. You can help too," she said.

"I always help," he countered, "unless I have to go somewhere."

"Yeah, right," she said. "That's just it, you always have to go somewhere."

"You're one to talk," he argued. "You're always going off to talk to your friends about all the boys."

"I do not!"

"Yes you do, especially about Ryan," he teased.

"Okay," I said. "That's enough. Hand me those beans."

I'd never understand why siblings had to tease each other so much. Did I really want to go on a family vacation with this going on all the time? Of course, if we were at a resort, we'd be pretty busy. Thinking about all the stuff we'd have to cram into a few days made my stomach hurt, and I wondered what I was thinking to even suggest it. I'd need to take a vacation after the vacation just to recuperate. How would Chris take it? Come to think of it, I wasn't sure which was worse, talking about a family vacation, or telling him about Uncle Joey.

I shouldn't have worried about it though, because when Chris got home, Savannah spilled the beans. "Hey Dad... did Mom tell you about our vacation?"

"What?" he asked.

"We want to go to Universal Studios in Orlando!" she gushed. "You know, Harry Potter? I looked it up on the Internet, and we can get some good deals if we book it now."

"Savannah!" I scolded. "I told you we'd talk about it."

"I know," she agreed. "That's what we're doing."

"No... I meant your dad and I would talk about it."

She knew that's what I meant, but she played dumb anyway. "Oh, okay. Well, think about it, because I'd really like to go. I've got some spending money saved up, and I could babysit more to help out." She gave Chris a hopeful smile, but didn't wait for him to respond. "I'm going to bed now. You can let me know in the morning what you decide." She gave him a big hug and a kiss on the cheek before running off to her room. Wow, she was really working it.

Chris pinned his gaze on me. "What's going on?"

"I just asked them where they'd like to go on vacation this summer," I explained. "And somehow it turned into a trip to Orlando." I shook my head. "What should we do?"

Chris shrugged. "Tell them they can either go to college or Orlando?"

I laughed. "Yeah, right. I think they'd pick Orlando. At least Savannah would." He nodded in agreement. "But I think I know how to handle this. Let's tell Savannah to get prices of everything we'd need, write it all down, and then add it up. She can present it to us when she's done, and we can decide if we can afford it right now."

"When she sees how much everything costs, it might make her think about it," he agreed.

"Exactly," I said. "Plus, I do have that money from Uncle Joey."

Chris sighed. Bringing up Uncle Joey's money irritated him. He made enough money to take our family to Orlando, even if it seemed like a waste, and using Manetto's money hit him the wrong way. Besides, he didn't feel like that money was ours. It felt like a pay-off, and using it seemed wrong.

"I know what you mean," I replied. When he didn't respond, I realized he hadn't spoken out loud. This time, it hit a nerve with me, and I decided if he didn't like it, too bad for him. "But on the other hand, after what I went through, I don't think using it for a family vacation would be so bad. Which reminds me..." I took a deep breath for courage, and let it out slowly. "I had to go to his office this morning."

"What? Why?" His surprise wasn't laced with anger at me, so I relaxed.

"He wanted me to 'listen' to his replacements for Johnny and Walter. You know... tell him what everyone was thinking, so he'd know who was loyal and all that."

"Just the usual, huh?" he asked, sarcasm tinting his voice.

"Uh-huh," I said. "Ramos was gone, and some other guy had taken his place."

Chris narrowed his eyes. "And why does that upset you?"

"Because I don't trust him. When Jackie introduced us, he was thinking – 'so this is Shelby' – like he already knew about me. Then, after everyone left, Uncle Joey and I were talking in the conference room, and someone was outside in the hall listening. I caught a glimpse of him as he took off, but we couldn't catch him."

"And you think it's this guy?" Chris asked.

"Probably not... but maybe. You know, now that I think about it, it could have been Rob Felt. He's been following me all day. Although there was this other guy, Nick, who was really interested in me and what I did for Uncle Joey."

"Who's Nick?" Confusion clouded Chris' mind.

"He took Walter's place in Uncle Joey's organization, along with Jimmy, who is Johnny's nephew." Since Chris didn't remember who Johnny was either, I answered his unspoken question. "The one that Walter murdered who owned the restaurant?"

"Oh, okay," he said. "So... do you think whoever was spying on you figured out what you do? That could be bad."

"I don't think so, and Uncle Joey said he'd take care of it, so we probably shouldn't worry."

"Right," Chris said, unconvinced. That made one more thing to worry about. Was there any more trouble I could get into? "What else did you do today?"

I decided to leave out the part with the FBI and the gang thing. I didn't think he'd like hearing about that. I could tell him if it came up, and if it didn't, he probably didn't need to know. Especially since I was not going to do it again. Instead, I told him about my visit with Emily, the owner of Novelty Creations, and how Dottie Weir had died about a year ago.

"So the shop is a dead end," he concluded.

"Not necessarily," I replied. I went on to explain about my visit with Detective Williams and the shipments of underwear that the police confiscated.

"But if the money wasn't in the shipment, it doesn't really matter who picked it up," Chris said.

"Yes it does," I disagreed. "What if it was Keith Bishop's partner looking for the stolen money pretending to be Dottie Weir's lawyer? If I talked to that person I would know if he was Keith's partner with my mind-reading ability."

Chris thought about it for a minute. "Okay, but how would you prove this person is the partner? In order to turn him in to the police, you need evidence for that sort of thing. And if he doesn't know where the money is, how would that help you find it anyway?"

"Geeze...don't be such a spoil-sport," I said, hotly. "Wouldn't it be good to find the partner whether he had the money or not?"

"Of course it would," he said, agitated. "I just don't want you to get into trouble with this person." He was thinking that I would probably give myself away somehow, and end up in a lot worse situation than I could handle.

"Hey," I smacked him on the arm. "I can keep my mouth shut when it's called for. And I can tell a good lie if I have to."

"Oh, yeah?" he asked, wrapping his arms around me with a tight grip. "What was the last lie you told?"

"That's not fair," I wiggled to get out of his hold. It didn't work. His lips tilted in a wicked smile, and he loosened his arms.

"Why not?" he asked.

"Because... it makes me look bad." He was thinking, *well duh,* and it made me mad. "But I'll tell you one thing for sure, when it comes to lying or dying, I'll pick lying every time."

"Good," he said, knowing there was more to the story I wasn't telling. "So what happened today?"

I sighed. Now I had to tell him the truth. "Uncle Joey was worried that I'd use what I knew about him to put him away, and I had to tell him that I would never do that, although, if I got the chance, I might."

"That's not lying," Chris said.

"It's not?"

"No... it's self-preservation. It's being smart."

"Okay," I smiled. "In that case I can't remember the last time I told a lie." I had him right where I wanted him, and he knew it.

"That doesn't mean you can lie to me," he said, backpedaling.

"I don't lie to you." It was true. I didn't lie to him... I just left things out. That's totally different. "I told you my powers came back," I reasoned. "Even though I knew you wouldn't be happy about it. That would have been under self-preservation, right?"

"Nope," he said. "Your powers were never gone. So that means you lied to me twice. First when you told me they were gone, and second, when you didn't admit you still had them."

"That's only once," I said, defensively. Not wanting him to get mad about it all over again, I continued. "Besides, I only brought that up to prove a point; that I do tell you the truth, even when it seems hard. And you forgave me remember? So it's all good."

Chris was thinking that I drove him crazy, but it was one of those things he loved about me, so he couldn't be too mad about it. "So what's your next move with the stolen money?"

"I don't know," I said. "Go back to the shop? Look around? I think it's got to be tied up in the shop. Maybe there was another shipment that got lost, or maybe the police missed something."

"I think there's a way you can find out who signed for the shipment. The police should have a record. Maybe that person was dumb enough to sign their own name. Usually you have to show your ID to get the evidence released to you. With a name, you can track him down."

"That's a great idea!" I smiled up at Chris. "I'll check it out first thing Monday morning."

"Just be careful if you find him," Chris said. He was thinking *don't do anything stupid.*

"I won't. I mean... I promise to be careful."

Chris shook his head, gathered me in his arms, and sealed the promise with a kiss that was so good, I was bound to remember it for the rest of my life.

Chapter 4

The weekend went by fast, with Chris spending a lot of time in his office. The only glitch was Savannah, since we wouldn't give her a definite yes on the trip, although once she understood her assignment, she warmed to the idea. She even spent time talking to her friend's mother who was a travel agent. I told her to present her findings to us after she'd done her research, and peace was restored.

Monday morning, I left for the gym, picking up my friend Holly. It was good therapy to talk about our kids and family vacations. Since she'd been to Orlando before, it got me excited about our trip and made it something to look forward to. I got home a little later than normal, but after a shower and quick breakfast, I was ready for the day.

My first stop was the police station to check on who signed for the confiscated underwear. I was disappointed that Dimples was out on a case, but with my badge, it was easy to get admitted to the evidence room. I was a little nervous about being there, since it wasn't a police case I was working on, but what good was this badge if I couldn't use it?

Everything was tagged and entered into the computer by case number. I talked to the officer in charge of evidence, and found the entry for the crates of underwear. "Is there a signature for the person who retrieved them?" I asked.

She shook her head. "Not that I can see. That means they must still be here."

"Really?' Detective Williams said someone from the family came and got them."

She checked again. "No... I don't have a name or date of that ever happening. Do you want to see them? I can take you back."

"Sure," I said. "That would be great."

"Let me just get the ID number." She wrote down the number on a sticky note and unlocked the door to the room.

Inside, the room was layered with rows of shelves filled with all kinds of things. One side alone had about fifty skateboards all tagged and neatly placed. It looked more like a thrift store than an evidence room.

"The crates should be in the back where we keep the large items," she said.

I followed her into another section that looked like a warehouse. This was where the big stuff was kept, like bicycles, machinery, tools, and lots of boxes. The numbers on the tags got bigger as we neared the end of the row. The officer stopped, and I hurried to her side, eager to see the crates, but the space was empty.

"They should be right here," she said, puzzled.

My heart sank. I was so close! Had someone stolen them? The security here was pretty tight. I couldn't believe just anyone could walk out of here with evidence unless they had clearance. So it had to be someone in the police department. But why would they want a bunch of underwear? And how could they get the crates out of here without anyone noticing?

"Are you sure?" I asked, just to be safe.

She checked her note again. "Unless they got misplaced," she said. She was thinking it wasn't likely, and it made her nervous that someone in the department had taken them. It was her responsibility to keep that from happening, but sometimes things got 'misplaced' and it didn't take a brain surgeon to know it was one of their own who did it. But why would anyone want a bunch of underwear?

She started checking the boxes on either side, and I plunged in to help. No underwear in sight. "Maybe someone did pick them up, and it didn't get recorded," I said.

"Yes," she agreed. "That's a possibility, especially since that's what you were told. Let's go back and check the computer again. Maybe I missed something." She knew she hadn't, but it didn't hurt to double-check. "This is so strange."

As we retraced our steps, I kept an eye out for anything that looked like the missing crates. "What happens to all this stuff if it's not claimed?" I asked.

"We hold auctions, and sell it back to the community. You can get some really good stuff for cheap. Especially the bicycles and skateboards, but we have cars, boats, and even houses."

"Wow, that's nuts. Do you have auctions very often?"

"It depends, but usually when we need to clear out space. As you can see, it gets pretty crowded in here."

"Do you think that's what happened to the crates?" I asked.

"Maybe, but it should have been marked on the computer. We keep very meticulous records so things don't get lost." She couldn't figure it out. Someone must have made a mistake. Maybe they were picked up, and it wasn't recorded. Or maybe they were scheduled for auction, especially if they'd been here for a long time. That made the most sense to her.

We made it back to her desk, and she checked the computer again. "That's strange," she said. "On this column it says they were brought in and labeled. This column has the tag number, but this column has a check on it. That usually means they were released, but there's no signature of who signed for it. Maybe someone picked them up after all, and just forgot to record the name. You said they belonged to a business?"

"Yes," I nodded.

"Then maybe you should check with them, and see if they know who picked it up."

"Yeah... okay." I sighed, discouraged they weren't there.

She was eager to close the books, and decided that was what happened. It made sense to her, and explained why they were gone, better than if someone in the department had taken them. She'd also double-check to see if they'd already been auctioned off, or on the schedule for the next auction.

I managed a smile. "Thanks for your time. If you happen to find out where they are, could you call me?" I handed her one of my cards. "I'd really appreciate it."

"Sure." She took the card and wrote 'underwear' on the back, hoping that would help her remember.

"Thanks." I sure hoped they hadn't been auctioned off. I took the long way back upstairs where the detectives had their offices. Without a name, I didn't have much to go on, but I could still check with Emily at Novelty Creations, and see if she had any records of the shipment being picked up.

Passing by the detectives' offices, I caught a glimpse of Dimples and decided to stop by and ask how his date on

Friday went. With his back to me, I was hoping to 'hear' something about me so I could surprise him again, but he was thinking of a time-line in an urgent case he was helping with.

I hated to interrupt, but I also felt funny leaving without saying something. I mean, what if he saw me? Wouldn't he expect me to say hello if I was there? I took a few steps in his direction. Right then, the police chief stepped out of his office, and headed straight for Dimples' desk. He was thinking of asking Dimples how the case was coming, and hoping he was making progress since the story was big news, and the press kept calling for updates. They needed to find some answers quick. Maybe this was the type of thing Shelby Nichols could help with.

Me? He was thinking about me? I stood there, not knowing what to do, feeling like a kid caught with his hand in the cookie jar. It was one thing to play a joke on Dimples, but quite another to do it to the police chief. That's when I caught the 'missing child' part, and knew I couldn't hesitate.

"Hey," I said. They both turned to me, and I gave a little wave. The police chief's jaw dropped open before he gathered his wits and snapped it shut. "What's up?" I asked.

"Hey Shelby," Dimples answered, more used to me showing up unexpectedly.

"I don't mean to interrupt, but is there something I can help you with?" I asked.

"Yes," they both answered. They glanced at each other, then the police chief motioned me over.

"We've got a little girl missing," he explained. "Last anyone saw her was about an hour ago. She was at a friend's house and left to go home, but she never made it. Her mother called it in about..." he checked his watch, "twenty minutes ago."

That meant that she'd been gone for almost an hour and a half, and I had a bad feeling, but it didn't stop me. "I need to talk to everyone involved."

"Let's go." Dimples didn't hesitate, and the police chief nodded his thanks.

We hurried to Dimples' car, and pulled out into traffic with the siren loudly blazing. "Tell me about the case." I yelled over the noise.

"She lives in an apartment complex over by Lincoln Park. Right now we've got about twenty men knocking doors."

"Does the friend live in the complex too?" I asked.

"Yes." He was thinking the odds were pretty high that someone in the complex grabbed her as she walked by, or lured her into their apartment. He just hoped she wasn't already dead.

My stomach clenched. I did not want that to happen. If there was anything I could do, I had to do it. Dimples pushed on the gas, and I was grateful when all the cars pulled over to let us pass. It was sliding through the red lights that gave my heart a workout. By the time we pulled up to the complex, it took me a minute to peel my hand off the handle above the door.

My legs shook when I stood, but I managed to keep up with Dimples. "We need to start at the friend's place, and take the route the girl would have walked," I said.

He nodded, and found an officer to take us there. He introduced me to Officer Wilcox, mentioning that I was there at the Chief's request. There were uniforms everywhere, and Wilcox was thinking they had already covered that ground twice, and knocked on all the doors between, but he was willing to do it again to find her.

"What's her name?" I asked him.

"Shayla," Wilcox said.

"Did her friend say anything to you? Did she know if Shayla went straight home?"

"No, she was afraid to talk to us, but her mother told us they often played at one house or the other. It's just a few minutes' walk between apartments, and they do it all the time."

That ruled out the friend's house, and I didn't want to waste time questioning them when she was probably somewhere else. "Is there someone you suspect right now that you've already questioned?"

"Yes," he said, surprised that I'd asked.

"That's where I want to start," I said. "The first one on your list."

He nodded, and took us to an apartment on the second floor toward a young man who was leaning over the railing, watching our progress. He wore a white sleeveless t-shirt that showed off a tattoo, and puffed on a cigarette. He eyed me with distrust, thinking I looked like one of those caseworkers for the social services department. It reminded him of all the foster homes he'd landed in, and how alone he'd felt.

He was barely eighteen and on his own, and he liked his independence. If they thought he had anything to do with that girl's disappearance it would ruin what he'd tried to make of his life. This couldn't be happening, but he supposed he should expect it. He understood that he fit the mold of a messed-up kid, and he was always getting blamed for things he didn't do.

Sure, he saw those little girls playing together. He liked watching people, especially children, because they were always laughing and having fun. But he'd never hurt them. Never. Children should be protected. But he didn't think the cops would ever believe him. They had their minds made up, and it was hopeless to even try and reason with them.

I glanced in his eyes, and saw the vulnerability before he covered it with a glare of defiance. "Hi," I said, putting as much warmth in my voice as I could. "Is there someone... anyone that you've noticed around here... that would grab a little girl?"

He took a step back, visibly shocked that I didn't accuse him of the crime. He'd been so focused on himself that he didn't think about who could have done it. Now his thoughts raced. "You know, there is this guy, he's an older dude, and I've seen him talking to those girls now and then. He gives them candy."

"Where does he live?" I asked.

"Just over there." He pointed to an apartment that wasn't anywhere close to the route Shayla would have taken to get home.

"Thanks," I said.

I started toward the apartment, with Dimples and Wilcox trailing behind. Wilcox was amazed that I believed the kid, but if what he said was true... it was the only lead we had.

"Let me talk to him," Dimples said. His instincts told him we were on the right track, and he didn't want me to get hurt if anything happened.

"Okay," I agreed. "But just remember that no matter what he says, if I say she's in there, then you've got to believe me."

"I will," he said. "Wilcox... follow my lead."

"Yes sir." Wilcox was a bit confused, but didn't question Dimples' authority.

We arrived at the door, and Dimples rang the doorbell. A man opened the door a crack. Seeing the uniform, he took off the chain, and opened it wider. His brows drew together in concern. "Can I help you?" he asked. He had expected the police to come, but not this fast.

"Yes," Dimples answered. "We're asking everyone if they've seen a little girl. She's about seven years old, and her name's Shayla. She's been missing for a couple of hours."

"Yes, I heard about that," he said, his voice dripping with concern. "I can't believe something like this would happen here. Can I help? I would be glad to knock on doors with you." He was thinking that no one would suspect him if he joined in the search.

"Where is she?" I shouted.

"What are you talking about?" His thoughts turned to the closet in his bedroom.

"She's in the bedroom closet!" I shoved him out of the way, and rushed into the apartment, my heart in my throat. I couldn't tell if he thought of her as dead or alive, and dread tightened my stomach.

"Shelby, wait!" Dimples rushed in behind me, and I slowed to get my bearings. At the door I could hear the man straining against Wilcox's hold, and yelling that we were trespassing.

The bedroom opened on my right, and I flew inside, slamming the closet doors apart. Dimples saw her before I did. She was slumped in a ball, with her hands tied, and a piece of plastic wrapped around her head. Her mouth was open, and she was trying to breathe, but the plastic wouldn't let her get any air. Dimples grabbed her, put her in my arms, and ripped the plastic away from her face. She gasped in air, and after a few tense seconds, her red face turned white, and she started to cry.

"It's okay baby," I said. "It's okay." I held her in my arms, and patted her back while she cried. "Just breathe, honey. I've got you. You're all right now." Her little body quivered, but she soon settled down. I kept whispering to her, holding her tight. Dimples left, telling Wilcox to cuff the guy, and radio that we'd found her alive. A few tense minutes later, her mother was there, pulling her away, sobbing with relief.

I let her go and wiped my eyes. She was safe, and I needed to get out of there. I found Dimples in the living room, talking to a cop. He excused himself, and hurried to my side. "Are you okay?" he asked.

"No."

He grabbed my arm, and pulled me outside, leading me away from the crowd. He kept his arm around me while I calmed down. "That was close," I managed to whisper.

"Yeah," Dimples answered. "But we did it. You did it."

I shook my head. "No," I said forcefully. "We did it together."

"If you say so," he said, knowing from my tone I wasn't comfortable taking the credit. "Yup... we did good. We did something real good. Focus on that, Shelby. Focus on that."

I took a deep breath, and let his words work on me. My legs were a little wobbly, but I was finally able to stand on my own. "Thanks Dimples. I'll be okay now."

He nodded and let me go. "I'm just going to talk to them for a minute, but I'll be right back, and we can leave."

"Okay." I watched him go, grateful for some time alone. The police had cleared an area to keep the crowd at bay, but it was filling up with reporters and cameras. I did not want to go anywhere near them.

I glanced up, and noticed the young man still standing on his balcony. I waved him over, and he soon joined me.

"She was really in there?" he said, with a touch of disbelief.

"Yeah, she was," I said. "You saved her life. Don't ever forget that."

He glanced at me, his brows drawn together with a question. I waited like a normal person for him to ask. "What made you believe me? That cop thought I did it. That's why you came over. I fit the profile for your basic criminal. So what made you change your mind?"

I smiled at him and shrugged. "Just a hunch I guess. Kind of like the hunch you had about that guy. Have you ever thought about being a cop or a detective? I think you've got the chops for it."

He laughed. "Actually... no."

"Hmm... that's too bad. You'd make a good one."

Dimples joined us and gave the kid his card. "You saved that girl's life. Could you come down to the station and make a statement?"

"I guess," he answered reluctantly.

"Show them the card at the desk, and tell them I asked for you personally," Dimples assured him. "No one will hassle you, I promise."

"Fine," he answered.

"Great... I'm Detective Harris." He held out his hand, and the kid took it.

"Tyson," he said.

"Good, see you soon." Dimples turned to me. "You ready to go?"

"Yes. Let's get out of here." We skirted around the crowd of people, and made it to the street where the car was parked without drawing attention. As we pulled away from the curb, I caught a glimpse of the kidnapper being led to a police car. I shivered as the events washed over me again, grateful that I had made a difference in the outcome. It was close, but we'd saved her, and that was what mattered.

We pulled into the police station, and Dimples turned off the car, but made no move to get out. He was thinking that things were going to change for me when word got out about what I did, and he wasn't sure it would be good.

"I was wondering," I said. "If you could keep me out of your report. Or at least change it just a bit?"

"Like how?" he asked.

"Just say I accompanied you, but not that I knew she was in the apartment. Maybe that the way the guy was acting was suspicious or something, and that's why we went inside. That would work, right?"

Dimples smiled, and turned his gaze on me. "Sure, I can do that. I'll keep it between you and me. I'll see if I can persuade Wilcox to do the same. Besides, no one would believe us anyway, right?"

"Exactly," I agreed.

"How did you know?" he asked. "I mean... do you get images or something? It's almost like you can read minds."

I let out a nervous chuckle. "It's mostly premonitions or something close to that," I explained. "It's best not to think about it too hard, though."

"Yeah, you're probably right," he said.

"Well, if you don't need me for anything else, I'm going." I jumped out of the car before he could stop me. "See ya!"

He got out, thinking he needed to get my statement, but couldn't bring himself to make me come back. He'd write up a report, and have me sign a statement later. Now all he had to do was decide what to tell the Police Chief.

I hopped in my car, grateful that was his problem and not mine. I'd done enough for today and was ready to go home. I had planned to stop at Novelty Creations on my way, but not now. I could check that out tomorrow. Right now all I wanted was to go home and hug my kids.

Chris was late getting home again. The trial he was working on had started, and he still had a lot to do for the next day, but I didn't mind. Savannah and I spent the evening figuring out our vacation to Orlando. We decided it was better to stay at a hotel on the resort because of the benefits of getting into the park before the crowds. We even got Josh involved, and picked the week we wanted to go.

It was hard not to book the reservation right then and there, especially since Chris had thought that we had plenty of money for the trip, but I convinced Savannah and Josh that we needed to talk to him first.

Since I was so enthusiastic about it, they weren't too worried about the outcome. They were right about that. I was bound and determined to take this trip together as a family and have some fun. I was sure I could get Chris to agree.

With no sign of Chris, I decided to watch the ten o'clock news. The kidnapping was the top story. The news crew had been there the whole time and, after showing a mug shot of the man responsible, they did a time-line of events. I was shocked to see myself walking across the lawn with Dimples and Wilcox. I was glad I'd worn the navy jacket over my white shirt and jeans. With my ID dangling around my neck, it made me look official, like I belonged.

The reporter was talking about the police presence while we were talking to Tyson. The camera went back to the reporter, and we took off toward the kidnapper's apartment. The reporter was still talking when someone shouted that the police were running somewhere. The camera panned in on the apartment, and showed Wilcox grappling with the kidnapper.

The camera zoomed in on the kidnapper's face, and a shiver went up my spine. Wilcox cuffed him, and the police converged, blocking the view. Next, the child's mother ran with an officer into the apartment, and the reporter was saying that the girl had been found, but they didn't know if she was alive.

It was several tense seconds later that the news reached them that she was alive and well. The camera panned back in toward the apartment, and showed me standing with Dimples, leaning over to catch my breath.

"Mom? Is that you?" Josh asked. "You were there?"

"What is it?" Savannah joined us. Her attention riveted to the footage of me and Dimples standing outside the apartment. The camera zoomed out to focus on the crowd and catch a glimpse of the kidnapper. The footage cut to a later image of the kidnapper being put into a police car, then showed footage of the mother and child being escorted to a waiting car. The story ended, and I clicked the TV off.

"Come sit down, and I'll tell you what happened," I said. I explained how I helped Dimples catch the kidnapper, and how scared I was. I told them about the good tip we got that led us to her. "Thank goodness she was still alive. So it all worked out."

Josh didn't buy my explanation. "Did you know she was in that apartment because of your premonitions?" I'd told the kids that I helped the police, but he'd uncovered the premonitions part himself.

"Yeah," I said, trusting him and Savannah with that much of the truth. "But it's not something I want people to know, so let's keep it to ourselves, okay?"

"Sure," he agreed, smiling. He was thinking it was almost like having a super power. How cool was that?

"You guys better get to bed," I urged.

"But what about Dad?" Savannah asked. "I want to book our trip before it's too late."

"I'll talk to him tonight. We can book the trip tomorrow. One more day isn't going to make a difference."

She sighed. "Okay. Goodnight."

I got ready for bed, and Chris still wasn't home. It was almost eleven-thirty and he usually called if he was going to be this late. Had something happened to him? I called his cell, but it went straight to voicemail, so I left a message to call me.

The case he was working on was big, but that was all I knew about it. Still, with it being this late without a phone call, my stomach knotted with concern, sending a spike of fear down my spine. I called his office line, just in case his phone was out of juice. It went straight to voicemail.

I decided to give him ten minutes or so to call me back, and got out my book to read. Ten minutes turned into twenty without a word. I had been reading the same paragraph for the last few minutes, and couldn't concentrate. I snapped the book shut and picked up the phone.

It started ringing in my hand, and I jerked from surprise. Fumbling it in my fingers, I sighed with relief. It was Chris' cell number. "Chris," I snapped. "Are you all right?"

"Yes, I'm fine, but I'm at the hospital." His voice was strained.

"What's wrong?" I asked.

"It's Gary. Someone beat him up. Can you come to the hospital? I rode in the ambulance with him, and my car's still at work."

"Sure, I'll be there in a few minutes." I threw on some clothes, and grabbed my keys. Then I decided to write a quick note in case the kids got up, and jumped in my car. It seemed to take forever to get there. Due to the late hour, the parking lot was practically empty. I parked the car, and hurried inside to find Chris waiting in the main lobby.

"Hey." I sat down beside him, and took his hand. "What's going on? What happened?"

"Hi," he sighed, giving me a quick kiss. "Thanks for coming."

"Is Gary going to be all right?" I asked.

"He's stable now. He's got a broken jaw and some internal bleeding, but he'll be okay. He got beat up pretty bad. His face is a swollen mess. I can't believe this happened."

"Tell me about it," I said.

"I stayed to help him finish up some things for the trial tomorrow," he began. "I wasn't quite done, so I told him I'd finish up and he could leave. When I got to the parking garage about a half hour later, his car was still there. It didn't make any sense, so I went over and found him lying face down on the concrete, with blood all over him. I thought he was dead."

"Oh no. How awful," I said.

"I checked for a pulse and realized he was just unconscious, so I called nine-one-one. The police think it's a mugging because his wallet is gone, but I think there's more to it."

"Why?"

He glanced around before answering. "Gary showed me a note he got a few days ago. The note threatened that something would happen to him if he continued to defend our client. It said he needed to make sure our client lost the trial, or he'd be sorry."

"Didn't he take it seriously?" I asked.

"Not really. He's had threats before, but nothing's ever come of them. It just makes him more determined to win, and he didn't think this case was any different, but now I'm not so sure."

"Did you tell the police?"

"Yes." He sat forward, exhausted. "They're looking into it, but I doubt they'll find anything."

"Let's get you home." I tugged on his arm, and he stood up. I put my arm around him, and we walked slowly to our car. "At least Gary will be okay, but what happens with the trial?"

He snorted. "That's the kicker. It's mine now. I have to take Gary's place." Chris shook his head, worried that now he was a target.

This was not good. "I don't understand. Why would someone want your client to lose? Who is your client anyway?"

"Adam Webb, of Webb Enterprises."

Chapter 5

"You're kidding me," I exclaimed.

"No. Why?"

"Because Uncle Joey mentioned a trial he was worried about, and he mentioned Webb Enterprises. It has to be the same one."

"Do you think he had anything to do with beating up Gary or threatening him?" Chris asked, appalled.

"I don't know," I said. "But I don't think so. I'm pretty sure he's on your side." I tried to remember what he had said about the trial, but could only come up with a name. "Do you know who David Barardini is?"

"Yes," Chris answered, immediately suspicious. "He's an accountant working on the case with us. He's pretty important to our case. Why? How do you know him?"

"He's Uncle Joey's man," I said, relieved. "So... at least that means Uncle Joey's on your side. He's not the one responsible for Gary's injuries."

"That's good... I guess," Chris said. We drove to Chris' office in silence. Chris had plenty on his mind, but he didn't say anything, so I kept my mouth shut, and tried not to listen. I did pick up that it was the bookkeeping that would make or break their case, so I had to figure that David Barardini, and what he did, was huge. It also bothered him that in a roundabout way, Chris must be working for Uncle Joey.

Yikes! He was right. How did that happen? But when I thought about it, it made sense. I mean... Uncle Joey had ties with the firm of Cohen, Larsen, and Pratt, especially considering his association with Stephen Cohen, one of the first partners. I hadn't even told Chris that it was Uncle Joey who'd really killed Stephen Cohen.

The fact that Kate, Stephen's daughter, was hired to work there was probably not a coincidence. It was to appease Uncle Joey's guilt, as well as have a lawyer in his pocket. So it only made sense that Uncle Joey used Chris' firm for not only himself, but his 'associates' as well.

With Stephen Cohen dead, it was John Larsen and Gary Pratt who ran the firm. With Gary in the hospital, that left Chris as the defending attorney since he was helping on the case. It also made him the next target for whoever wanted them to fail, and I was sure it had everything to do with Uncle Joey.

I pulled into Chris' parking garage and waited while he unlocked his car and got in. I made sure he was following behind as I began the drive home. If Chris was in trouble, I was bound and determined to get to the bottom of it before anything serious happened to him. Good thing I had an in with Uncle Joey.

⁊᙮᙭

The next morning came too early. Chris was in the shower when I dragged myself out of bed. We hadn't spoken much once we got home last night. Chris was exhausted, and I didn't want to pester him with questions. I also didn't want to let him in on my plans concerning Uncle Joey. He had enough to worry about with the trial.

I called the hospital and talked to Gary's wife for an update. She said he had awoken during the night, and was now sleeping peacefully. His injuries would keep him there for a few more days at least, maybe even a week.

I whipped up some eggs and toast for Chris' breakfast, and gave him the update while he ate. He finished up, in a hurry to leave and make sure all was ready for the day's arguments.

"Do you want me to come?" I asked.

He stopped in his tracks, just now realizing what I meant. "I'll have to think about it, but it might be a good idea. What are your plans for today?"

"I was thinking of going back to Novelty Creations for a bit, but I could come if you needed me." I hadn't updated him with the progress of my case, or told him about the kidnapping. It was on the tip of my tongue to tell him I'd saved a little girl yesterday, but there wasn't time now.

"I'll call you," he said. He gave me a quick peck on the lips and turned to leave. "Oh, and thanks for breakfast!"

The door shut on my response, which he wouldn't have heard anyway. Oh well. Now it was time to get the kids off to school. Savannah came downstairs, eager to talk about booking our trip. Which of course, I hadn't talked to Chris about either.

"I'll talk to dad at lunch," I promised. "And we'll book it tonight." That seemed to do the trick, and she went to school happy and eager to tell all her friends. I didn't have the heart to tell her to wait until we knew for sure. It made me a little bit angry, and I decided that I'd better make it a priority to talk to Chris about it today. All I really needed to do was check his schedule and make sure he was clear for the week we wanted to go. I could call his secretary and find out before I talked to him. That way, he wouldn't have a reason to wait on a decision or say no.

I got ready for the day, knowing I needed to look my best if I was going to court. Not only that, but I planned to pay Uncle Joey a visit to see if I could find out just exactly what he had to do with Webb Enterprises. I realized that I didn't even know what they were on trial for. I should've asked Chris, but I was too busy thinking of other things. Although, it didn't really matter, I just hoped they weren't guilty.

This time I wore some dark slacks with a short-sleeved white fitted blouse, and a gray vest. I had a fedora-style hat that matched, but I didn't want to look like I worked for the mob, so I left it at home. My four-inch black pumps rounded off the outfit, and I looked hot.

My first stop of the day was Novelty Creations. I found a parking place, and opened the door to go inside. The bell above the door jingled, and Emily came out of the back. "Hi," I called to her. "Remember me?"

"Yes," she smiled. "The pink teddy. How can I help you today?"

I closed the distance to the cash register where she was standing, and leaned against the counter like I had a secret to share. "Do you know anything about a shipment of underwear that the police confiscated as evidence to Keith's guilt?"

Her brows scrunched together, and surprise lit her eyes. "No. When did this happen?"

"I think it was before your mother died, or right after. I don't have an exact date. But when I talked to the police detective, he thought your mom's lawyer may have picked them up from the evidence room shortly after she died."

"My mom's lawyer?" Emily didn't know what I was talking about. "I didn't even know the police took a shipment, but there was so much going on at the time with her death, and Keith being arrested, it's kind of a blur."

"Could we check the books?" I asked. "Maybe it would show up there."

"Probably, but why is this important? What does the shipment have to do with anything?"

"Detective Williams thought the money might be hidden in the shipment. That's why it was confiscated in the first place, but he didn't find anything. He told me that your mother's lawyer might have picked the shipment up, but when I went to the evidence room, no one had signed for it. I thought it was still there, but when I checked, it was gone. The person in charge of the evidence room thought it must have been returned to you, and someone forgot to have the paperwork signed. So that brought me back here, to see if you knew anything about it, and if your records would tell you what happened to the shipment."

She was confused. This was the first she'd heard about a confiscated shipment. And she couldn't see her mother's lawyer picking it up. What was going on? "I can check our records, but I don't know if they will tell us much. As far as I know, everything I have balances out. Uncle Dean never told me anything, and I think he would have noticed a lost shipment."

The bell jingled, signaling another customer, and Emily pulled away. She frowned, thinking I wouldn't be happy to see who had just walked in.

"Morning ladies," Rob Felt said. I sighed and turned around. Oh great! How was I going to get rid of him?

Emily was wondering the same thing. "Can I help you?" she said.

"No, just looking." He made a show of examining the underwear on the closest table. He was thinking that he wasn't about to leave while I was still there. He could look at underwear all day if he had to, anything to find out what I was so interested in.

I turned back to Emily, and she shrugged. "I can let you look at the records on my computer, if you like," she whispered. "I'll stay here, and keep an eye on my customer."

"That would be great," I said.

"Let me just find the right place on the computer, and then you can go back."

I nodded, and she disappeared through the back door to the office. Waiting, I listened in on Felt's thoughts. He didn't hear what Emily said to me, but figured we were up to something so he came closer.

Emily came back, and nodded to me. I hurried around the counter and into the office, shutting the door firmly behind me. Sitting at the desk, I studied the records on the screen. Once I figured out what I was looking at, it was easy to understand the system. The records were meticulously done. Emily had pulled up the shipments around the date of her mother's death.

I was especially interested in the ones Keith had signed for, going back a little further in the records to see if there was a pattern. Nothing was out of place, and there was no sign of a confiscated shipment anywhere. I scrolled down closer to the date of Keith's arrest and found nothing missing. It didn't make sense.

I looked at the spreadsheet, and changed the window from shipments received to shipments sent. There were quite a few Internet orders listed here. Most were personal orders sent all over the country. Scrolling back to the time Keith worked there, I found more than one entry for shipments sent to the same address. Could this be it? I double-clicked on the shipment, and it brought up a purchase order. Under the company name it read Betty's Bra Bar, with an address right here in the city.

I'd never heard of them, but that didn't mean they didn't exist. Could that be where the stolen money was shipped? I checked one more time, and counted three shipments sent to that address, all within a six-month time span. The last was right before Keith was arrested. My heart raced with excitement, and I eagerly wrote down the address, determined to find out.

Emerging from the back, I found Emily following behind Felt, fixing the messes he made at each table. She was relieved to see me, and hurried around the back of the counter. "Did you find anything?" she asked.

"Not any missing shipments," I whispered. "But I did find several shipments Keith sent to Betty's Bra Bar. Have you ever heard of them?"

Emily's face turned red. "No... well... maybe." She was thinking she'd heard the name before. Keith joked that if he ever had his own store, that's what he'd call it, but it didn't exist. He'd just made it up. She was sure of it. "You have an address?" she asked.

"Yes," I answered, keeping my voice low. Felt had inched closer while we talked, and was now less than three feet away. Probably close enough to hear what we were saying. I pulled Emily into the office, and closed the door. "I'm going to check it out. You want to come with me?"

"Yes," she said. Glancing at the clock on the wall, she grabbed her purse and keys. "It's close enough to call this a lunch break, but you know, the nice thing about owning my own business is that I can take a break whenever I want."

"True," I agreed. I liked her spunk. "But Felt will probably follow us."

"Not if I can help it," she said with determination. "Stay here. I'll get rid of him and lock up. We'll go out the back and take my car. That should put him off long enough for us to make our escape."

"All right," I said. She left the door ajar, and I heard her telling Felt that she was closing the store for lunch. He didn't protest, just left in a hurry. I glanced around, looking for a back way out, and found a door that opened into a large room filled with plastic-covered inventory hanging on rolling racks and stacked on tables.

"Is this the way out?" I asked Emily, motioning toward the double-doors where trucks unloaded merchandise.

"One way, but not the way we're going. Right down here..." she motioned ahead, "is a staircase that leads to the underground parking lot that connects with the hotel behind my store. We have parking privileges since we were here first."

"Ah-hah." I chuckled. "Now I understand how we're going to lose Felt."

She smiled, and I followed her down the stairs to a door that opened into the parking garage. "My own private door," she said, holding up her key. "And the key to let me back in."

She led the way to a little red car parked nearby and unlocked the doors. We settled inside, and I told her the address. "It looks like it's across town on the west side close to Spring Hill. Do you know this area?"

"No," she shook her head. "Keith moved around a lot, so maybe he lived there. But even then, he's been gone for over a year, so I can't imagine anything of his still being there."

"True," I said. "But that doesn't mean the money couldn't be hidden there somewhere."

She nodded, thinking how awesome it would be to find all that money. Of course, she couldn't keep any of it, but still... maybe there was a reward? She glanced at me, thinking she'd have to share it, but half was better than nothing. How much money would she get?

I tuned her out. Thinking about getting a lot of money for nothing, and what you could do with it, was never a good thing. I had five million dollars once, and all it ever brought me was trouble and a couple of near-death experiences. Just thinking about it gave me the shivers.

We turned the corner onto a street with lots of little shops and fast food joints. "It should be right in there," I said. And there it was, Betty's Bra Bar. I could hardly believe it was real. The tiny storefront featured a small window with Betty's Bra Bar painted across the top and showing bras strapped around torso mannequins. "It's really here," I said with surprise. "I thought for sure it would be bogus."

"Me too," Emily said. She was thinking the layout looked a lot like her store, and it was making her mad. Had Keith set up a store just like hers, using her inventory? This was outrageous!

"I don't think it's as nice as your store," I said. "And it looks pretty small too. Plus, they probably just sell bras."

"Yeah, maybe." She sniffed. She was eager to go inside and see who was running the place. The parking to all the shops was in the back, and we found a place by some dumpsters.

"Before we go in, we need a game plan," I cautioned. "We should pretend we're customers, and we're checking the place out. Let's not give ourselves away, or have any confrontations. Okay?"

"Sure," she agreed, eager to proceed.

We went inside to the familiar sound of a bell jingling over our heads. A pretty woman with dark hair and eyes came out from the back. "Hi. Can I help you?" she asked.

"We were just driving by and noticed your store," I answered. "We thought we'd come inside, and take a look at what you've got."

"Well, take your time. The tables and racks have all the sizes you'd need."

"Thanks," I said.

She smiled, and rearranged the papers and pencils on the counter. She hadn't been expecting her client for another half hour, and was relieved that we were real customers. She hoped one of us would buy something. It made things more legitimate that way. "That table in the middle is fifty percent off today and tomorrow," she called, acting on impulse. "It's a great bargain if you find something you like."

I smiled, and moved to the middle table to check it out. There were some pretty nice things here and, at fifty percent off, I could get a good bra for less than fifteen dollars. When I found the push-up bras, I knew I'd hit the jackpot. These looked like the bras that sold for fifty dollars at another store.

I picked a couple of them up, and took them back to the counter. "Do you have a fitting room where I can try these on?"

"Yes," she smiled. "Right over here." She ushered me to a small room in the back corner, and I hurried inside. A twinge of guilt went through me as I caught the thought from Emily that I was a turncoat, but her thoughts ended when I shut the door. Oops, probably not the best move on my part.

I tried them on as fast as I could, worrying what Emily might do or say without me there. I came out of the room, barely put together, and found things just as I'd left them. The proprietor was still standing behind the counter, and Emily was looking through the racks.

"How did those work for you?" the woman asked.

"Good... really good," I said. "They fit perfectly. I'll take them."

She smiled, hoping she'd made a customer out of me. At the same time, she shouldn't be selling her inventory so cheap. But it was worth it for a sale. She could easily fix the books to look like I paid the proper amount, and supplement it with the earnings from her real job.

She swiped my credit card, and I signed the receipt while she bagged my bras. Her eyes narrowed as she looked at Emily. What was she doing? I glanced over my shoulder to find Emily with nearly the whole table of bras in her arms. She had done the math, and knew that buying these bras at fifty percent off was better than the cost she could get from her supplier. If this lady was stupid enough to sell them for that price, she wasn't about to pass up the opportunity to dish out some serious pain to her competitor.

"I'll take all of them," Emily said, dropping them on the counter.

"Oh... I'm so sorry," the owner responded. "I forgot to tell you the deal is limited to three bras per customer. I hope you understand."

"Yeah, I get it," Emily sighed with defeat. She knew it was too good to be true. What was this lady up to? "Since she bought two, I'll buy four. That should even it out." She smiled, but her eyes held a challenge in them.

"Sure," the lady nodded. Maybe her little ploy had been too overboard. She should have said they were only twenty-five percent off. Now she was stuck with making up the difference for six bras out of her own pocket. Good thing she had plenty to cover it. She didn't know how anybody could make it in this business.

Glad we were done, she rang up Emily's purchases. Her client would be there any minute, and it was always best not to have any witnesses. Emily took her purchases, and we walked to the door. "Thanks for coming in," the woman said with a cheerful wave.

"That was weird," Emily said. "She won't make any money selling her stuff that cheap. I wonder what's really going on."

"Me too," I agreed. "Let's drive around the block and park across the street for a minute. I want to see who her next client is."

"What next client?" Emily asked.

Oops. "I just want to see if she has more clients, and if no one comes after a few minutes, we can go."

"Okay," Emily agreed, thinking I was kind of odd. It was like I was making things up just to stick around. "But only for a few minutes. I have to get back to my store."

After she parked across the street, we sat quietly. "So... did any of those bras look like they came from your inventory?" I asked.

"No," she said. "But they looked like knock-offs from Victoria's Secret. Either that, or the real thing. I don't know how she does it, unless they were stolen or something."

"Look," I said, motioning toward the store. "Someone's going in."

A man dressed in jeans with a jacket, baseball cap, and dark glasses rounded the corner from the parking lot, and entered the store. A minute later the shop owner glanced out the window, and turned the open sign to closed.

"I don't know what she's doing," Emily said. "But it's not selling bras."

What if her store was a front for something else? That might explain the reason she wanted to sell some bras to us. But what did she do? I could imagine all kinds of things, but I wouldn't know for sure unless I got close enough to hear the thoughts of that guy who'd gone in.

"We'd better get back," I said. "I don't know what's going on over there, but I intend to find out."

"When you do, will you let me know?" Emily asked. "It's got to be related to Keith somehow. And I'd like to know what's going on."

"Sure, but I can't guarantee anything."

We got back to her store in less than ten minutes, and I was hoping I could make it back to the shop before the man left. I figured that if I stood in front of one of the shops beside Betty's Bra Bar, I could follow him to the parking lot and hear his thoughts. He could get in his car, and I could get in mine. It should work as long as he didn't suspect me of following him.

I exited from the front door of Novelty Creations, and hurried to my car, making it back to Betty's Bra Bar in record time. Pulling into the parking lot, I hoped I hadn't missed him already. I jumped out, and walked around the back of the store beside Betty's to the front sidewalk. This was a hardware store, with lots of knobs and handles. I glanced next door, and was relieved to see the closed sign still up. That meant he was still there.

I leaned over, examining the display in the window with great care. From the corner of my eye, I glimpsed the man leaving the shop. He walked straight toward me, instead of going to the parking lot. As he passed I 'heard' him thinking how funny it would be to give my butt a swat since it was sticking out so far.

I straightened, but kept my indignation to myself, and waited until he was a few yards ahead before I started following. I didn't know how long I could stay behind him before he noticed, but my luck held out as he turned toward the convenience store on the corner. This was perfect. I could get a Diet Coke, and listen to him at the same time.

There were several other people in the store, but I concentrated on him and tuned the others out. He moved to the cooler and grabbed a six-pack of beer, thinking it was time to celebrate. What he had in his pocket held his freedom, and it was worth every penny.

He noticed me standing nearby and grew suspicious. Was I following him? I grabbed the package of beef jerky in front of me, and made my way to the soft drink dispenser. After filling my cup with Diet Coke and two squirts of cherry flavoring, I stood in line to pay. He stayed in the back of the store watching me. He'd noticed me looking in the hardware store window, and was thinking that if I was following him, or knew what he was up to, he might have to kill me. If I stuck around or tried talking to him, it was almost a sure thing. Out of habit, he stroked the knife in his pocket.

I quickly paid and hurried out, practically running to my car. Out of breath from hurrying so fast, I jumped inside, and immediately locked the car doors. As I fastened my seat belt, I watched to see if he was following. With no sign of him, I started the car, and pulled out of the parking lot. I had to stop at a red light, and there he was, waiting to cross the street. I kept my face forward, only turning my eyes to see if he recognized me. Before I could tell, the light turned green, and I pushed on the gas. Watching him in my rearview mirror, I noticed his head turning to follow my progress.

A chill went down my spine. That was too creepy. It was probably best from now on to concentrate on the lady in the shop and leave her clients alone. If only I knew what she was up to. The client had thought something about his freedom being worth the cost of what she had given him. But what could that mean?

I checked the time to find it was nearly twelve-thirty. Usually, court was recessed anywhere between noon and one for the lunch hour, so this was my chance to stop and see if I could talk to Chris. If David Barardini was there, I could also check on him, and hear what he was thinking. For Chris' sake, it would be helpful to know what was going on.

I got there just in time. The gavel sounded, and the judge dismissed everyone for one hour. Chris was seated in the front with his client, and I had to fight against the crowd to get to him. His head was bent toward the defendant, who had to be Adam Webb, and there was another man I didn't know seated next to him.

I slowed my steps, not wanting to interrupt, and worried that Chris wouldn't be happy I was there. I should probably wait until they got up to leave before I barged in on them. Sliding into a back seat, I tried to untangle their thoughts amid those of everyone else in the room.

The man next to Chris was thinking the trial was going well, and the evidence from the books corroborated his story. There was a glitch that no one had picked up on, but if the prosecuting attorney found it, he was prepared to set his plan in motion. It would be better if he didn't have to though, because he hated framing an innocent man. Of course, it was better than the alternative.

This guy had to be David Barardini. He looked just like Nick, only with graying hair. I wondered if Chris knew anything about this 'glitch' in his defense. I couldn't pick up what Adam Webb and Chris were talking about as easily. It was something to do with... food? Ah... where they were going for lunch. It was a safe bet I could probably interrupt them now.

I stood just as Chris and Adam slid their chairs back. The courtroom was nearly empty by now, and Chris spotted me when he turned around. Surprise at seeing me turned into pleasure, and I smiled with happiness. His left brow lifted, and he smiled slowly, thinking I looked hot in my outfit.

Adam and David noticed his slow perusal, and turned curious stares in my direction. David wondered who I was, running through a list in his head of who I could be; never once thinking I was Chris' wife. Adam was more perceptive, thinking I looked even better in person than the photo in Chris' office. He totally understood why Chris was happy to see me. I gave him a bright smile in response, and decided I liked him.

Chris greeted me warmly, and introduced me to David and Adam. David smiled, keeping his surprise to himself. Then his eyes narrowed as he remembered that I was 'that Shelby' who worked for Uncle Joey. He hoped I wouldn't give him away to Chris. That might complicate things. Oops, too late for that.

"Do you mind if I borrow Chris for a moment?" I asked. "I won't keep him long."

"Not at all," Adam said.

"I'll meet you in the food court," Chris assured him, and turned toward me with a questioning glance. "What's up?" he asked.

"I just wanted to talk to you for a minute. How's the trial going?"

"Pretty well," he said. "It's a good thing I've been so involved with the case already, otherwise I could be in trouble."

"Have you heard anything about who beat up Gary or why?" I asked.

"No. In fact, it doesn't make a lot of sense," Chris answered. "I've been trying to think who would gain if we lose, and the only thing I can come up with is someone with a personal grudge against Adam."

"But if Adams loses, won't that put Webb Enterprises on the line? You should ask Adam who his competition is, or find out if he has any enemies. But you're right. It could be a personal thing too."

"That's a good idea," Chris said. "I'll ask Adam what he thinks."

"You should include David as well. He might know better than Adam, especially since he has connections with Uncle Joey."

"Umm... yeah, I forgot about that." Chris considered what I said, but was convinced that David knew what he was doing with the books. It was all legal and admissible in court. He checked his watch and scowled. There wasn't much time to eat and he was starving.

"There is one more thing I need to ask you before I go," I said. "Savannah and Josh are really looking forward to going to Orlando. I promised Savannah I'd talk to you today so we could book our vacation tonight. I can check with your secretary about the week we want to go, and make sure your schedule is clear. Is that all right?"

"Yeah, I guess so." Chris tugged me out the door, thinking I could walk him to the food court. A sigh escaped him. He felt pushed into a corner about the vacation, but since he hadn't been around much, it was probably his fault. Plus, he felt guilty for not spending much time lately with the kids or me, so it was probably the right thing to do. Who knew, it might even be fun.

I smiled, happy he was resigned to his fate. "I'll go by your office on the way home and clear it with your secretary."

"Okay," he said. "By the way, how's your 'case of the stolen money' going?"

"I'm making progress," I said. "I'll have to tell you about it when we have more time."

"Okay." He felt bad that he had been gone so much. "It's a quick walk from here to the food court. Do you want to grab some lunch with us?" Chris didn't think the others would mind, especially since they'd gone over everything they needed to cover in the trial for the rest of the day.

"Sure. That would be nice," I agreed, happy that he wasn't ready to say goodbye. We entered the food court and got in line for a sandwich. Carrying our trays, we found the others, who were happy to make room for us.

"I'm glad you joined us," Adam said to me. "It's always nice to have a pretty face to look at. Helps with the digestion." He was thinking I was like a breath of fresh air. This trial was getting to him. He couldn't wait until it was over and he could breathe again.

I was surprised that none of the stress showed on his face. He didn't want to think about the trial, so I asked him about his family. Mild curiosity about me came from David, but his thoughts centered mostly on our conversation.

It was time to leave before I knew it, and I walked with Chris toward the courthouse before taking a detour to his office. We said goodbye, and he was walking away when I heard it. Someone was thinking about Chris, and how he was the other lawyer they needed to take out. Unless he agreed to lose the case. He'd start with threats, but if that didn't work, he'd hurt him lots worse than the other guy.

"Chris!" I called, my heart pounding. He glanced over his shoulder, hearing the panic in my voice. As he reached my side, the threatening thoughts faded into the distance. The person was gone... for now. "What's wrong?" Chris asked.

"Someone was here," I whispered. "Watching you. Thinking about taking you out. They're going to threaten you first, give you some time to respond, but then they're going to hurt you worse than they hurt Gary." I clutched him. "Chris... I'm scared. This isn't a joke."

"I can see that," he said, frowning. "At least it sounds like I have some time. I'll be all right for now, but I've got to go. I can't walk in there late."

"Okay," I said. "But watch your back, and if you can, try and figure out what is going on."

He nodded, gave me a quick kiss, and rushed toward the courthouse. I watched until he disappeared inside, worry tightening my stomach. I had to find out what was going on. I had a feeling it had everything to do with Uncle Joey, and it made me mad.

Why did he always have to be involved in our lives? Although, for a change, this didn't have anything to do with me, and upon further consideration, I was in the perfect position to get to the bottom of this. Uncle Joey or not, no matter what I had to do, or who I had to do it to, anyone threatening my man was going to be sorry.

Chapter 6

I entered Chris' office and talked to his secretary about our plans for Orlando. We chatted about our vacation, and she was happy to clear his schedule for the week we wanted to go. Savannah would be thrilled.

That accomplished, I decided to pay a visit to Uncle Joey. He'd wonder why I was there, and I had to decide if I should tell him what I knew about the trial, or listen to his thoughts and figure it out that way. Of course, when I thought about it, I really didn't know anything about the trial. And it was probably better to level with Uncle Joey, since we were on the same side anyway.

As I pulled into the parking garage, it suddenly occurred to me that Felt wasn't following, and I didn't have to worry about him. Yay! At least something had gone right today.

I got off the elevator on the twenty-sixth floor, and entered Thrasher Development. Jackie wasn't at her desk, and I worried that I'd missed Uncle Joey. Maybe they were at lunch? I probably should have called first.

Trying to figure out what to do next, I was startled by a bulky figure ambling down the hall. Doug. Since Doug had taken over Ramos' security job, maybe I could persuade

Ramos to be my husband's bodyguard once he came back. Of course, Chris would hate that. Probably Ramos would too.

"Hi, Shelby," Doug greeted me. Caution was the only thing that filtered through his thoughts.

"Hi," I said. It almost seemed like he was guarding them. Now why would he do that?

"Is Uncle Joey here?" I asked.

"No," he answered quickly. "He and Jackie are gone somewhere.

"For lunch?"

"Yeah, for lunch." He was thinking that I complicated things, but it... He cut his thoughts off with an effort. "They should be back soon. Do you want to wait?" He hadn't meant to say that, but I flustered him.

"Sure, I'll wait."

He didn't expect me to say that either. "Okay. You can wait in his office if you like."

I shrugged. "Fine. Have you heard anything from Ramos?" I asked.

"No." He was thinking *yes*, and when I raised my eyebrows, he changed his answer. "I mean yes... he'll be back soon."

"That's great," I said.

"Um... I've got to get back to my office." He backed away from me, then turned and hurried down the hall. From what I could gather, he didn't like being around me very much. Now why was that?

I turned in the opposite direction toward Uncle Joey's office, and went inside. I liked the décor in here, and the view from the window was spectacular. After watching the people and traffic below without a sign of Uncle Joey, I decided to give him a call.

He answered after the first ring. "Shelby... what can I do for you?"

"I'm at your office," I explained. "I need to talk to you about something. When do you think you'll be back?"

"I'm on my way right now," he said. "I'll be there in about ten minutes."

"Okay, see you then." Knowing I had a few minutes, I decided to see if his safe was in the same place as it was before the remodel, and tugged on the landscape painting hiding it. I figured it would swing out. Instead, the painting practically flew off the wall. I reached out to grab it before it crashed, but the corner hit the floor, and a piece of the frame broke off.

Damn! At least the glass didn't break... but still! I searched the floor for the broken piece, then got on my hands and knees to look under the couch. I finally found it lodged beneath the couch, and strained to reach it. With a grunt, I clasped it in my palm just as the door opened behind me.

A deep chuckle sounded. "Babe. What are you doing down there?" It was Ramos!

I scrambled to get up, chagrined that he caught me in such an embarrassing position. "I... uh... accidentally knocked the painting off the wall. I'm just trying to put it back together before Uncle Joey gets here."

"Let me see." He held out his hand for the piece. With a red face, I plopped it in his palm, and turned to heft the painting onto the couch.

"It goes right there." I pointed to the bottom corner. "Maybe we can fix it with some superglue, and he won't know."

"I won't know what?" Uncle Joey said, coming into the room.

"You said ten minutes," I blurted. He fixed a pointed stare at me. Oh great! Now I had to tell him the truth. "Um... that I accidentally knocked the painting off the wall, and the frame broke. But I can fix it. See... I just need to glue this piece in here..." I took the piece from Ramos, "and it will be good as new." I pushed the piece into the corner and it held, but it looked pretty bad. It was easy to see it was broken. "Well... almost as good as new."

"Don't worry about it," Uncle Joey said, his voice tinged with amusement. "Looking for the safe, huh?"

What could I say? "I was just wondering if it was still there." I glanced at the wall. "Guess not."

Uncle Joey's lips twisted in amusement. Ramos was thinking that he hadn't minded the view, and I gave him a dirty look. His eyes widened, and then he smiled even bigger. Yup... he was right, even if I wouldn't admit it.

No matter how hard I tried, I couldn't keep my exasperation from showing, so I quickly turned my back on him.

Uncle Joey put the painting back on the wall, thinking this wasn't the first time it had fallen. He had the painting situated just right on the hanger, so that if someone moved it, it would fall off. That corner piece had broken several times now. He should probably get it fixed, except that he always knew if someone had moved it from how it looked after. Kind of like an alarm, only better, because he usually knew who had been in his office. And the look on my face...

"Argh!" I said, throwing my arms up. He knew I was listening, and I called him a few dirty names in my mind. Thank goodness he couldn't hear me.

"So... how come you're in my office?" Uncle Joey asked.

"Doug told me to wait for you in here."

"Doug?" Uncle Joey frowned. "He was here?"

"Yes," I said cautiously. "Why?"

"Because I told him to clear out this morning. He was gone when I left to get Ramos from the airport. I wonder what was he doing back here?" He glanced at me. "Did you pick up anything from him?"

I glanced pointedly at Ramos, but he just grinned. Uncle Joey didn't seem to notice, or care that Ramos was listening. I pursed my lips. I could play this game too. "He told me you and Jackie went to lunch, although now that I think about it, I insinuated that that's where you were. He just kind of went along with it. He didn't want to talk to me. After telling me to wait in your office, he hurried back to the security room." There... I hadn't given myself away.

Uncle Joey knew I hadn't exactly answered his question. He turned to Ramos. "You'd better check the office and equipment for any kind of tampering." Ramos nodded and left.

"Why did you fire Doug?" I asked.

"The guy who recommended him didn't realize that Doug's last employer was missing a few thousand dollars the day after Doug quit his job."

"So Doug stole it?"

"He couldn't prove it, but it looked that way to him." Uncle Joey shrugged. "I don't want anyone in my office that I can't trust, especially with my security. So I had to let him go." He paused, and pinned me with his gaze. "What was he thinking? You can answer now that Ramos is gone."

I smirked, but it wasn't worth arguing about. "That's the strange thing. It was almost like he was guarding his thoughts. I know he didn't like being around me. I flustered him. But that's all I got. It's too bad you didn't wait until I was here before you fired him. I would have known if he really had stolen that money."

Uncle Joey sighed. "It doesn't matter now. He's gone. Ramos is back. I don't need anyone else."

"Did Ramos find out anything in Seattle?"

"Only that Kate isn't there."

"Does he think she's dead?"

"No," Uncle Joey shook his head. "She was there, but she left about the same time Hodges was killed, and Ramos couldn't find any trace of her."

"That's too bad," I said. "Do you think she'd come back here?"

Uncle Joey huffed. "Not likely. She knows I want my money back. This is the last place she'd come. I guess I'll have to hire a good private investigator to find her. You know anyone?" He thought maybe I'd want the job, since I had my own agency.

"Oh no... I don't want the job. My agency is a consulting agency, not a private investigator thing. There is this guy who's been following me though. He might take the job."

"You mean that same guy from the Museum Gala that Chris used your stun gun on?" He chuckled with derision. "I don't think so. Why is he following you?"

"I'm looking for the stolen bank money, and since that was his job first, he won't give up. So he follows me around, thinking I'll lead him to it, and he can get the reward money."

"Sounds exasperating. Maybe he could have an accident and end up in the hospital for a while. It could be arranged." He was serious. He'd do that for me?

"Tempting... but no," I said quickly, before I took him up on it. "But that reminds me of why I'm here. It's about the trial you were concerned about? The one with Webb Enterprises?"

Uncle Joey shuttered his thoughts. "Yes. What about it?"

"Did you know someone beat up Adam Webb's lawyer?"

"Yes, I heard." He was wondering how I knew Adam's name.

"Do you know why?" I persisted.

"Why do you want to know?" his eyes narrowed with suspicion.

"Because Chris took over the case, and now he's a target. I was there earlier, and I heard someone thinking about threatening him to lose the case, and if he doesn't... well, they'll hurt him. Worse than they hurt Gary. Why would someone want Chris to lose the case?"

"Hmm..." Uncle Joey knew the answer to that, he just didn't want me to know.

"It's because of you," I said, picking up some of his thoughts.

"Yes," he huffed. "But that's not for you to know. I'll take care of it. I'll find out who it is and stop him." He was thinking about having him ground into fish food. He owned a plant.

"Okay," I said quickly, before I heard any more. "Then I'll try not to worry about it, but if you need my help with this, you've got it."

"Good," he nodded. "I'll keep that in mind."

"Well, I guess I'll go then."

"Wait. There is something you can do for me." He was thinking that he needed to shake things up, especially if someone was after him. He took a seat at his desk, and pulled a manila envelope with a substantial bulge from the bottom drawer. "I want you to deliver this for me. The address is on the top. Give it to Nick, and come back here. I want to know what he's thinking."

"What is it?" I asked.

"It's better you don't know," he said. "Take my word for it. But don't worry. You'll be safe. It's nothing dangerous."

"Okay," I said, a little nervous. I didn't want to become his 'mule'. "What if Nick's not there? Should I leave it with someone else?"

"No... bring it back here." He handed the package to me. It wasn't as heavy as I thought. "Will it fit in your purse?" he asked. "That would be best."

"Yes, probably." I crammed it in, but couldn't zip my purse up.

"Good." He checked his watch. "See you in about half an hour."

I left the office, seeing no sign of Ramos or Jackie on my way out. Where was everyone? I got in my car, and pulled out of the parking garage. That's when I realized I didn't have the address in front of me because it was on the package. I turned right, and managed to drive while wrestling the package out of my purse without looking down. I heard a rip and cringed. Had I just torn the damn thing?

I left it alone until I came to a stoplight. The package was halfway out of my purse with a gaping hole torn down the side. Dammit! I wasn't supposed to look inside, in fact, I didn't want to look inside, but I couldn't drop it off like that. I needed tape. I could probably fix it without looking inside.

I found a supermarket and parked in the corner. Taping it might not be the best thing. They'd know it was tampered with. Maybe I should just buy a new manila envelope, and repackage it. If I did that, I'd know what it was. But Uncle Joey wouldn't know that, and neither would Nick.

I pushed the package under my seat and locked the car. In the store, I found the manila envelopes and the packing tape, and bought them both, still unsure how to proceed. Knowing what was in the package could give me leverage where Uncle Joey was concerned. That would be a good thing. It would also help me decipher Nick's thoughts. Another good point. On the bad side? I might be breaking the law, and it would be better if I didn't know.

I heaved a sigh, and pulled the package out from under my seat. The rip was on the bottom. If I shook what was inside to the top, I could fold the envelope, and tape it up without looking. I pulled out the tape, straightened the envelope, and looked. I couldn't help it. I figured it was drugs or money, so what did it matter?

Only it wasn't drugs or money. It was a hard-drive from a computer. At least that's what it looked like. Dang. Feeling bad because I had no self-control, I quickly folded it up, and put lots of packing tape around it. This package was not going to rip again.

I plugged the address into my GPS system and followed the instructions, arriving at a building called Global Interactive. The building seemed fairly new, with massive steel beams and glass windows. I entered the double doors into a large mezzanine with a security officer standing guard and a reception desk in front of a security checkpoint. There was no getting inside to the elevators without the proper ID. Kind of like the FBI. What kind of an organization was this?

I smiled at the receptionist, told her I was there to see Nick Barardini, and gave her my name. She asked me to take a seat while she let him know I was there. A small sitting area with some chairs and a couch were arranged nearby. I sat in plush leather, enjoying the comfort, and looked through the magazines strategically placed on the coffee table. They were all about new technology and science. Not quite my cup of tea. A few minutes later, Nick came through the security checkpoint toward me. He smiled with pleasure to see me, and I stood to greet him.

"Hi Shelby. Please sit down. What brings you here?" He sat on the edge of the couch and leaned forward, his elbows resting on his knees, and giving me his full attention.

"Uncle Joey sent me with a package," I said nervously. "It's in my purse. I don't know if I should just hand it over, or if there is some protocol I should follow."

Nick stifled a laugh, thinking it was funny how I was being all spy-like. But he could play along. "Ah, the package. Yes. Good thinking, we don't want anyone to see you give it to him." He glanced at the security guard while he thought up a plan. "This is what we'll do. When you stand up to leave you'll give me a hug with the purse between us. I'll reach inside, take the package, and slip it into my jacket. Stay close until you know I have it. I'll kiss your cheek as a signal." That last bit was pure inspiration.

He stood up, but when I didn't move, he sat back down. "Shelby? Is something wrong?"

"I know what you're thinking, but it's not going to work." Did I really say that? I took the package out of my purse, and handed it to him. In a blink, it disappeared inside his jacket. "You do know what it is, don't you?"

"Yes, Mr. Manetto called and told me you were bringing it." He was disappointed. "What gave me away?" he asked.

I smiled. "You were enjoying yourself at my expense a little too much."

His eyes narrowed, I was pretty shrewd, but I was wrong about the package. It really was better that no one saw me give it to him. He smiled, noticing my widening eyes. If he didn't know better, he'd think I realized I'd almost blown it. "Tell Mr. Manetto thanks. I hope he sends all of his correspondence this way."

"Sure," I said. "But don't count on it." This guy totally disconcerted me.

He chuckled, and we both stood. I held my purse like a shield in front of me, and he leaned in for a quick hug before turning away. I let out my breath, and left the building a little light-headed. What was that all about?

It wasn't until I pulled the straps of my purse over my shoulder that I heard something crinkle. I glanced down to find a small envelope tucked inside. How had he done that? Probably when he hugged me. What had I just done? It felt like stuff I saw on TV with spies and espionage. Of course, I could be wrong, and Uncle Joey was just sending his hard drive for Nick to fix since he worked with computers. That's probably all it was.

Feeling better, I drove back to Thrasher Development. I arrived to find Jackie sitting at her desk. "How are thing's going?" I asked. "Has Miguel settled in?"

"Yes," she said. "He loves it here." She was thinking everything would be perfect if Carlotta, Miguel's mother, was out of the picture. She hated her. "Joe enrolled him in a private school and he's doing quite well. He wants to go into business administration." She was so proud of him, like he was her own son.

"I'll bet Uncle Joey's happy about that."

"Yes, he is." She was thinking things were going well, at least with Miguel. She couldn't say that for the rest of it. The trial, firing Doug, and wondering what Kate was up to was worrisome. Of course, there was always something to worry about. That was just business as usual.

"How did Doug take it?" I asked. "Did he seem surprised, like he'd been wrongly accused? Or guilty, like he'd been caught?"

"Um..." My question caught her off-guard, but she considered it. "He didn't defend himself, so I guess he took it in stride. But he wasn't happy about it. He controlled his anger, but I could sense it boiling under the surface. Does that mean he's innocent? I don't know. I'm just glad Ramos is back."

"Yeah, me too."

"Joe's in his office. He told me you were coming. You can go on back." She smiled, her thoughts turning to what Joe had told her about me, and how I'd knocked the painting off the wall. That would have been hilarious. She wished she could have seen it.

I turned away with a sigh. It wasn't that funny. I knocked on Uncle Joey's door and went in. He sat behind his desk and beckoned me to take a seat. Ramos was already there, fiddling with a device that looked an awful lot like the bug the CIA had planted in my house.

Uncle Joey stood and moved to the bookcase against the wall. He pulled the tip of a book down, and a panel on the book shelf below slid open, revealing a safe.

So that's where it was. After opening the safe, Ramos set the bug inside. Uncle Joey closed it. When everything was back in place, he turned to me. "Ramos found eight of those throughout the office. That one was in here. We left the others where they are until we decide what to do, but for now, this room is the only one where we can talk safely."

"Did Doug plant them?" I asked.

"Yes, we're certain of it," Ramos answered. "We just don't know who he's working for."

"That's not good," I said. "Is there some way you can track the bugs back to their source?"

"No," Ramos answered.

"Then you should just flush them all," I said. "I mean, since you fired Doug, he can't replant them. And it would be better if they were gone. Did you check the phones? Could they have a tap on them?"

"The phones are clean," Ramos said. "So that would rule out the FBI. It's probably not a government agency."

"Shelby's right. Get rid of them," Uncle Joey said. "I want Doug to know we're on to him. Getting rid of the bugs might be an incentive for him to come back, and we can take care of him then. I'd also like to know who he's working for."

"Sounds good," Ramos said, and quietly left the room.

"How did it go?" Uncle Joey asked. He was thinking of the drop to Nick.

"Oh, it went all right," I said. "I wasn't prepared for it though, and Nick was fooling around like it was spy stuff."

Uncle Joey's brows drew together. "So... you didn't look in the package?" He was thinking about the phone call he got from Nick, telling him about the tape job. He knew I'd looked. "I thought I told you not to look inside."

"You did," I said. "But it was an accident. When I pulled it out of my purse to see the address, it ripped open, and I had to tape it back together. I caught a just a tiny glimpse of it, but I didn't look real hard. I promise."

"That's a relief," he said sardonically. "But don't worry. It's not that big of a deal. Nick fixes my computers, and I just needed him to take a look at my hard drive."

"Oh," I nodded, relieved. "That's what I thought was going on." But it really wasn't. From his thoughts, I knew he was lying through his teeth. But I played along since this was a case of self-preservation. "It's great to have someone you trust to work on your computer."

"Yes," Uncle Joey agreed, hoping he'd fooled me. "So what do you think about Nick? Is he trustworthy?"

"Yeah, as far as I could tell. Oh... that reminds me, he left a little something in my purse." I pulled out the small envelope. "I think it's for you." I handed it to Uncle Joey, and he quickly pocketed it before I got a good look at it, but he was thinking it was the thumb drive he needed.

"Thanks." Uncle Joey realized I might have heard about the thumb drive, so he quickly changed subjects. "I've been thinking about the trial. I want to find out who's threatening your husband, and I've got an idea, but I could use your help." He knew I wouldn't refuse.

"Sure. What can I do?"

"I'd like you to come to Webb Enterprises tomorrow. I have a meeting at eight, and you could attend with me. There are a few people it might be good to have you 'listen' to. Then we'll know if any of them have a hidden agenda to thwart the trial, what their plan is, and why they would do it."

"All right," I agreed. "As long as it helps Chris. How are you connected to Webb Enterprises?"

He believed it would help Chris, but it would help him even more. "I'm a member of the board." He was thinking that he held most of the stock in the company. "What you hear will help Chris, but you can't tell him. He can't know what you're doing. It could ruin the case if he finds out you've been involved."

"But if I find out something useful that he needs to know, shouldn't I tell him?" I asked.

"No." Uncle Joey was firm on this. "Too much information might be harmful to your husband." He was thinking that it was just as harmful to me. "Sometimes, it's better to know as little as possible."

"I think I've heard that from someone," I said. "Oh yeah... it was you."

He smiled, not at all bothered that I was displeased with him. "That's not all," he continued, pushing me even further and enjoying every minute of it. "I might need your help at the club. You'll have to pretend you're one of my security people. But it should work." He was thinking it would be worth it to see the looks on his associates' faces when he brought me into their prestigious little club. He could get away with it if I pretended to be his bodyguard.

"I'll give you a call about that one," he continued. "It will be soon, probably tomorrow night. You'll have to sneak out, but you can do that, right? Just tell Chris you have to go to a meeting or something. Or you're going out with your friends. I'm sure he'd understand."

"You want me to lie to my husband?" I asked. "I'm not sure I can do that." I had to draw the line somewhere.

Uncle Joey could see that he'd pushed me a little too far. He decided to put it back on my shoulders and not be so helpful, especially since I didn't appreciate it. "You can handle it how you like. Either way, I need you to be there. Just remember... this is Chris' life we're talking about."

My stomach clenched, and I nodded. "If it means saving him, I'll do whatever it takes." Lying to Chris was nothing if I could save him from getting hurt. I'd just have to make sure he didn't find out.

"Good. I'll see you here in my office at seven-thirty tomorrow morning. Don't be late."

I left Thrasher Development with a huge weight on my shoulders. I knew that Uncle Joey was using me for more than helping my husband. Because of that, I worried about the meeting in the morning.

When Uncle Joey thought about owning most of the stock in the company, he seemed to be gloating, like he'd pulled one over on them. So, if he'd gotten all those shares by illegal means, he wouldn't want anyone to know. Plus, he'd want to know if anyone did know, because they would be the person who'd want him to go to prison and want Chris to lose the trial. He certainly wouldn't want Chris to know that.

Of course, I could be totally wrong, and maybe Uncle Joey had done nothing illegal. But I wouldn't bet on it. So did that mean the person threatening Chris wanted to expose Uncle Joey? If that were the case, did that make him a good guy? What would I do then? There had to be more to it, and thinking about it like this was driving me crazy. I'd just have to wait and see what happened tomorrow.

I pulled into my driveway just as Savannah got home from school. I told her the good news about our vacation, and we spent the next hour planning. She'd done some more research on places to stay, and we talked to her friend's mom who was a travel agent. It was seriously exciting to finally book our hotel and airfare. It also lifted my spirits to have something to look forward to and take my mind off my troubles.

Chris called to tell me he'd be late. "That's fine," I said. "Just make sure you have someone walk you to your car. Maybe you can call the security people from your building. They shouldn't mind, especially since Gary got beat up there."

"I'll be careful," he said.

Since I couldn't read his mind over the phone, I didn't know if that meant he'd get security or not. "Are you sure?" I prodded.

"Yes. I have it covered."

"What does that mean? That you're getting security, or something else? Can't you be more specific?"

"Shelby," Chris said sternly. "David and I are leaving together. Okay? I told him about the threats, and we're both prepared."

"Is he packing?" I asked, knowing I probably shouldn't.

Chris sighed. "I don't know, but probably. I'll see you soon." He disconnected.

That didn't go so well. Now I knew why I didn't like to put my shields up around Chris. We communicated better when I could read his mind. I huffed, realizing that reading his mind had made our relationship better in some ways. Not all the time. He hated that I knew his thoughts, but lately, I'd learned how to keep things to myself. I was getting used to it and using it to my advantage. He may not like it, but we were making it work. Now I just had to figure out how to tell him about my involvement with Uncle Joey and how it related to his case. It pained me to realize this was one of those times I might have to lie to him.

After dinner was all cleaned up and put away, it was a relief to hear the back door open and know Chris was home safely. Savannah heard it too, and rushed to tell him about our vacation plans. His face slackened with bewilderment, and I realized I should have warned him over the phone.

With Savannah's enthusiasm bubbling over, it didn't take him long to warm up to the idea. My heart softened to see them with their heads together. Josh entered the conversation, and we all migrated to the computer to check the Internet for all the fun things we could do in Orlando. The kids went to bed happy, and contentment warmed my heart.

Chris pulled me into his arms. "I think I'm excited for our trip," he said, surprised. "You must have cleared the dates with my secretary."

"Yup. First thing I did after I left you today. How did the rest of your day go?"

"Pretty well. What about you?" He couldn't discuss the case with me, so he changed the subject. "Find the stolen money yet?"

"No. But I think I'm getting closer."

While we got ready for bed, I told him about staking out Betty's Bra Bar and the good deal I got. "I think the shop is a front for something else, but I'm not sure what. I'll just have to keep digging."

Chris thought that sounded ominous and wondered if there was more to the story. I quickly got into bed and changed the subject. "I went to Uncle Joey's to ask him about Webb Enterprises, and why someone might want them to lose."

"What did he tell you?" Chris climbed into bed, but left the bedside lamp on.

"That he'd take care of it," I said.

His brows rose. "What didn't he tell you?"

I smiled. "He thinks the less I know, the better. Which is probably for the best. He's involved with the company, but I don't know how. But at least he promised to get to the bottom of it."

"Without your help?" Chris asked. He knew I wasn't telling him something.

"Not exactly," I admitted. "But I'm not supposed to tell you about it."

"Since when do you do what Manetto tells you?" He could see I was struggling with this. "Shelby, you don't seriously mean to say that you're not going to tell me what is going on." When I didn't answer he continued. "Remember how that didn't work so well last time? I need to know so I can help you figure this out. You don't need to do this alone."

"Okay," I capitulated, knowing I could tell him most everything, except for my suspicions. "I'm supposed to go with him to Webb Enterprises tomorrow morning, and see if there's anyone there who'd want Adam Webb to lose. If I can hear something like that, we'll know who's behind this and how to stop it."

"So he thinks it's a personal attack on Adam?" That's what Chris believed.

"I guess," I shrugged. "Maybe someone is setting him up? Isn't that what you think?"

"Well... yes. But you're not supposed to know that."

"What can I say?" I quirked a smile and shrugged. "It's dangerous being around me."

"That's for sure." He sighed. "Okay. This could be helpful, and I don't think you'll be in any danger."

"Not considering I'll be with Uncle Joey," I said. "I'll let you know if I find out anything. In the meantime, you need to watch your back."

"Don't worry about me." He pulled me into his arms. "I mentioned the threat to David, and he's taking it pretty seriously. It reminded me what you said about him being Manetto's man. What exactly does that mean?"

"I don't know. He didn't explain it, and I couldn't exactly ask."

"That's too bad. If you talk about David, listen to Manetto's thoughts, and maybe you'll find out. I'd like to know."

"Yeah," I sighed. "But it's more complicated than that. You're forgetting that Uncle Joey knows I can read minds. It kind of puts a damper on our conversations and makes him suspicious of everything I ask or say. He's learning how to block his thoughts pretty well. Kind of like you."

Chris huffed, thinking that having that problem in common with Uncle Joey was disconcerting. It made him dislike Manetto even more.

"How much longer do you think the trial is going to go?" I asked.

"Hopefully, we'll be done sometime next week." He was thinking it might even be by the end of this week, but he didn't want to get my hopes up.

"That means the person threatening you will have to make his move soon."

"I don't plan on giving him that opportunity," Chris said. "If he can't get to me, then he's out of luck."

"Or he might think of something else. Maybe you need me at the courthouse."

"See what you find out with Manetto first, then we'll decide what to do after that." He was thinking he could take care of this himself, and he didn't want me in the middle of something dangerous. "Oh... that reminds me," he said. "Why didn't you tell me about the little girl?" He was thinking it was embarrassing to find out about it from one of the police officers at the courthouse. Especially since they'd told him to tell me thanks, and he didn't know what they were talking about.

"Oh... well, if you remember, that was the night you stayed late, and ended up at the hospital with Gary. I wanted to tell you, but it was really late, and you were too distracted with all that stuff going on."

"So, it's my fault you didn't tell me?" he asked.

"Did I say it was your fault?"

"No, but you sounded upset."

"So did you," I said. "Plus you were thinking that you were embarrassed that you didn't know. That sounds a little like you're blaming me, doesn't it?"

"Yeah," Chris replied, and rubbed my arms, instantly contrite. "But I want you to tell me things like that, no matter how out of touch I might seem. It's important. I mean... you saved a little girl's life. That's pretty amazing. Sure I was embarrassed. But I felt left out too."

"Well... sometimes you're just so busy with your work that I feel like I can't impose on your time. Kind of like I have to take a back seat because what you're doing is more important."

"Oh," Chris said, thinking that if I felt that way, it was probably true. It was a shock to think he acted like such a jerk. But there were also times he got the distinct impression I wasn't telling him everything either, and that bothered him.

"But I should have told you," I said, not wanting him to feel bad, especially since he was right that I didn't tell him everything. "I was going to tell you the next morning when you left for work, but you were in a hurry, and it was late. Then with everything else, it slipped my mind. Probably because it was awful to think about finding her... with her head wrapped up in that plastic... and not knowing if she was going to live or die. It was pretty traumatic."

"I'll bet," he said. "Tell me what happened."

I snuggled next to him in bed, and told him everything. It felt so good to share my feelings, and I realized I needed this moment with him. And Chris needed it too. He didn't want to be left out of my life, no matter how busy he was. I finished my story and he held me close.

"I'm so proud of you," he said. "Maybe reading minds isn't all bad. Just... some of it's bad."

"Oh, really?" I pulled away.

"You know what I mean," he tugged me back. "It isn't easy for me, and I know it's been hard for you. But for now, I'm glad you have it."

"Wow, I never thought I'd hear you say that," I said.

"Well... enjoy it, because tomorrow I might feel differently." He leaned over and gently kissed me, smothering the protest coming from my lips. "And I want you to know that I'll always have time for you. You're the most important person in my life. Don't ever forget that."

I met his kisses with passion of my own, letting him know how much I loved him. Much later I fell asleep, feeling safe and secure in his arms.

Chapter 7

I startled awake at four in the morning from a bad dream. My heart pounded with fear, and my stomach clenched with remorse. I knew it all stemmed from guilt. There were things I'd kept from Chris, and no matter how much I thought it was for his own good... guilt, and worrying if I'd done the right thing, deeply troubled me.

Knowing how early I had to get up didn't help either, but I managed to doze on and off until my alarm went off at six a.m. I shuffled into the bathroom and turned on the shower while shedding my clothes. The spray hit my face, jolting me awake. Not being a morning person, getting up after such a bad sleep did awful things to my system, especially since I was already cranky.

It made me question things. Like... what was I doing with my life? Was this how I wanted to live? Having my own business seemed cool at first, but now I wasn't so sure. Instead of getting answers and staying on top of things, it seemed I was just getting sucked deeper and deeper into trouble.

I was making some progress into finding the stolen bank money, but it might be dangerous and even life threatening, considering that guy who thought about killing me. Did I want to go back to Betty's Bra Bar? Not exactly. Where did that leave me? Maybe I should just give all my clues to Rob Felt and let him get killed instead of me. I smiled. That thought lightened my mood a bit.

The more important issue, of course, was keeping Chris safe from whoever wanted to beat him up. At least I was doing something about that. This was one of those times I was grateful to have my mind-reading skills. What I did was a good thing. I needed to focus my positive energy on saving Chris, and not worry so much about lying to him.

Feeling more at peace, I rushed to get ready for my day. I decided to wear a blazer and pencil skirt ensemble that made me look more like a professional. Chris was dressed and finishing breakfast when I joined him in the kitchen. "Are you leaving already?" I asked.

"Yeah. I've got some things to go over at the office before we head to court." He set his dirty dishes in the sink and pulled me into a hug. "You look great," he said. "And smell even better. Good luck today. Let me know if you find out anything I need to know for the trial, okay?"

"Sure." I smiled, pleased with his compliments. "Is anyone else going to be in the office besides you?"

"Yeah, don't worry about me."

"You know, you can say that all you want, but it isn't going to happen. I'm going to worry. I can't help it. Hey... I know... why don't you take my stun-flashlight? You can have it until I order a regular stun gun for you. What do you think?"

"All right, sure." He was thinking it was a waste of money, but if it made me feel better, he'd do it.

I grabbed my purse and took out the stun-flashlight. "It should fit in your pocket. Do you think you can get it past security in the courthouse?"

"Maybe," he said. "I'll put it in my briefcase and see what happens."

"Okay. I'll give you a call at lunchtime."

"Good." He kissed me and hurried off.

As I finished getting ready, Josh and Savannah came downstairs and grabbed something to eat before leaving for school. Between getting them and myself out the door, I panicked that I wouldn't make it to Uncle Joey's on time.

I pulled into the parking garage with only two minutes to spare, and dashed to the elevators. I exited on the twenty-sixth floor, hoping Uncle Joey wasn't a clock-watcher, and wouldn't be angry with me.

Ramos stood with his arms crossed, waiting at the doors to Thrasher Development. "Oh good, you're here," he said. "I'll get Mr. Manetto." He was thinking that I'd barely made it. Manetto hated waiting for people. Of course, in my case it was different. Manetto had a soft spot for me, which was a good thing, since Ramos did too. Had I just heard that? He glanced at me, and I turned so he couldn't see my face. My satisfied smirk would have given me away for sure.

Uncle Joey left his office with Ramos trailing behind. "Let's go," he said to me. I followed closely and tried to pick up what he was thinking, but the only thing I heard was that he was glad I'd dressed up, and that I looked good. After that, he successfully blocked the rest of his thoughts, and I wondered if he was hiding something. Ramos drove, and I took my place in the back seat beside Uncle Joey.

"You can sit in on the first part of the meeting, but you'll have to leave when we vote since you're not a member of the board," he said. "I'll introduce you as my personal assistant. Here's a binder from the last board meeting so you can follow along. It's typically the same agenda each time."

"Okay," I said, taking the binder. I shuffled through the pages to get familiar with the topics they would be covering. "Is this a summary of expenditures and profits?"

"Yes," he said. "You will be excused at the end when we decide if we want to keep going the way we are or diversify. Several of the members will make proposals that we will vote on. Those are the ones I want you to listen to carefully."

"Okay," I said, puzzled. "How does that help Chris' case?"

He wasn't expecting me to question him, and his brows rose. "It will help us know if someone wants the company to fail. Before the vote, we'll take a break and you can tell me what you've picked up. Then I'll know how to vote."

"Okay," I said. This was getting strange. Why would anyone on the board want the company to fail? These people held stock in the company. It wouldn't make sense. They'd lose money. "I don't get it, but I'll do it."

"Good," he said. A trickle of anticipation slid past his barriers. Having me there was going to be tremendously helpful.

Ramos pulled the car in front of the building, and opened the door for us. My stomach did nervous little flip-flops, and I worried about what I was getting into. I realized it was a natural reaction whenever I showed up someplace with Uncle Joey.

Webb Enterprises was located on the fifth floor, and we entered the suite behind several others who had arrived before us. With our entrance came a polite greeting from the secretary, and others acknowledged Uncle Joey with a handshake. While not enthusiastic, most seemed resigned to having Uncle Joey there.

He introduced me as his personal assistant, and I picked up a stray thought from a younger man. He was thinking that Manetto had never brought a personal assistant before, so maybe I had other duties. Duties like... I sucked in my breath and frowned, narrowing my eyes at him until his leering smile dissolved. Take that, you pervert.

Several others were curious as to why Uncle Joey needed a personal assistant. One man thought he was the type to flaunt his standing in the company, and this was just another way to say he was better than the rest of them. That came from the man in charge, and I decided to keep my eye on him.

We followed the secretary through several corridors to a large conference room. Uncle Joey took his seat, and a chair was brought in for me to sit behind him. I took out my pen and noted the names of the people from their nameplates, and where they sat around the table. There were twelve in all, and I hoped I could keep their thoughts straight.

The first part was pretty straightforward and boring. It wasn't until we got to the proposals that it got interesting. I was shocked to realize that Uncle Joey held almost half the stock in the company. He had the most power and control in the room. But the others were still eager to see the company succeed.

Nothing seemed deceitful with the proposals, and I wondered what Uncle Joey had expected me to find. Then someone asked about the trial. They were all worried about the outcome. If Adam Webb was found guilty, it would ruin them. Most all of them figured it had something to do with Uncle Joey, and they blamed him for the charges in the first place.

My head began to pound from the strain of listening to all of them at once, but I knew this was my chance to hear something important. I focused on them, one at a time, but could find no evidence of guilt, or deception from their thoughts.

I even listened to Uncle Joey. He wondered which one of them had betrayed the company and turned over the initial evidence to start an investigation. He knew they didn't like him, but to take down the whole company over the way he was compensated was stupid. If it weren't for his initial investment, there wouldn't even be a company. He hoped I could figure out who did it.

Now I knew he suspected one of them, but he was wrong. None of them had done it, I was sure of it. So who wanted Chris to lose the trial? Who would benefit? It didn't make sense to me, but maybe Uncle Joey would know. He must have a lot of enemies. It could be any of them. But how did they know he had underhanded dealings with Webb Enterprises? It seemed like only someone in his organization would know that, someone who wanted Uncle Joey out of the picture. On the other hand, it could be someone who just had a beef with Adam Webb, and maybe it didn't have anything to do with Uncle Joey.

The meeting adjourned for a ten-minute break, and Uncle Joey escorted me out of the room. We walked out of the office and down a corridor until we found a place away from anyone who could hear us. "Well?" he asked. "Who is it?"

I twisted my lips, and shook my head. "It isn't any of them. They all want the company to succeed. They're worried about the trial, and they think it has something to do with you, but they don't want the company to fail. That means the threats must be coming from someone else. Think about it. Who would gain if Adam Webb lost the trial? Would losing the trial expose you? Could you go to jail?"

"Those are good questions," he said, his brows furrowed in contemplation. That's why he had David Barardini working on the trial, so he wouldn't go to jail. "You're sure it isn't anyone on the board?" It was still hard for him to believe.

"Yes," I said decisively.

He frowned, disappointed that finding the culprit wasn't going to be as easy as he thought. "Okay," he said, resigned. "Let's get back."

I followed him back to the conference room, but when we arrived, I wasn't allowed back inside. The secretary gave me a tight smile and told me I could sit on the couch in the waiting area. She returned to her work, but not before thinking she was glad there were rules for people like Manetto, who'd just break them left and right if they could get away with it. Then there was me. No respectable person would work for a guy like Manetto. What I did for him probably took the position of personal assistant to a whole new level. Cheap trash.

Anger washed through me, turning my face red, and I unconsciously drew my fingers into clenched fists. How dare she? Who gave her the right to judge me? I wasn't any of those things. Why did everyone assume the worst? I mean... sure I was with Uncle Joey, but that didn't make me his plaything. I wanted to tell her to get her mind out of the gutter, but that was out of the question. Instead, I focused on the pictures on her desk.

"Are those your little boys?" I asked, trying to sound calm.

The question surprised her. "Yes," she said. "But this picture is out of date. They're teenagers now."

"Oh really? I have a fourteen-year-old son myself. He's always hungry. I swear that kid eats more food than a horse."

She laughed, and we shared a few stories of what it's like to have teenage boys at home. Before we knew it, the meeting was over, and it was time for me to go. "It looks like they're done," I said. "It's been nice chatting with you. Good luck with your boys."

"You too," she answered, thinking what a nice person I was. She must have been wrong about me.

I smiled, feeling lots better. Uncle Joey came out talking to Ramos on his phone, and we walked to the elevator with some of the other board members. This time, I put my shields up. Hearing stray thoughts I could do nothing about was taking a toll on me. That meant I couldn't hear Uncle Joey either. But so what? I didn't need to know what he was thinking all the time.

We exited the building and waited for Ramos. Uncle Joey glanced at me, a faint smile on his face. He raised his brows like he was asking a question, and I realized I'd missed something. I dropped my shields. "Oh, I'm sorry. I had my shields up. Did you think something?"

"You put your shields up?" He could hardly believe it. What was I thinking? He thought I was force to be reckoned with, and here I'd put up my shields? Maybe he shouldn't worry so much about what I'd pick up from his mind after all, although he thought I was smarter than that.

"Well... yeah," I said defensively. "You wouldn't believe what a lot of the people in there think about me and you. It's pretty disgusting."

"What do you mean?" He stopped cold, wondering if he'd have to break somebody's arms or legs.

Oops. I should have kept my mouth shut. "It doesn't matter," I said. "What did you want to tell me?"

His eyes narrowed, and he pursed his lips. He had a reputation to uphold, but he couldn't start beating people up because of their thoughts. He glanced at me, trying to remember what he was going to say. Oh yeah. "Since the threat isn't coming from Webb Enterprises, there's another source we'll need to check."

We were interrupted when Ramos pulled the car to the curb. As we climbed into the back seat, Uncle Joey was thinking about a match of some sort, and I couldn't figure out what he meant by that. Ramos started driving away, and he continued. "There's an event at my club tonight. I mentioned it yesterday. We might be able to find out what's going on there."

My heart sank, knowing I'd have to decide if I should lie to Chris about it, like Uncle Joey wanted me to. "What time?"

"We generally meet about nine," Uncle Joey answered.

"Nine? That's kind of late." What was I supposed to tell Chris? He wouldn't believe I'd go to dinner with my friends that late.

"You're right," he agreed. "I'll see if we can go a little earlier, around seven. That should make it easier for you."

"Gee, thanks," I said. "Why will meeting with them help?"

"You'll see," he said cryptically, his mind blank. "Be sure and wear black. I'll have Ramos outfit you after you arrive. In fact, come to the office first, and we'll go to the club together."

Ramos pulled into the parking garage and cut the engine. He was thinking that having me there was going to make things interesting. As long as I kept my mouth shut. He'd have to make sure I knew not to say anything that would get me in trouble, and maybe I should wear my black wig. My blond hair was a little too noticeable and made me an easy target if things got out of hand.

"Meet us here at six-thirty." Uncle Joey got out of the car and waited for me to exit. He patted my arm and smiled conspiratorially. "And Shelby, this is to be kept in the strictest of confidence. No one, especially Chris, is to know about this little meeting. His life, as well as yours, may depend on it. Got it?"

"Sure," I said. He was freaking me out, so I made a joke of it. "You're making it sound like we're meeting with a bunch of monsters, like werewolves and vampires." I laughed, but neither of them even cracked a smile. "Okay. Well... see you later."

I started toward my car, listening to their thoughts as they walked to the elevators. Uncle Joey was getting good at shielding his thoughts, but Ramos was easy to pick up. He was thinking that I was in for a surprise, and chuckling about the werewolves and vampires joke I'd made. He couldn't wait to see my reaction tonight. It was going to be...

The elevator doors shut, cutting off his thoughts. Damn... I hated when that happened. Now I had to wait on pins and needles to find out what was going on. I stomped my foot with frustration. Why couldn't they just tell me, instead of being so cryptic? It's not like I couldn't keep a secret. I had a sneaking suspicion that they were enjoying my discomfort a little too much. Almost like they were teasing me. Thinking of it that way settled me down some. Whatever was going on tonight, I could handle it.

I got in my car and sat for a moment, trying to decide what to do with the rest of my day. My options included staking out Betty's Bra Bar, and going to the courthouse to watch out for Chris. I wasn't ready to go back to Betty's, and if I went to the courthouse, I'd have to tell Chris about the dead end Webb Enterprises had turned out to be. Plus, I couldn't tell him about tonight, so where did that leave me?

I needed to figure out who was threatening Chris, and the best way to do that wasn't going to some meeting tonight with Uncle Joey. It was following Chris until the guy made his move. If I could catch him, I could listen to his thoughts, and we'd know what was going on and why. Problem solved. Seemed pretty simple to me. The big question was if I could catch the guy before he attacked Chris. Was I willing to risk Chris' safety on that? What if there was more than one guy?

I pictured Chris and me, standing against three big guys holding bats with brass knuckles on their fingers. The odds of that working out didn't look so good. It was probably best to go to the meeting first before taking matters into my own hands.

I had an hour before lunch and decided I might as well use it to sit in front of Betty's Bra Bar. I might find something interesting, and I didn't have to actually talk to her. I started the car and zoomed out of the parking garage.

I pulled up across the street from Betty's Bra Bar and turned off the engine. Taking out my phone, I clicked on my time card app and started the clock. It was a bit of a shock to see that I'd used up almost all of my first twenty hours. That meant I'd need to talk to Blaine Smith soon about my progress. I was pretty sure he'd want to keep me on the case after I told him what I'd found. But I wished I were closer to finding the money.

I glanced at the shop, making note of the 'open' sign, and settled in for a wait. After fifteen minutes and no customers, I put the seat back slightly to get more comfortable. My eyelids began to droop, and I struggled to keep them open. It was hard considering my restless night, and the early hour I'd gotten up.

A loud rapping on my window jolted me awake, and I jerked upright, nearly smacking my forehead against the door. A shock of fear raced down my spine, but it was quickly replaced by anger to find Rob Felt bent over, glaring at me. What was he doing here? How had he found me?

I rolled down my window and caught the look of mirth on his face, but that was nothing compared to his thoughts. He was gleeful that he'd scared me and was having a hard time keeping the laughter inside where I couldn't see it. His lips quivered, but he managed to keep a straight face.

"Well if it isn't Shelby Nichols," he said. "Have a nice nap?"

"What do you want?" I straightened my seat and glared at him. Instead of intimidating him, he took my glare as a compliment that he'd seriously rattled me. The jerk.

He took his time answering, and a wave of self-satisfaction rolled off him. I'd humiliated him, and it was nice to have some payback. "That's an interesting shop. Find anything useful inside?"

"Yeah," I said. "She has some great buys on bras. Why don't you go in and check it out?" I wanted to add that I didn't think she had anything in his size, but that would have been snarky, and I didn't want to stoop to his level.

He was thinking that he already had, since he'd followed me the day before. After I'd given him the slip, his patience had paid off when I came out of Emily's store, and he'd followed me here. I probably didn't even know it. What surprised him was my detour to get a soda and the man who had watched me leave. He'd followed the guy to a run-down apartment complex, but left when nothing came of it. Somehow, it was all tied up in that shop. I'd confirmed it by coming back, and his hunch to watch the place had paid off. Now if only he could get me to talk.

Wow, that was impressive. Maybe he was better at this job than I thought. Of course, he never would have gotten this far without following me, so I couldn't give him too much credit. I checked my watch. Thankfully, I'd only been asleep for about twenty minutes.

Felt was blocking my view of the shop, and with him standing there, it might draw Betty's attention. I couldn't have that. "Can you go away? You're blocking my view."

"Sure. If you'll tell me why you're watching that shop." He was thinking it had to be tied to Novelty Creations somehow, since they both dealt with underwear. Was it the same supplier? How did that tie in with Keith Bishop?

"I just have a hunch, that's all. Isn't that why you're here?"

"Well, yeah. But..."

"Wait," I interrupted. "Something's happening." Someone inside the store was turning the sign to 'closed.' "Hurry, get in the car. You're going to draw her attention standing there like that."

Felt quickly opened the back door and slid inside. We waited with anticipation for the first few minutes. That quickly gave way to tedium as time stretched out to ten, and then fifteen minutes. It didn't bother Felt. He'd been on enough stakeouts that he knew most of the time it was boring as hell.

"Watch it," I said. Oops.

"Watch what?" he asked, confused.

"The store. I've got to check my phone," I improvised.

He shook his head, thinking I was weird, and kind of uptight. Once this case was over, he'd be glad if he never saw me again.

I sniffed. At least his thoughts matched mine in that department.

"A car just pulled up," he said, excited. Two men got out of the car and went inside. "What do you think they do in there?" he asked.

"I'm not sure," I answered. "Maybe we can follow them when they leave."

"I think I'd better do it. You're too obvious. Why don't you stay and watch the shop after they come out? I'll follow them and call you if I see anything." He was thinking it was better to ditch me now. He could always call if nothing turned up, and see if I saw anything he could use.

"Okay," I agreed, mostly because those guys looked scary with their shaved heads and scruffy beards. They were wearing jackets, even though it was warm, and I figured they were carrying guns of some sort. "As long as you call me if you find out anything interesting."

"Sure," he lied, already dismissing me. He jumped out of the car and crossed the street. His car was parked down the block from the shop, allowing him to easily pull out into traffic once their car passed him.

It wasn't a moment too soon. The men came out of the shop and got in their car. They drove away, and Felt pulled out behind them. Soon, they were gone from sight, and relief that I wasn't following them flooded over me. Even if Felt didn't want to share where they went, I was sure I could pick it up from his mind the next time I saw him. As long as they didn't know he was behind them, he was probably safe enough.

I turned my attention back to the shop, wondering if anyone else was going to show up. Instead of turning the sign back to 'open,' Betty came out of the store. After locking the door, she turned the corner to the alley and got into a parked car.

My heart started hammering in my chest, and I knew this was my chance to follow her. Lucky for me, she pulled onto the street going the same direction my car was facing, and I slipped into traffic behind her. I tried to keep one car between us, so she wouldn't suspect a tail, and barely made it through the light.

My hands began to sweat from the stress of keeping up with her and making it through all the intersections. I let out my breath when she pulled into a coffee and bagel shop. I kept going down the street, and stopped at a metered parking place. I grabbed some change I kept in the cup holder and went to the meter, taking my time so I could watch her without looking suspicious.

Instead of going inside, she sat at an outside table under an awning. It seemed as if she were waiting for someone, so I put a quarter into the meter, and hurried back into my car. I couldn't risk her seeing me, but I felt pretty safe since it was close to lunchtime and the coffee shop was getting crowded.

Several people wearing police uniforms converged on the shop, and I realized the police station was just up the street. It wasn't long before a man broke from the crowd and approached her. I could only see his back, but from her smile, he was the one she'd been waiting for. Who was he? He wasn't wearing a uniform, but his jacket and trousers seemed familiar. A wave of dread clenched my stomach. He turned his head, laughing at something she said, and I gasped. It was Dimples!

Chapter 8

I watched in stunned silence as she took his arm, and they entered the coffee shop. How did Dimples know her? Then it hit me. She had to be the woman he'd told me about. The one who'd spilled her coffee, and he'd ended up getting her number. I never did ask him how their date went.

From the looks of things, it must have gone pretty well. I sighed, knowing I had to go over there and pretend to bump into them so I could find out what she was up to. By now, I was convinced she was doing something illegal in her shop, and I didn't want Dimples to get caught in the middle. She was probably using him, and my heart sank to think how hurt Dimples would be when he found out.

With reluctance, I pulled on the door handle, but stopped when my phone rang. The caller ID said it was Chris. I quickly answered, relieved to put off talking to Dimples for a little longer. "Hey honey. What's up?"

"We're breaking for lunch," Chris said. "Can you come to the courthouse?"

I hesitated, hating to leave Dimples without knowing what was going on. Chris spoke into the silence. "I really need you here," he said, his voice low.

That got my full attention, and my heart sped up. "Is something wrong?"

"Not exactly... but I can't explain right now," he answered.

"Okay, I'll be there in a few minutes." I started up the car, knowing if Chris needed me, Dimples' predicament would have to wait.

It was only a few blocks to the courthouse so it didn't take me long, only I couldn't find an open parking spot anywhere on the street. I finally went to Chris' parking garage and walked to the courthouse.

I got through security and hurried up to the courtroom. Only a few people were still in the room, and I found Chris with David beside him gathering their papers at the defendant's table.

I hurried to Chris' side, and he glanced at me with a show of surprise. "Hi Shelby... what brings you here?" I scrunched my brows together in confusion before I picked up his thought of *play along with me*.

"Oh... um... since I was downtown, I thought maybe we could go to lunch together." Chris was thinking alone, so I continued. "Just the two of us. Unless you're too busy?" I glanced between him and David, picking up that David thought Chris wasn't acting like his normal self, and wondered what was going on. Maybe lunch with his wife would do him some good.

Chris glanced at David, and smiled apologetically. "Is that okay with you?"

"No problem," David answered. "I'll see you back here in about... twenty-seven minutes." He smiled at me, grabbed his briefcase, and left.

Chris concentrated on getting his papers into his briefcase while thinking *just act normal*. I relaxed my stance, and waited for him like a dutiful wife. Before he closed his briefcase, I noticed that my stun flashlight was missing.

"Where's my flashlight?" I asked.

Chris huffed. "They wouldn't let me bring it in, so I had to leave it with security. I guess even lawyers aren't allowed special privileges."

"Bummer," I said. "Who would've thought?"

"Yeah," he smiled wryly. "We can pick it up on our way out, and you can put it back in your purse."

"Okay." We left the courtroom and walked down the hallway to the elevators. "Now can you tell me what's going on?" We got on the elevator, but halted our conversation when another man got in with us. Chris was thinking *just act normal until we're alone*. It kind of rubbed me the wrong way since I wouldn't have said anything with the guy there anyway. But I could tell he was rattled, and it worried me.

We exited the elevator and stopped at security for my stun flashlight. At least they were nice enough to hold it for him, and it felt good to have it back in my purse where it belonged. Once we left the building, Chris visibly relaxed, and took a deep breath of fresh air.

"Someone in the courtroom placed an envelope next to my papers," he began. "I didn't see who put it there, but it had my name on it. I waited until the next recess to open it up."

"Was it a threat?" I asked.

"Not exactly, but it certainly wasn't what I expected. It said that David worked for 'The Knife' and that I shouldn't trust him. It also said my client was guilty of making unlawful payments to 'The Knife' and if I was a good citizen, I would lose the case so justice would be served. What do you make of that?"

"It sounds like they're trying a different tactic to get to you," I said.

"Yeah, they're making it personal."

"But it's more than that. It's like they know you, and figure that you'd want to take Uncle Joey down. They're telling you this is the way to do it." I glanced at him with concern. "Do you think they know I work for Uncle Joey?"

"That would certainly be a good reason for me to lose the case," he said. "So yeah, they must know."

"But it's not anyone in his organization. I'd know."

"Okay, but what about David? How is he involved? You said he was working for Manetto, but do you know how?"

"Not really." I wracked my brain for anything that might help and remembered one of his thoughts. "David thought about a glitch with the trial the other day. But he was prepared to handle it. I don't know how, but he hoped he didn't have to put his plan into motion because it might hurt someone."

"Why didn't you tell me that?" he asked.

"At the time, it didn't seem like it mattered, and I kind of forgot," I said. "Would it have made a difference?"

Chris sighed. "Well... no, but it would have been nice to know. I mean, you have the inside scoop on something that's pertinent to my case, and you don't share it. What's the point in having your abilities if you don't share stuff like that with me?" He was thinking I told Manetto everything I knew, but not my own husband. That was just wrong. It made him feel angry, and even a little betrayed that I'd held out on him. How could I do that?

"Hey... you're blowing this way out of proportion. I tell you the important stuff. I know we're in this together, and I'm sorry I didn't remember to tell you about it."

"Well, it hardly matters now. We both know that Adam Webb is guilty," Chris said, hating to admit it out loud.

"Why else would Manetto have David working with me on the case? Manetto doesn't want to get caught."

"That's true," I agreed. "At Webb Enterprises this morning, Uncle Joey was thinking that was why he had David helping you."

"Then maybe I should lose the case," Chris said. "If it would get rid of Manetto, it might be worth it."

"You can't," I disagreed. "It's tempting, but it's too risky. You don't know what he would do to you. Or to our kids or me. We can't do that."

"What if I found a way to make it look like it wasn't my fault?"

"It will never happen. Not with David keeping an eye on you." How could he even think about it? I had to convince him it wouldn't work.

Chris glanced at me. He was thinking that I was so involved in Manetto's life that I couldn't think straight. I was more loyal to him than I realized. Couldn't I see that this might be our one chance to get out from under him?

"Chris don't..." I shook my head. "I might feel indebted to him, but it's not as simple as you think. Let's talk about it later. Okay? After we've had some time to think it through."

"All right," he said, relenting. He knew he was too emotional to make a good decision at the moment, and I probably was too. "I'll be home late again tonight, probably around eight. We can talk then."

"Sounds good," I agreed. I took a breath to tell him about my meeting with Uncle Joey tonight, but I couldn't do it. It would just give him another reason to do what he wanted without knowing the huge risk involved. "Believe me, if there's a way to get out of this mess, I'm all for it."

"Good," he said. "Keep thinking that, because it just might happen."

He smiled, and I cringed at his enthusiasm. He was dreaming if he thought we could double-cross Uncle Joey and live to tell about it.

"Don't look so worried," he chided.

"Yeah, easy for you to say." I caught his gaze. "Just promise me you won't do anything stupid."

Chris chuckled. "Hey, wait a minute... that's my line."

I smacked his arm. "Just be careful. This person threatening you could still beat you up."

"All right," he agreed, checking his watch. "I've got to get back."

"What about lunch?"

"I'll just grab a sandwich and eat it on the way."

"Okay. I'll come with you."

Luckily, Chris made it back to the courthouse with time to spare. I couldn't go in with my stun flashlight, so I kissed him goodbye before hurrying to my car. I couldn't stop thinking about how he was considering losing the case. Uncle Joey had too many schemes in place to lose for real. The only way he would lose was if Chris sabotaged the trial. Not only were our lives on the line, but Chris' job was too.

I hoped by the time I talked to him tonight, he would realize that the risks outweighed anything we could possibly gain from it. If Chris still didn't understand that, then there was only one thing left for me to do, and that was tell Uncle Joey about the threat. Could I do that to Chris? Maybe if I said it was David who saw the note and told Uncle Joey, it could work, and he'd never know it was really me. I hoped it wouldn't come to that, but it was something I had to consider.

By the time I got home, my stomach was tied in knots. It was one of those times I had to drink Mylanta straight from the bottle. After my stomach settled, I changed into jeans and a t-shirt and rushed to get ready for the meeting with Uncle Joey and his club.

I found my black wig stashed in the back of the closet along with my black pants and boots. The black shirt that completed the outfit had been ruined the last time I wore it, bringing back the memory of when Ramos killed Mercer to save my life. I thought I was over it, but remembering the sickening splatter of blood across my face and shirt made my stomach clench. Suddenly, I had to take another swig of Mylanta. At this rate the bottle would be empty before I left for the meeting.

Shopping usually helped me feel better, and since I needed a new black shirt, I decided to make a run to the mall. This time I was buying something cute. Just because it was black didn't mean it had to be plain. I found the perfect blouse. It was short-sleeved with a collar, and it buttoned up the front with some tucks around the waist that really flattered my figure.

Next, I stopped at the jewelry shop where they sold fake eyeglasses and decided to get another pair. My last pair got smashed when Uncle Joey's car was bombed, and since I didn't want any of the people at Uncle Joey's club to know who I was, being extra disguised seemed like the best way to go.

I got home and concentrated on fixing something healthy for dinner, knowing I needed the distraction. I checked the fridge and freezer, then the cupboards, before looking in the fridge again. After about ten minutes of this, with my mind a total blank, I gave up and ordered pizza.

At five o'clock the pizza arrived, and I called the kids to dinner. Josh's friend was here, and I invited him to stay and eat with us. We had plenty to go around since I could only manage a few bites before I had to take another swig of Mylanta.

"Mom... that's gross," Savannah said, her nose wrinkled in disgust.

"Not if it works," I said. "Don't worry, I just drank the last of it, so you don't have to watch me drink any more tonight."

"Eww." She shook her head. She was thinking how awful that stuff tasted, and couldn't imagine anyone taking a spoonful, let alone drinking it from the bottle. It couldn't be good for me.

"So, what are your plans tonight?" I asked, wanting to change the subject. "Got homework or anything you have to do?"

"No..." Savannah tilted her head and raised her brows. "Don't you know?"

"Know what?"

"School gets out next week. We're basically done with our work. Geez Mom, where have you been?"

I tried to cover my blunder with a smirk. "Of course I knew that. What I didn't know was... oh never-mind." Calling Savannah a smart aleck was probably not a good idea right now. I got up from the table and put my dishes in the dishwasher. I knew Josh and his friend were playing video games tonight and wouldn't even know if I left for a few hours, but what about Savannah?

I listened to her thoughts and was relieved to hear her thinking about going to her friend Ashley's house. She worried that I wouldn't let her go since it was a school night, and she had one last assignment to finish up, but I didn't know that, and she was pretty sure I bought her explanation.

What? She'd lied to me? Now what should I do? I couldn't let her lie to me and get away with it. Of course, if I couldn't read her mind, I wouldn't know she'd lied, and right now knowing was working against me. So, maybe this one time it was okay that I let it go.

Savannah brought her plate over. "Ash wants me to come over to her house for a while. Is that okay?"

"I guess... since you don't have any homework." I watched her closely, hoping she'd show some kind of guilt or remorse for lying to me.

"Nope," she said smiling. She was thinking it was a stupid assignment anyway, and she could finish it up before she went to bed, and even if she didn't, she was getting an A in the class, so it didn't really matter.

"All right," I agreed half-heartedly, discouraged that she didn't show even a smidge of guilt for lying. "As long as you're back by nine-thirty."

"Sure." She was thinking nine-thirty was later than normal to let her stay out on a school night, but she wasn't about to tell me that.

I sighed, wondering if I could ever get being a mom right. I mean, even when I let her do something she wanted, she was thinking that I shouldn't. How crazy was that?

By five-thirty, dinner was cleaned up, the boys were downstairs, and Savannah had left for Ashley's. That gave me plenty of time to get ready before I had to leave at six so I could be to Uncle Joey's by six-thirty.

I got dressed in my all-black ensemble and realized I'd have to wait until I got there to put on my wig. Then it hit me that I couldn't remember if Uncle Joey had told me to wear my black wig, or if he'd just been thinking I should wear it. Or was it Ramos who'd mentioned it? Oh well... it didn't matter now. I was wearing it because I thought it was a good idea.

I carefully placed it in my bag along with my glasses and glanced in the mirror. I looked kind of pale and sick. Just like I felt. I put some blush on my cheeks and decided to go with red on my lips since it was a power color. I rubbed my lips together and struck my sassy 'don't mess with me' pose. That was more like it.

"I'm going to the store," I yelled down to Josh. "I'll be back in an hour or so."

"K," he called back.

I fervently hoped I'd get back before Chris got home. There was a good chance I would with the late hours he'd been keeping so far. Hopefully, my luck wouldn't run out tonight. I started my car and was soon on the freeway to Thrasher Development.

I pulled into the parking garage, and got to the office five minutes early. This was perfect since I needed some time to put on my wig. I walked into the office and found Ramos sitting in Jackie's chair. He was dressed in black, and I couldn't help but notice how nicely the snug t-shirt showed off his rippling pectorals.

"Hey babe," he said. "Good timing. We were hoping to leave a little early." He was thinking I looked different, then decided it must be the red lipstick. My shirt was nice. Too bad I couldn't wear it.

"What do you mean?" I asked.

His lips quirked up in a rueful smile. Ha, he caught me.

I backtracked to his earlier statement of leaving early. "I can't leave until I get my wig on, but it won't take me more than a minute."

"You brought your wig?" he asked. "What made you do that?" He was thinking it was probably because he'd suggested it.

"Didn't you tell me I should?" I asked, confused, and a little suspicious at his question.

"Yup," he said. But he was thinking *only in my mind.*

I clenched my teeth. He was baiting me, and it was making me mad. I tried not to let it show, treating it like I did when my kids pushed my buttons. He was not going to get the best of me. I scrunched up my eyebrows. "Funny... I thought it was my idea." I took a deep breath. It was time to push back just a little. "You know... I like you Ramos. Don't spoil it. I'll be back in a minute."

"Wait," Ramos said, sheepish that he'd pushed me into a corner. He realized that he'd gone too far and respected that I'd put him in his place. Not many people could do that. "Sorry, but you'll have to put these on too." He held up a t-shirt similar to his in one hand, and a ball cap that said 'security' across the front in the other.

His 'sorry' wasn't meant for the clothes, but for how he'd been acting. I sighed, but gave him a quick smile to let him know we were good. I took the clothes to the restroom to change. I was kind of mad that I couldn't wear my cute blouse, but usually when I did stuff like this, my black clothes got ruined, so maybe Ramos was doing me a favor.

The t-shirt was stretchy, but tight, so I tucked it into my pants, glad I'd worn a belt. I pulled my hair back and pinned it down before slipping on my wig. With it in place, I slid on my glasses and hat, pleased to find that I looked like a totally different person. Plus, the red lipstick balanced out all that black. Now all I needed was a gun to make me look like a kick-butt security person.

I hurried back into the office and found Uncle Joey quietly conversing with Ramos. They stopped talking to admire me in my outfit. Ramos was thinking he liked the results, but Uncle Joey thought I'd gone too far. He thought the glasses ruined the look, since he didn't think a security person would wear them. Wouldn't they just get in the way if a fight broke out? Not that it would, but still.

"I'm wearing the glasses," I said. "If a fight breaks out, Ramos can handle it. I'll use this." I motioned to my waist where I had clipped my stun flashlight. "Don't forget it's got one million volts of shock-stopping power, and will drop anyone in their tracks."

"Good," Uncle Joey said, smiling. He was thinking that he liked my initiative and my willingness to play along in this role. Since both he and Ramos were packing, it might come in handy to have me armed with something. Who knew? Maybe by the end of the night I'd need it. "Let's go. I'll explain what I want you to do in the car."

I wasn't too nervous about tonight until I heard that. What kind of a club were we going to anyway? I got my answer as we drove out of the parking lot. "The club belongs to one of my associates, Lanny. It's a boxing club... among other things, and he keeps up on the major movements, or happenings, in the city. He's a good friend to have if you need 'eyes and ears' on things. That's why I go to the club regularly. He likes my business, and I like his info. That's where you come in. As part of my security detail, he won't be suspicious of you. It's like you'll be invisible, which, for a woman in that place, is invaluable."

"Why? What are most of the women like?" I asked, but quickly changed my mind. "Wait, never mind."

He smiled. "You'll see soon enough. Anyway, I'll have to place some bets and mingle a bit. Hey... you could actually help me with the bets." He was thinking I could 'listen' to the fighters, or their managers, and see who was throwing the fight, or who was supposed to win. He could actually make some money for a change. Wouldn't that be nice?

"Do people actually throw the fights?" I asked, surprised.

"Most of the time. When I come around, Lanny always gives me a suggestion on who to bet on. But with his advice, I never know if I'm going to win or lose. That seems to be my price for the info he gives me. But with you there, I can have you or Ramos place the bets for me on the right people. It should work out great."

"Yeah," I said, a little sarcastically. "But the main reason you need me is to help you know what's going on in the city, right? Because Lanny doesn't always tell you everything?"

"Right." Uncle Joey's thoughts went quiet, like he didn't want me to know that was only part of his plan.

I sat back, wondering if this was a waste of time. Was I actually risking my marriage to help Uncle Joey win some bets? How would knowing what was going on in the city help Chris' case? The person threatening Chris had to be someone close to Uncle Joey, not some new thing going on in the city. In fact, the person who could help me the most was probably Uncle Joey. But I couldn't tell him about the new threat.

Maybe I could phrase it in such a way that he wouldn't know the truth? I'd have to figure out what questions to ask that would make him think about what I wanted to know. In the meantime, I had my work cut out for me, and I might as well make the most of it. I could pick up lots of things that might be helpful to Uncle Joey, and I could use them to bargain my way out of a mess if I needed to.

With this much to figure out, it was going to be a long night. I wished I had a small notebook or something in which to write down my findings. Keeping it straight was going to be a challenge. Just thinking about it made my stomach clench. Too bad I'd finished off all the Mylanta.

Ramos pulled the car around to the back of a warehouse-type building. A chain-link fence surrounded the property, and a guard stood in front of a tall gate. Ramos rolled down his window and handed him a card. The guard studied it, glancing inside to get a look at Uncle Joey. Satisfied, he pushed a button to open the gate, and we drove inside.

Ramos parked the car in an open space near the back of the lot. As he turned off the engine, he glanced at me. If he had any doubts about what I did, my conversation with Uncle Joey had effectively erased them. But he would keep it to himself, for now.

"Shelby," Ramos began, "even though you're only acting the part, I need you to keep alert. Watch where people put their hands. If it looks like anyone is going for a gun, don't hesitate to tell me."

"Really?" I asked.

"Things have been known to get out of hand here, but we should be fine," he replied.

"Okay," I nodded. From his mind, I knew Ramos wasn't kidding, and the sick feeling in my stomach got worse.

Ramos eased out of the car to open Uncle Joey's door. I scrambled out the other door, and rushed to flank Uncle Joey as we walked to the entrance. Ramos glanced at me and frowned, thinking I looked too scared for a security agent, and hoped I would get a grip. I quickly schooled my features into what I hoped portrayed cool detachment.

A burly guard at the door looked us over and, apparently satisfied, pulled the door open to let us in. Uncle Joey went first, with Ramos and me on either side of him.

The interior of the warehouse was an open room, and we stood at the top of a small arena. From here we could see the boxing ring below. To our right was a ticket counter where people lined up to place their bets. A schedule of the evening's fights was posted next to it on a marquee, with the odds listed beside them.

The left-side corner contained three offices. A man quickly emerged from the closest one, and headed straight for us. He was pleased to see Uncle Joey, thinking it had been a long time since 'The Knife' had visited his establishment. He was equally surprised to find two bodyguards, and eyed me with curiosity. A woman for a bodyguard was unusual, but he supposed that Manetto had his reasons. Still, he would keep his eye on me, since something about me didn't quite fit the part.

I straightened my stance and tried to keep from fidgeting or chewing on my lip like I normally did when I was nervous. I realized this guy was dangerous, and more observant than Uncle Joey gave him credit for. Nothing got past him.

"Mr. Manetto, good to see you," he said, shaking his hand.

"Thanks, Lanny. You too," Uncle Joey replied. He leveled Lanny with an ice-cold stare that spoke volumes. "Just thought I'd stop by and see how things are going. Maybe try and earn some of my money back."

Lanny smiled, but there was a nervous twitch in his left eye. "Good. We've missed you around here." He liked Manetto's money, but the man still managed to give him the willies. The last time Manetto was here, he'd lost quite a bit of money. From the looks of things, the information he'd gotten might not have been worth it. He'd better make sure he didn't lose tonight.

"I know," Uncle Joey grimaced dramatically. "I've been a bit sidetracked lately, but I'm back now. Do you have anything of interest for me?"

"I do," Lanny spoke with enthusiasm. "Come sit with me, and we'll discuss it." He was thinking that if Manetto won a few bets, he'd still have enough information to earn a payoff without telling him too much.

Lanny led us around the arena to the other side of the building where a staircase led to a glass enclosed room perched above the seats below. We entered into posh luxury quite different from the wooden benches on which everyone else sat. The room held many amenities, including a wet bar in the back and lots of scantily clad women bearing trays of food.

"Care for a drink?" Lanny asked Uncle Joey.

"Of course," he replied.

Lanny signaled to a server, and soon had a glass of scotch in Uncle Joey's hand. He motioned Uncle Joey to a corner table and sat, with Ramos and me standing protectively behind. Another woman descended with a platter of food and, after filling his plate, Lanny suggested Uncle Joey place a bet while he was there. The fight below had barely begun, and there was still time to pick a winner and make some money.

I picked up from Uncle Joey that this was a ritual they went through, but this time he had me to help him out. Lanny gave him a rundown of the fighters' various strengths and weaknesses, and left it to Uncle Joey to decide. He was hoping Uncle Joey chose Razor, because he was sure to win, but this match could go either way. So nothing was a sure thing.

Uncle Joey turned, handing me five hundred dollars. "Place the bet for me will you?" he asked.

"Um... sure. I mean, yes sir," I fumbled. Panic gripped me. Didn't he know I'd never done this before? He turned his back but was thinking that all I had to do was go down to the box office, and say five hundred on whoever would win the match, and place it under his name.

I nodded absently, glancing at Ramos since he was thinking the same thing, and made my way out of the room with the money clenched in my hand. I was halfway to the box office when it dawned on me that I'd heard the name Razor before. I stopped to watch the match, and recognized the young man as the kid I'd seen. He was the gang member I'd listened to at the FBI office. What was he doing here?

As I watched, I heard someone thinking about me. He was wondering if he'd seen me before. I looked familiar. *Oh right, she looks like that psychic that came to the office. Only with black hair and glasses. That was sure weird.* His attention went back to the match, and I quickly headed straight to the box office. The undercover FBI agent was here too?

With my heart racing, I placed the bet on Razor. The bookie gave me a ticket, and I turned to leave, nearly bumping into the guy behind me.

This guy was thinking that I'd made the right call, and he could let Lanny know he didn't have to fix the match for Manetto to win. I stifled a groan and stepped around him, barely managing to keep the surprise from my face.

On shaky legs, I made my way back to Uncle Joey, alert for trouble. This time, I spotted the undercover FBI agent standing at the top of the stairs and carefully steered clear of him. What was he doing here? I remembered him thinking about a club. This must have been it. I hurried around him, grateful his mind was on the match and not watching for me. None too soon, I was back at my place behind Uncle Joey. I took a deep breath to settle my nerves and handed him the ticket.

"Here you go, sir," I said.

Uncle Joey gave it a fleeting glance and turned his attention to the match. Razor was taking a beating, and it turned my stomach. Blood was running from his nose and he had a cut on his face. Sweat was flying everywhere. Yuk. I hated boxing. It was just too brutal for me. If he was favored to win, he was sure making a mess of it.

At the last minute, Razor broke free of the ropes, and in a fast move, landed a one-two punch that threw his opponent to the floor. The crowd roared with approval, and with the countdown, the match was over. Razor had won.

Relief swept over me, magnified by Lanny and several other people in the room. The right person had won. I hoped now that this part of the negotiations were over we could get down to business. I couldn't wait to get out of there. After congratulating Uncle Joey, Lanny finally got around to telling him what he wanted to know.

"There is something going on with the gangs," Lanny began. "The shot callers of the two major rival gangs have been killed, along with several top gang members. Someone is moving in on their territory, and doing a lot of recruiting." He was thinking that taking in Razor had paid off in many ways. "Whoever it is has connections to lots of drugs and guns, and they've started selling."

"What about you? How are you handling this?" Uncle Joey asked, knowing full well that Lanny's operation could be in jeopardy.

Lanny swallowed. Manetto was smart, and he'd better play this right. "I'm taking in the misplaced gang members who will work for me. Keeping it tight. Trying to find out what I can."

"So... who is it?" Uncle Joey asked, pushing the stakes higher.

"I don't have a name," Lanny said. Nervous sweat trickled down his back. What game was Manetto playing? Lanny wasn't picking sides yet. Not until he had a guarantee of protection from one or the other. "But I'd be willing to find out for a fee, and some protection."

Uncle Joey nodded. He'd been expecting this. "You know Lanny, I just got back from Mexico, where I took out a drug cartel who was threatening me. If you have something to tell me, I'd suggest you do it."

"Word is they're after you." Lanny was thinking that he'd said a hundred times more than he'd planned, but it was Manetto. You didn't mess with him. "That's all I know."

Uncle Joey's jaw tightened, and he fixed Lanny with a furious stare. "You find out any more, you come to me. Got it?"

"Yeah... sure," Lanny said, breaking eye contact and lowering his head. "I'll let you know."

Uncle Joey stood, then leaned menacingly forward with his hands braced on the table, invading Lanny's space. "Keep my winnings as payment for any information that comes your way. I'll be in touch."

Chapter 9

Uncle Joey stalked out of the place like he owned it, and people were quick to get out of his way. He wasn't happy with the information from Lanny. If it was correct, things were worse than he thought. He mostly stayed away from the gangs and the drugs, focusing mainly on his lucrative business arrangements. But it was always good to keep abreast of what was happening there.

It was a bold move for someone to shake up the gangs to get a toehold into his city. It would take someone with inside information, and a lot of firepower, to do the job. Not an easy proposition. On the other hand, it would give whoever was in charge an instant crew to take on anyone who opposed them, like himself, of course. He'd have to get the South End on the job to find out exactly what was going on, and tell them they were looking for an organization a lot like his own.

We exited the building, and Ramos left to get the car while we waited. "What did you pick up? Uncle Joey asked. "Was he telling the truth?"

"Yes," I answered. "He wanted you to win the bet on the match, and was hoping he could spoon feed you enough information that you'd pay him for it. But you ended up forcing his hand, and he told you a lot more than he wanted to."

"Good," he said, pleased with himself. "Anything else I should know?"

"Not really. He told you what he knew, and no names came to his mind." I considered telling him about the undercover FBI agent, but decided against it. It wouldn't go over too well if he knew I'd helped them, even if it was only once. Plus, I couldn't see it changing anything. The FBI was probably more in the dark than Uncle Joey.

"Hmm... so this person is coming after me," he said. "Who would be that stupid?"

An involuntary chuckle escaped my lips. "Yeah, you got that right."

Uncle Joey smiled, pleased at my reaction. His thoughts went to the trial, and he wished it were over so he could focus all his resources on this new threat. "Heard anything new about the trial?" he asked, thinking about Chris.

"Chris isn't worried about losing," I said. The way I said it caught Uncle Joey's attention.

"What is it?" he asked, suddenly suspicious that I wasn't telling him everything.

Damn! Now what? I couldn't tell him the whole truth. "He's just concerned with the threats I told you about. But it's nothing he can't handle. I'm the one who's having a hard time with it. I don't want Chris to get hurt."

"David will watch out for him," he said. "You don't have to worry."

"That's good to know." I kept my tone earnest, but light so he wouldn't question me again.

I sighed with relief when Ramos pulled up, and we got into the car. I checked the time, encouraged to find it was only eight o'clock. Luckily, I could still make it home before Chris.

Uncle Joey was thinking about how to find out who was threatening him. I tuned him out after the first scenario he came up with included kidnapping and torture. Ripping someone's nails off, or cutting off their fingers a little at a time made my stomach queasy.

I almost told him to stop with the torture part, and just let me listen to the guy's thoughts, but stopped myself. If he didn't think about me helping him, then why should I volunteer? Especially when he was in the mood to use torture anyway. I did not want to see that.

I put up my shields and kept them secure until we reached Thrasher Development. After parking the car, we all got out and, grabbing all my things, I quickly said goodbye. Uncle Joey glanced at me with confusion. "Where are you going?" he asked.

"Home. I want to get there before Chris so I don't have to explain where I've been."

Ramos was thinking that was a good idea, even though it was wrong to lie to my husband.

Uncle Joey wasn't finished with his diabolical plans, but he'd figure them out with Ramos and get my input later. "I might need your help tomorrow..." He glanced at Ramos, who kept a straight face, even though he knew what Manetto wanted me for.

Uncle Joey turned his gaze to me, thinking how handy I would be for his planned interrogations. I tried not to roll my eyes. Was he really going to kidnap some kid from a gang? "I will help... as long as it doesn't involve torture," I said. "Just give me a call."

I turned away before he could argue, and rushed to my car. After getting in, I pulled off the hat, wig, and glasses, relieved to scratch my itching head. This was big. Who in their right mind would want to take on Uncle Joey? The only person that came to mind was Kate, but she'd already tried that and lost... big-time. Plus, she didn't have the resources to pull it off. I mean... she had some money, but not the manpower to take on the gangs. It couldn't be her.

This was something I needed to talk to Chris about. He might not be happy I went to the club, but knowing about a possible threat to Uncle Joey could be useful. I doubted it would help his case, but it might make him back off from his plan to send Uncle Joey to prison. Especially since any plan that included sending him to prison was sure to backfire.

I arrived home, and pulled into the driveway. Finding the garage empty, I let out a breath of relief. I'd made it home before Chris! I rushed into the house, and yelled a quick hello to Josh before running to my room and changing my clothes.

I was pulling my hair into a ponytail when I heard the back door open. I stashed the wig and clothes into the back of my closet, and hurried downstairs to greet Chris.

"Hi honey!" I said, giving him a big hug. He held me for a moment before pulling back, and I noticed the circles under his eyes, along with the haggard line of his lips. "Are you okay?"

"Just tired," he answered. "I've been going over the case, and I can't find an easy way to lose. I've done too good of a job. I can't lose unless someone changes their testimony or I get new evidence of some kind. But that's just not going to happen."

"If that's the case, then it's better you don't lose. Uncle Joey would know, and he's not someone you mess with."

"But this could solve all our problems!" He sank into the couch and leaned his head back against the cushions. "I think I know what Manetto's been doing that's illegal, but with David working so closely with the company's files, he's probably got a backup plan that would implicate someone in the company who is completely innocent, and that person would end up in jail instead of Manetto. David's a wiz with computer programs and software. He could fix anything."

"That makes sense," I said, taking a seat beside him. "His son, Nick, works at a software company, and Uncle Joey just put him at the top of his organization."

"Manetto's got his fingers in everything that goes on in this city," Chris said. "It's kind of scary when you think about it."

"Yeah, that's for sure," I agreed. Now that Chris seemed to realize how powerful Uncle Joey was, it made it easier to tell him what I'd been doing. Only I found I didn't really want to. He was feeling bad enough already, and my involvement at the club would make it worse. Still, I had to tell him, regardless of how it made him feel.

"Did you have any dinner?" I asked instead, knowing he was always in a better mood when his stomach was full. "I could make you an omelet."

"Oh, no... I ate already. But thanks."

I nodded and was ready to tell him about my evening when he asked me a question. "Do you think you could come to the courtroom tomorrow? I think whoever's threatening me will be there. Maybe you can spot who it is."

"Um... that should work," I said. "I don't think I can be there the whole day though. What time would be best?"

"Morning," he said. "Maybe you could come between ten and noon. The note was left at that time today, so they might be there around the same time tomorrow."

"Okay, I'll come," I agreed. I thought it was a long shot, but what could it hurt? "I'd like to see the note. Do you have it?"

"Um... yeah. I think I put it in my briefcase. Let me look." He rummaged through the case at his feet. "Hmm... it's not there. Maybe it's in one of my pockets." He checked all his pockets, emptying out everything inside, but couldn't find the note. "I know I had it."

"Maybe you left it at work," I said.

"Yeah, that's it. I think I put it in my drawer. I'll check first thing in the morning."

"Okay," I said. "As long as someone didn't take it. Did it have your name on it?"

"Yes," Chris answered. "But no one would go through my drawers, and I always lock up before I leave. It's safe. I'll be sure and bring it home tomorrow, and you can look at it. I just wish this person would come forward instead of leaving notes. If they have evidence that would prove Manetto's guilt, I'd use it in a heartbeat. But then they wouldn't need to threaten me. They could just go straight to the prosecution."

"True," I agreed. "But it's got to be someone who knows you, and knows you'd want Uncle Joey to go to jail. How many people fit that description?"

"Only one," Chris said, his eyes lighting up. "Kate." He glanced at me with new determination. "It's got to be her," he continued. "She's the only one with inside information that could possibly know about Manetto's dealings with Webb Enterprises. She also knows about your involvement with Manetto, and that alone would give me the motivation to lose the case."

"That makes sense," I said. "But if she really wants Uncle Joey to go to prison, why doesn't she just turn state's evidence and testify against him?"

"She must still be harboring the ambition to take over his organization."

"Hmm... you could be right," I agreed. "But there's something we're missing. She's got to know it would never work."

"Not necessarily. She might not know anything about David, and what he does for Manetto. Without David, Manetto's vulnerable."

"There's more going on here than you realize," I said. Now was the time to tell him about my evening. "Uncle Joey needed my help earlier tonight." I explained that we went to an exclusive boxing club, and how the owner had said someone was taking over the gangs in the city. "They're coming after Uncle Joey next. That doesn't sound like Kate. She doesn't have that much influence, or enough money to buy the manpower and drugs it would take to pull something like this off."

After Chris' initial shock at what I'd done had worn off, he could see my reasoning. "You've got a point," he agreed. He stifled his dismay at my actions and asked, "You went as a security guard? With Ramos?"

"Yes," I admitted. "I was perfectly safe."

"Right." He was still trying to wrap his head around what I'd done without getting upset about it. "What was the club like?" He was thinking if he focused on that part, he wouldn't be as upset with me.

I told him the details of how we got in and out, and what the arena looked like. His interest spiked when I told him about the fight, and the special room above the arena in which we were entertained. By the time I was through, he was wishing he could have been there. Go figure. I wanted to tell him I'd trade places in a heartbeat, but that wouldn't be true. Having him in the kind of trouble I was in all the time would drive me nuts.

"Back to Kate," I said. "Now you know why I don't think it's her."

"Unless she found a partner," Chris interjected.

"Who would go to all that trouble for her? I mean... with both her previous partners dead? Not to mention her infatuation with you, and how selfish and mean she is. Besides all that, it would have to be somebody pretty stupid to agree to take on Uncle Joey."

"All right, you've made your point," he said. "But that doesn't mean we should say she's not involved at all. Who knows? She might have something to do with it."

"You're just flattered to think she'd go through all of this for you." As soon as the words were out of my mouth, I knew I shouldn't have said them.

"That's not true," he defended himself. "If you weren't so jealous you'd see that."

I hated when he was right. Why was I making such a big deal out of it? I thought for sure I was over it. "I guess I'm still upset about what happened with her. And the fact that she could be back just makes my blood boil." I had bad thoughts about her, which probably made me a bad person. But since her partners were both dead, how come she couldn't be dead too? It just wasn't fair.

Chris pulled me into his arms, and I rested my head against his shoulder. He was thinking things were complicated enough without adding Kate to the mix. She brought back all those feelings he'd hoped I would forget. Plus, he couldn't help feeling a little guilty, since he was the one she was after. But seriously, he couldn't help it if he was ruggedly handsome, and sexy as hell. What woman could resist? Women practically fell at his feet, and were always so disappointed to find out he was married. It was...

"All right! Stop. That's enough." I smacked Chris' shoulder.

"Ouch!" he said, feigning pain. "Hey, if you're going to listen, I might as well make it good. Am I right? Huh?"

"Yeah, yeah. You think you're so funny." I tried not to smile, but couldn't hold it back.

"I know, but at least you're smiling now." He pulled me back into his arms. "We'll get through this. You'll see. The trial's going well, and tomorrow's Thursday. I have both Thursday and Friday to present my case. After that we'll have the weekend to regroup. By Monday or Tuesday, we should have a verdict." He was thinking that tomorrow and Friday were going to be the toughest days of all, and he hoped he was ready. If Kate were going to carry out her threats, the next few days would be the time to do it.

"You really think it's Kate?" I asked, dismayed.

He sighed. "Now that the possibility is in my head, I can't think who else it would be. So yeah, I guess I'm assuming it's her. Which, for me, makes it easier for some reason."

"Yeah, that's because you don't think she'd beat you up and ruin your ruggedly handsome face."

"You're probably right." He chuckled and squeezed me. "So, you'll come tomorrow?"

"Yes, I'll be there." Something occurred to me. "If it is Kate, she's not going to be there. She'd have someone else leave the note."

"I know," he agreed. "And if she has a partner, it could be him." He noticed my frown and continued, "But even if it's not and you can pick up their thoughts, it will still tell us something about who it is. That's better than what we have now."

"I'll do what I can," I said, knowing it was still a long shot. "I'm also going to talk to Uncle Joey and see what he thinks about it being Kate."

"Why not?" Chris shrugged. "It will be good to know what he's thinking too."

I chuckled. "Anyone else?"

"No. That should do it for now."

"Good." I jumped up. "Because all of a sudden, I'm starving. Want some ice cream?"

"Sure!"

The next morning I got to the courthouse by nine-thirty. Although it was closer to ten before I got in the courtroom, since I forgot to take my stun flashlight out of my purse and had to go back to my car. I slipped it into the jockey box and hoped I'd remember it was there later.

I sat in the back corner where I could see the door, and who went in and out. The prosecution rested its case, and it was Chris' turn to present his defense. I was a little nervous, but Chris was doing a great job. So far, the only thing I'd picked up was that the prosecuting attorney was worried he'd lose. His evidence was good, but Chris had managed to find documents that made him look like a big bully. The jury was bound to empathize with Webb.

I thought about listening to each jury member to see who was leaning what way, but after scanning the first two, I started to get a headache. It was incredibly hard to pick out certain thoughts and block out all the others in the room. I could probably do it if I had to, but from what I could pick up, not one of the jurors had made a decision one way or the other. I'd talk to Chris and try again later if he thought it was necessary.

My phone vibrated, and the caller ID said it was Uncle Joey. I'd been expecting a call from him, so I gathered my things and hurried out into the hall. "Hello," I answered softly.

"Why are you whispering?" Uncle Joey asked.

"I'm in court, helping Chris with the case."

"Oh," he paused. "You're helping Chris? How's it going?"

"Pretty good," I answered. "I have some questions for you. Can I come by in about fifteen minutes?"

Silence answered me, followed by a quick breath. "That will be fine," he growled. He disconnected, leaving me confused. What had I done to offend him? Was he worried about what I was telling Chris? He had told me not to tell Chris anything, but if it helped his case, why not?

It was nearly noon, and I was pretty sure Chris wasn't going to get another note until it looked like he would win the case. Right now, it was still up in the air, so the person threatening him would have to wait a little longer to know how it was going to go. Since I hadn't 'heard' anything useful, I might as well leave now.

Walking to my car, I got another phone call. This time it was from the bank manager, Blaine Smith.

"Hi Shelby," Blaine said. "I'd like to go over your progress with the stolen money. Do you have a minute today?"

"Sure," I answered. "I've got an appointment right now, but I can come over after that."

"Good. I'll be in my office all afternoon."

We disconnected, and I realized something was off. The normal warmth in his voice was missing. He'd seemed tense and cold. I also hadn't expected to talk to him until tomorrow, or at least next Monday. Had something changed?

Then it hit me that I hadn't seen or heard anything from Rob Felt since he went after those guys yesterday. Usually he was following me everywhere I went, but not today, or last night. I should be grateful... and I was, but did that mean he was in trouble? Was he lying dead somewhere? Was it my fault? Alarm tightened my chest. I should probably try and contact him, just in case. Maybe Blaine had his cell number.

I pulled into the parking garage of Thrasher Development and hurried to the elevator. Knowing I was about to face Uncle Joey sent a chill up my spine. Uncle Joey's response to my involvement in Chris' case worried me. As I contemplated why he could be upset, I rubbed my arms against the sudden cold. I was doing everything he wanted. It didn't make sense for him to be upset with me.

I got off the elevator and entered Thrasher Development. Jackie sat at her desk and gave me a polite smile, but there was an underlying menace to it. She was thinking that I'd better not double-cross her man. What? Where had that come from?

"Hi Shelby," she said without warmth. "He's in his office waiting for you."

"Thanks." Puzzled, I turned down the hall, and met Ramos coming toward me. He could hardly look at me, and was thinking that after saving my life more than once, it was hard to believe I'd double-cross Manetto.

"Hey," he said, leaving out his usual 'babe' greeting. He just didn't have it in him. He worried about what would happen next, and hoped I'd be able to explain my way out of it.

By now, my stomach had clenched into a tight little ball. "What's going on?" I asked. "Why so glum?"

"I'll do what I can for you," he said softly. "Even if he wants you dead, I promise I won't let that happen." He couldn't face losing me, even if it meant going against Manetto.

As my legs went weak he opened the door. What the freak! I swallowed, finally summoning the strength to move into the office. Uncle Joey's eyes went from sad to hard so quickly I might have missed it if I hadn't been watching so closely.

"Come in Shelby." Taking in my bewildered expression, Uncle Joey softened, thinking it had to be a big mistake. As Ramos followed me into the room, he held up his hand. "Give us a minute, Ramos."

Ramos was caught between his allegiance to Uncle Joey and his concern for me. Before it became too apparent to Uncle Joey, I glanced at him, and with my eyes, motioned him out. His brows creased together, but with an imperceptible nod, he left.

Turning back to Uncle Joey, relief coursed through me to find he hadn't noticed our little exchange. I squared my shoulders and faced him. "I don't know what's going on, but I swear I haven't done anything wrong. So let's get this cleared up. We have a lot of work to do."

Uncle Joey straightened, narrowing his eyes. A glint came into them, and his lips turned up into a grudging smile. I never failed to surprise him. He liked that. "Good. Then you can explain this note." He threw the folded piece of paper toward me, and I eagerly picked it up.

I read through the contents, realizing it was the threat sent to Chris the day before. David must have given it to Uncle Joey last night. Now I knew why Uncle Joey was upset. He thought I was working with Chris to lose the case.

"I can't believe you think I'd be that stupid." I quickly sat down, relieved to know what was going on. "Chris got this note yesterday, and he might have been tempted to follow through, but I convinced him it would never work. Last night he agreed.

"It's part of why I wanted to talk to you today," I continued. "We think it had to come from someone who knows that Chris would want you in jail, mostly for my sake. Anyone like that come to mind?"

"Yes... Kate," Uncle Joey said, chagrined that he hadn't thought of it sooner.

"That's exactly what we thought. First, she knows you're after her for the money and jewels she took. Second, she probably wants revenge for her father's death. Which she believes you caused," I added hastily, careful not to let on that I knew he'd killed him. "Third, she might still want to run your organization. And last, she hates me and is after my husband. Those are all good reasons for her to risk coming back."

Uncle Joey shook his head. "But that doesn't explain everything. How could she manage all of this? With the gangs and everything?"

"Well, she'd have to have a partner," I used Chris' reasoning. "You know she's got a lot of money. Maybe by stirring up existing circumstances, she's hoping to offer protection to people you've harassed all these years. At least until you're out of the picture." I nervously licked my lips, hoping I hadn't offended him about the harassment part.

Uncle Joey considered it. "She does have ambition, I'll give you that. But I'm just not sure with her limited resources she could pull it off."

"You have a point," I agreed. "But it is possible." I couldn't believe I sounded just like Chris.

"Sure," he said, unconvinced. "Lots of things are possible." He was thinking Kate would have to have a pretty smart partner to get this far. Even then, it was a stretch. "So our next step is to find her. Or if it's not her, find whoever it is. That hasn't changed."

"Right," I answered.

He was thinking that he could still go through with his plan, and just take out the part where he locked me up until Chris came around.

"So... you weren't going to kill me?" I asked.

"Hell no. Whatever gave you that idea?"

"Well... Jackie was pretty upset when I came in. So was Ramos."

He snorted. He knew Ramos would never hurt me. Not after all the times he'd saved my life. No... if Uncle Joey wanted me dead, he figured that with all the trouble I got in, he'd just stay away and let it happen naturally.

"Seriously?" I grumbled. "Most of the trouble I get in is because of you."

"Pretty much," he agreed. "And I'm always there to bail you out." He let the implications of that sink in. "But don't worry, Shelby. I don't think it will ever come to that."

What could I say? Thanks so much? I don't know what I'd do without you? He could tell he'd hurt my feelings, but he decided to let it go. It wouldn't do if I thought he really cared or something. No... it wouldn't do at all. Damn... had I just heard that?

Keeping his head down, he silently berated himself for the irony, thinking it was time to work harder at protecting his thoughts. Someday he'd do it, but for now, it wasn't worth the trouble.

"So, what's your plan?" I asked, steering him back to Kate, and hoping he'd never take the time to learn.

"I need you and Ramos to follow a lead with the South End. After I notified them of what was going down last night, they found a dealer with ties to this new gang. I need you and Ramos to go check it out, see what you can 'hear' from him. I don't want them to know we know anything about them yet. So you have to be discreet." He was thinking maybe I could dress up like a hooker and buy some drugs or something. Ramos would go with me for protection. I'd be fine.

"No way! I'm not doing that."

He was afraid I'd say that. "Do you have a better idea?"

"Yeah. Get Ramos and some of these South End guys to grab him, and bring him here to the basement for questioning. You could keep him blindfolded so he'd never know who you are, and even if he didn't answer your questions, I'd hear them and tell you."

Uncle Joey sighed. If he did that, the guy was a dead man. No way could he let him go back and warn his gang that someone was asking questions about them. He'd have to make it look like an overdose so they wouldn't suspect anything. He could do it if he had to, but it would cost him.

Thoughts of this guy's death on my hands weren't any better. "Isn't there something else we can do?" I asked.

"Well... I guess we could keep the dealer locked up somewhere until this is over."

"That could work," I said with relief. "Hey... what about the police? We could tip them off and have him arrested. I could talk to him at the police station with Dimples. That would be even better. No one would suspect you had anything to do with it."

"Hmm... you know... that's a good idea," he said. "Let's ask Ramos, and see what he thinks. He should be out in the hall. Would you mind getting him?"

"Not at all," I said. I pulled the door open to find Ramos standing guard across the hall. "We're good," I said with a smile. "And we need you," I added.

"Took you long enough," he grumbled under his breath. He was thinking that life was much easier before he met me. Being Manetto's number one man gave him power, respect, and a lot of money. He never questioned Manetto's orders, and the job suited him just fine... until I came along.

Well, maybe that wasn't entirely true. The job still suited him just fine, but it was me who drove him crazy.

"What's up?" Ramos asked.

Uncle Joey filled him in on our conversation about the note and my suspicions about Kate. Ramos was thinking Kate being involved was a long shot, but stranger things had happened. Letting the police know about the drug dealer shouldn't be a problem. But getting them to actually arrest him might. "Walter used to be our contact with the police," Ramos said. "Whose job is that now?"

"I've given that to Ricky," Uncle Joey said. "He's been in touch with our contact." Uncle Joey glanced at me, careful not to think of the police detective's name. I shuttered my mind to block his thoughts. That was one thing I did not want to know.

"Maybe it would be better for me to tell Dimples," I said. "Then I could be involved. Otherwise, it might not work."

Uncle Joey frowned. "How would you do that?" he asked.

"Well," I took a breath. "Dimples thinks I have premonitions about things, and I could make up something about this drug dealer that would make him check it out."

"What... like he sells drugs?" Ramos chuckled.

"It's a little more complicated than that." I frowned to show my displeasure. "But yeah, basically. It might have to be connected to another case I'm working on with Dimples." I was already thinking I could tie it into my interview with the undercover FBI agent, and Razor, whom I'd seen at Lanny's. "But... I'll figure it out and talk to him this afternoon. Maybe we can bring him in sometime today."

"You really think that's going to work?" Uncle Joey said, skeptically.

"Sure. Just tell me his name and where he is."

Ramos shook his head. "If you show up with a cop, he's going to be long gone before you can talk to him. I don't think that will work. I have a better idea." He turned to Uncle Joey. "How about I pretend I'm an undercover cop, and I grab him?

"Shelby could join me as my partner while I question him. Once Shelby knows who he works for, we could let him go with a warning that we're watching him, and he'll think it's the cops, not us, who are doing the harassing. When he leaves, we could even have someone from the South End trail him to find out where he goes."

"I like it," Uncle Joey said. "And following him would get us one step closer to the leader. Shelby?"

I pursed my lips. Ramos had a point, and not involving Dimples was probably a good idea. "Yeah, okay. When do you want to go after him?"

"I'll call my contact and see where he is right now," Uncle Joey said, keeping his mind blank. He glanced at me. "Why don't you wait in the other room until we finalize things?"

"Okay," I said, slipping from the room. There was a lot about Uncle Joey's organization I didn't know, and I was glad to keep it that way.

I wandered down the hall to Jackie's desk. She sent a piercing glance my way, thinking that if I was still here and unharmed, it must have turned out all right. Good thing, since she liked me.

I smiled at her. "Hey, do you have a Diet Coke around here someplace?" I knew she did since she was thinking about getting one for herself. "I can get you one too, if you'd like."

"Sure," she said. "You know the apartment down the hall, where Ramos stays sometimes? There's some in the fridge in the kitchen." She really wanted it with ice in a glass, but that was probably asking too much, so she didn't say anything.

"Right," I nodded. "I'll be back." I hurried down the hall and opened the door to the apartment. After closing it, I leaned back and let out a sigh, savoring the silence. Privacy and alone time seemed rare these days. The apartment was just as I remembered it. Clean and spotless, but more like a hotel suite than a home. I knew Ramos stayed here a lot, but where did he really live, and what was it like?

I could only imagine it being just like this. He didn't seem to have a life... only work. The fact that he would go against Uncle Joey for me... well, I wasn't sure how I felt about that. It might help if he knew Uncle Joey cared about me too. But I also knew that sometimes caring wasn't enough when it came to Uncle Joey. If I had double-crossed him... well, that would be the end, no matter how he felt.

I crossed to the kitchen and opened the cupboards until I found a glass. Then opened the fridge and got out the Cokes and ice. I took my time filling up Jackie's glass, in no hurry to get back. Waiting for the foam to go down, I wandered over to the huge windows to take in the view. If I could, I'd sit down on the plush couch and be content to watch the world go by. If only life were that simple.

I heard the door open and jerked like I'd been caught doing something wrong. As I turned to leave, Ramos walked in. He narrowed his eyes, wondering what I was doing there.

"Just enjoying the view," I said. "I mean... I came to get a Diet Coke for me and Jackie, and couldn't resist looking out the window."

He smiled, nodding with understanding. "Yeah, it kind of pulls you over, doesn't it?"

"Uh-huh," I agreed. "So what's the verdict? Are we leaving soon?"

"Yeah," he said. "I need to get ready. Change my clothes. Then we can take off."

"I'll get out of your way then." The changing his clothes part made me nervous, so I hurried past him to the kitchen. He disappeared into the bedroom, and I finished pouring the Coke, grabbed mine, and was out of there in record time. Ramos and I had a relationship that was totally platonic, and I didn't want to jeopardize that in any way.

Jackie smiled with surprise when I gave her the glass. How did I know? "I thought it would keep cold longer with some ice," I quickly explained. "But if you prefer, you can take the can, and I'll drink that."

"No," she said. "This is great. Thanks."

"You bet." I found a certain satisfaction when I got to use my powers this way. It made me feel good, plus it never hurt to be nice to people.

I moved to the sofa and sat, knowing I'd have to wait a moment for Ramos. Not surprisingly, the beginning of a headache was coming on, so I got some aspirin out of my purse, and washed them down with a swig of Coke.

A few minutes later, Ramos came down the hall, and my mouth dropped open in surprise. If I didn't know better, I wouldn't have known who he was. He wore a tight, black, sleeveless muscle shirt, worn jeans held up by a studded belt with a skull and crossbones buckle, and a navy bandana covering his hair. His ear had a big diamond stud in it, and his muscled shoulder was covered in a tattoo. To finish it all off, he sported a pair of dark glasses and was chewing on a toothpick. He smirked at my response, and I snapped my mouth shut.

"Nice disguise," I said, breathlessly. "Is that tattoo real?"

He nodded, thinking it would have been fun to dress me up too, but since I was playing the part of a straight cop, it wasn't necessary. "Let's go," he said. "I'll explain what's happening on the way."

Chapter 10

I followed Ramos to the elevator, grateful I was on his side; otherwise I'd find him totally intimidating.

"Our guys are keeping watch," he said. "But I'll have to drop you off where they're hiding so you won't blow my cover. They're in a building close to where the dealer's set up shop. Just stay with them until I bring the dealer there."

"You're bringing the dealer to the building?" I asked. "How are you going to do that?"

"That's my problem," he said, thinking he had a plan and I didn't need to know. Mostly because I wouldn't approve. "You just sit tight and wait for me."

The elevator doors opened, and we stepped out into the parking garage. "Over here," Ramos said, nodding toward the right. I followed him around the corner and jerked to a halt. The only thing in that corner was a flashy black motorcycle.

"That's yours?" I asked.

"Here." Ramos tossed me a helmet, which I barely caught. "It might be a little big for you, but we can tighten up the straps."

"But... my skirt." Since I was going to court that day, I'd worn my black boots with a black knee-length tiered skirt, a fitted white tee, and a sweet black vest with little chains on it. Around my waist, I wore an elastic black belt that hooked together with a silver buckle. Luckily, since my skirt wasn't tight, I might be able to straddle the seat without too much leg showing.

Ramos shrugged. "I'll be sitting in front of you. You'll be fine. But we need to go before the dealer leaves the area." He backed the motorcycle out and turned it around.

I slung my purse over my shoulder and stuffed my hair into the back of my shirt before pulling the helmet on. I found the strap, but couldn't find the snap on the other side.

"Here," Ramos said. "Let me do it." He quickly snapped the strap in place and did something that tightened it. "Okay, get on," he said, scooting forward.

With the big floppy helmet on, I could hardly see out of it, let alone find the foot pedal. How was I supposed to do this in a skirt and keep my dignity?

"Here, give me your hand, and slide your leg through to the other side." Ramos grabbed my arm to steady me, and I slid my leg over, but then I was stuck. I couldn't get all the way on. "Grab hold of my shoulders and pull yourself up."

I did what he said, and managed to get centered, but my feet were dangling, and my skirt was hitched up clear to my thighs. With his hand, Ramos guided my left foot to the pedal, and once I found where it was, I got my other foot situated.

"Ready?" he asked.

"No!" I yelped. "I've got to fix my skirt." I quickly stood on the pedals and with both hands, smoothed my skirt under me and sat, pulling it down my thighs as far as I could. I tucked it under me, hoping the breeze wouldn't blow it up too much. "Okay, I think I'm ready."

"Hold on," Ramos said. He pushed a switch, stepped down on the starter, and the engine revved, sending a ripple of excitement through me. He settled in his seat, and we roared out of the parking garage. I closed my eyes, grabbing Ramos' waist in a death grip.

We came to a stop, and I cracked my eyes open. We'd only gone from the parking garage to the street, and my heart was pounding to beat the devil.

Ramos glanced over his shoulder. "Put your visor down," he shouted. "On your helmet."

"Oh, right." I flipped the visor down, and Ramos made a right turn into traffic. As we zipped down the street, I decided it was best to keep my eyes open. Since I couldn't see much anyway, it was better to know what was coming. It kept me from freaking out.

A few minutes later, I started to get the hang of it, and my breathing settled down. I relaxed and let out a breath, finally enjoying the ride. My skirt was flapping in the breeze, but luckily, it was still tucked under enough to be okay. I hoped... since there was no way I was going to let go of Ramos long enough to fix it.

We rounded a corner, and I held on tight, catching my breath. Ramos yelled something over his shoulder, but I couldn't hear him well enough to understand what he was saying. He yelled again, but I still didn't get it. Then something strange happened. I could feel the muscles in his stomach wiggling. What was he doing? His shoulders started to twitch, and it finally dawned on me that he was laughing.

"What's so funny?" I yelled. Of course, with the helmet on, and the visor down, I doubted he could hear me.

About ten minutes later, Ramos turned down an alley that curved around to the back of a building and slowed to a stop, killing the engine. His stomach was still wiggling, so I quickly let go of him and scrambled off the seat. He caught my arm before I fell, and I managed to stand on both my feet with my skirt still intact around me.

Feeling a bit claustrophobic, I tugged at the helmet snap and pulled, but it wouldn't budge. With the helmet this big, I was ready to try pulling it off any way I could. Totally frustrated, I started tugging at it, but nothing happened.

"Here, let me help you," Ramos said. With a quick jerk he got the strap undone, and pulled the helmet off my head in one swift move.

My hair was full of static, and it covered my eyes, but I could still see Ramos' barely contained mirth. Was he laughing at me? I probably looked pretty awful, but still. I shoved my hair back and combed my fingers through to loosen the tangles. "What's so funny?"

Ramos shook his head. "You. Is that the first time you've ever ridden on a motorcycle?"

I wanted to deny it, but he knew it was true. "What gave me away?" I said instead.

He chuckled again, shaking his head. "Babe... I thought you were going to break my ribs."

"Oh... sorry," I said.

"It's okay," he assured me. "Just don't hold on so tight on the way back, okay?"

"Yeah, sure." I could feel my face going red with embarrassment.

Before I could say another word, he handed me the helmet and focused his attention on the building behind us. "Keep hold of this," he said.

I turned to see what had caught his attention, and found a scary looking dude coming toward us. Ramos faced the man, and his shoulders tightened with tension. The guy did something with his hands, and Ramos suddenly relaxed his stance. He turned back to me. "Come on." He was thinking something about the South End, so I figured they were with us, and it was all right.

I followed him to the door, and the guy held it open. His clothes were along the same line as what Ramos was wearing, only without the bandana. He was wondering what I was doing there, but since I was with Ramos, it must be okay.

The room we entered was filled with dirty cupboards and rusty filing cabinets. There was a desk in the corner along with a couple of old tattered chairs. Other than that, it was empty. There were two other guys inside, and with the addition of Ramos and me, the room seemed pretty small.

"Is he still there?" Ramos asked.

"Yeah, but not for long. We'd better get over there. He's got two guys watching his back, so we'll have to move fast."

"I'll approach from the street," Ramos said. "You know what to do."

The three guys left in a hurry, and Ramos turned to me. "Wait here." Without waiting for an answer, he walked out the door. His motorcycle rumbled to life, and I followed the sound until it was indistinguishable.

I frowned, wondering what I was supposed to do if he didn't come back. This was a side of Ramos I had never seen before. It was like he was in full Metal Gear Solid Mode, and his mind was focused and blank. I had no idea what he planned, or how he planned to do it.

Maybe that was a good thing. Did I really want to know all the gory details? Not really. At least I knew they were going to bring the dealer back here for questioning. I dusted off the nicest looking chair and sat down to wait.

After about ten minutes, I needed to find a bathroom. That Diet Coke had gone right through me, and I instantly regretted drinking it. Maybe there was a bathroom in the building. I found a door along the back wall and turned the handle. It opened, and I took a quick peek to the other side.

I was facing a wall, and to my left and right was a long hallway. Leaving the door ajar behind me, I stepped into the hall, and wandered down until I came to another door. It was locked, so I figured it was another office. I turned back the way I came, and at the end of the hall, I found it. Now if only it worked!

Opening the door, relief swept over me. The place was somewhat dirty, but not as bad as I thought. I flushed the toilet, just to make sure it worked, then wiped it down with a tissue from my purse. I'd learned long ago to keep tissues in my purse, and today was one of those days I was particularly grateful. Still, I didn't think I'd actually sit on it.

After finishing up, I washed my hands in the sink, drying them with another tissue. I pulled the door open, and took a step into the hallway, but froze. The door down the hall slammed open and a body flew into the hallway. I quickly retreated, knowing I was safer in the bathroom than out there.

"Where is she?" A voice I recognized roared.

I hurried out of the bathroom, just as Ramos raised a fist to hit the guy again. "What's going on?" I asked, hoping to distract him. Ramos lowered his fist, and glowered at me. Where had I gone? He'd told me to wait.

"Potty break," I said, motioning behind me. "So... is that him?"

Ramos growled, and dragged the guy back into the room. I followed, but kept my distance. Ramos dumped him unceremoniously into a chair, and cuffed his arms behind him. He glanced at the three South End guys and they left, casting surreptitious glances my way. I caught a stray thought about me and frowned. Of course, the way Ramos had acted probably made it seem like I was his girlfriend, but did they have to think I wasn't his type? At all?

I closed the door behind me and stayed there, content to keep out of the dealer's sight and let Ramos handle it. Ramos glanced at me, and I nodded. His questioning began. "The only reason you're still alive is because I need some answers. If you want to stay that way, you'll tell me what I need to know."

"You can't kill me," the dealer said. "Cops don't do that. Either take me in or let me go."

"Don't be so sure," Ramos growled. "Who'd care about another dead dealer found in some back alley or abandoned building? Not anyone I know. I'll start easy. You're new in town. Who do you work for?"

He kept his lips pressed together, but I heard the answer clearly.

"Not going to tell me?" Ramos said. "Then how about this. Where are you from? Why are you here?"

Again, he kept his mouth shut, but I heard his answer. Ramos glanced at me, and I nodded. His brows drew together on a frown. How could he let this guy go when he hadn't answered any of his questions?

"What's in it for you?" Ramos asked. "Is it worth your life? Or prison? Tell me what you know, and we won't press charges. You can leave a free man. You see... I'm not after you. It's the big guy I want. Just tell me what you know, and I'll let you walk out of here."

"No," he said. "Either take me to jail or let me go. I'm not telling you anything."

"Cut him lose," I said, knowing what I needed to do. I walked over to him and leaned into his face. "You think you're so smart, but you listen to me. We'll be watching you. Every move you make. We're going to take your boss down, and when we do, he's going to think it was you who ratted him out. How's that going to go for you?"

Fear shuddered through him loud and clear. I'd hit a nerve. He was thinking it didn't matter, because he was leaving this place. The free drugs, the money... all of it just wasn't worth getting mixed up in this war. The cops had no idea, and he was alive because he'd always known when to check his losses and move on.

I straightened, glancing at Ramos. With reluctance, he undid the cuffs and hauled the dealer out the door by the scruff of his neck. As soon as his feet touched the ground he was up and running. I knew we'd never see him again.

"Did you get the answers?" asked Ramos.

I glanced at him. Until now, we'd been dancing around my secret without admitting it. Once I told him the answers, it meant something would change between us. But since he'd already figured it out, maybe it wouldn't be so bad. I decided to trust him... out loud anyway. "Mostly," I said.

"Is it Kate?" he asked.

"Nope, at least not that I could tell. Remember the security guy Uncle Joey hired while you were gone looking for Kate?"

"Yeah," he said. "Doug Carter. He's the one that left all those bugs."

"He's part of it," I nodded. "But there's more. There's someone else, but that's where it gets tricky. I didn't get a name, but whoever it is scared the crap out of that guy."

"Huh," Ramos said, thinking he had his work cut out for him. "At least we have a name. What about the dealer? Do you think he'll warn Carter about the cops?"

"No. He's leaving town. Unless Carter gets to him first."

Ramos rocked back on his heels. This was serious. "We'd better get back."

This time, I got on the motorcycle before I put on the helmet. Ramos still had to help me snap the strap, but at least he didn't have to haul me over the seat. I started out holding onto his waist with gentle pressure until he sped up, and my gut reaction was to squeeze for all I was worth. I felt the wiggling of his stomach, and knew he was laughing again. He'd sped up on purpose. I shook my head, but couldn't help the smile that creased my lips.

We got back to Thrasher intact, and I found that I liked riding a motorcycle. I was almost disappointed to have it end. As Ramos punched the call button for the elevator, I checked my watch, surprised to find it was just after three-thirty.

"Shoot! I've got to go," I said. "Tell Uncle Joey to call me if he has any questions. Okay?"

Ramos frowned, unhappy I was skipping out on him. "I really think you should come with me."

"Why?" I asked. "You can tell him everything I know." He hesitated, so I went in for the kill. "It will really help me out. Please?"

"Where are you going?" he asked.

"To the bank. I have to talk to the manager about the case of the missing money I'm working on. If I leave now, I won't be late getting home."

Ramos shook his head. Manetto wasn't going to be happy. It always made him mad when I did stuff like this. Why couldn't I just work for Manetto, and not take all these side jobs? He could still hardly believe I worked with the police. Of course, it could come in handy down the road. Maybe the police had a record on Carter. Could I check that out? Manetto would be a lot more understanding if I agreed to do that.

"Sure," I said. "But probably not until tomorrow. Bye."

Ramos smiled, and stepped into the elevator. "See you tomorrow," he said.

I wasn't sure who won that round, him or me? I had a feeling it was him. I caught a fleeting thought from him before the doors closed, and reached up to touch my hair. Yes, it was a tangled mess, just like he'd been thinking.

By the time I got to the bank, I'd run my fingers through my hair enough times that it was presentable. Just not looking the best. I'd have to remember to stash a brush in my glove box for times like this.

Blaine stood when I entered his office, and motioned to the chair in front of his desk. His smile was brief, and I remembered the hostility I'd sensed from him over the phone. "Hi Shelby, thanks for coming. Have a seat."

He was thinking it would sure be nice if I had something good to tell him. Especially since Rob Felt had called to say he was close to finding the money. Blaine wondered why I hadn't told him anything. I was the investigator he'd hired. I should really keep him in the loop. Plus, he really didn't want to pay Felt the finder's fee. He'd much rather pay me for my time since it would be a better deal.

"How's the case coming?" he asked.

I was still reeling from that bit of information and didn't respond right away. "Um... good. I've made some really good progress."

"Wonderful," Blaine said, relieved and eager to hear my side of the story. "What have you found so far?"

"Just so you know," I added, "Felt's been following me everywhere. The leads I've had, everything I've done, he's been right behind me. Yesterday he caught up with me and we sort of staked out a store together. I haven't seen him since. Have you heard from him lately?"

"That's funny you should ask. He called me just before I called you today, and said he was real close to finding the money. Do you know what he's talking about? Is it true that he's close?"

"He can't be any closer than me," I answered, hotly. "Let me tell you what I've found, and we can go from there. First of all, there's an underwear shop called Novelty Creations that Keith's Aunt Dottie owned, and where Keith was working prior to the robbery.

"The aunt died right around the same time Keith got arrested. Her daughter owns the shop now, so I've been following up with her. During the police investigation, the police checked out the shop, but they never found anything. They did confiscate two crates of underwear, but I don't know exactly what happened to them. They may have been put up for auction or they're still somewhere in the evidence room. The daughter has no record of them being taken, so it seems to be a dead end, although I'm not so sure.

"I did trace a couple of shipments that Keith sent to another underwear shop the year before he was arrested. This shop is called Betty's Bra Bar, and it's the store I staked out with Felt yesterday. Betty mostly sells bras, but I think something else is going on there. Every once in a while, she closes the shop and people go in. A few minutes later, they come out, and she opens the store again. I don't know what's going on, but I think it might be tied to the stolen money."

"How? You think the money might be in her shop?" he asked.

I sighed. "I'm not sure. All I have so far is the link to Keith Bishop. I can't prove she has the money. But besides that, I think she's doing something illegal."

"Like what?" He was thinking she was probably a hooker.

"I don't think she's a hooker... if that's what you're thinking," I quickly added. "Mostly because of the people she meets with. There's something different about them. I just wish I could figure out what it is. Yesterday, I was watching the shop when Felt showed up. We saw three men go inside, and when they came out, he followed them. I haven't heard from him since. It's possible that he thinks they have the money hidden somewhere. But I don't believe that. I think it's got to be somewhere else." I decided not to tell him about Betty meeting up with Dimples until I had a chance to talk to Dimples first. That was my next step.

"Hmm..." Blaine said. "Well he must be okay since he called to tell me about his lead."

"Did he say what it was?" I asked.

"No," Blaine said. "He didn't explain anything, except for saying he thought he knew where the money was. He also said that I shouldn't believe anything you said because you have ties to some suspicious people with whom you could arrange to keep the money for yourself. He implied that these people would help you, for a fee of course, to launder the money so it couldn't be traced back to you."

"What?" That arrogant jerk was trying to set me up. "And do you believe him?" I asked.

"Not at all," Blaine assured me. He was thinking that the only person who could do that around here was Manetto, and since he owned most of the bank, that notion was ridiculous. But Felt's implication made sense if he thought I worked for Manetto. On one hand, Blaine couldn't be too mad at Felt for that, but he would hate to have to pay him the finder's fee. Especially now that he knew Felt was following me all this time.

"He wouldn't have anything to go on without you," Blaine continued. "I don't know why he would say those things about you, but I'm sure they're not true. I just wanted to give you a heads-up about what he told me. He might act like he's being helpful, but I think he'd leave you high and dry in a flash if he could."

"Yeah, I get that. I'll just have to see if I can use his 'helpfulness' to get him off my back."

"Good luck with that," Blaine said. Now that he knew what was going on, he felt much better. "So... how many hours have you used up so far?"

"Let me see." I checked the time-card app on my phone. "About eighteen."

"That's not bad. I'll authorize another twenty hours. How does that sound?" he asked.

"Works for me." I stood to leave, and Blaine extended his hand.

"Keep me in the loop," he said. "I'd like to know if you catch a break, or if there's anything at all I can do to help."

"I will." We shook hands and, after pulling away, I hesitated. "There is one thing you can do. If Felt calls you again, will you let me know?"

"I can do that," Blaine agreed.

"Good. Thanks so much. I'll see you later." I left his office, working to get control of the anger simmering beneath the surface. And I had been concerned for Felt? Ha, that was a joke. And now he thought he knew where the money was? Is that why I hadn't seen him today? I'd show him, that worthless piece of crap.

By telling Blaine that I was involved with Uncle Joey, he'd gone too far. I couldn't let that go unchallenged. Thank goodness Blaine knew better than to believe him. Then I realized that as much as I didn't want to talk to Felt again, it was the only way to find out his plans, but after that, sending him off on a wild goose chase would be sweet revenge.

I got in my car and tried to decide what to do next. My first thought was to find Felt and beat him up, but I should probably save that for later. I also needed to talk to Dimples about Betty, and find out what he knew about her. I could check on Doug Carter at the police station for Ramos at the same time, but now that Uncle Joey knew about him, he'd probably have more success finding him that I would.

My stomach chose that moment to growl, and I realized I'd missed lunch. I rummaged around in my purse until I found a granola bar that had probably been there for a few months. The wrapper was smudged, and the bar was smashed on one end, but I was too hungry to care.

The most important thing right now was probably Chris. I'd kind of ditched him this morning, and I was feeling a little guilty that I'd left without a word. I could go back to the courthouse and see how the trial was going. By now, if it looked like he wasn't purposely losing the case, the bad guy might make his move. He'd probably forget about writing another note, and just go straight for the jugular. I'd better get over there and protect him.

In a state of growing panic, I started the car and took the quickest route I could find. Instead of wasting time trying to find a parking space, I parked in Chris' garage. I jumped out, hurrying up the stairs, through the square, and across the street. Huffing and out of breath, I took a seat in the back of the courtroom, relief coursing over me to see that Chris was all right.

I relaxed into my seat and caught my breath, realizing the stress of the day was getting to me. Too much was going on, and I wasn't sure I could handle it all. Was this how I wanted to live my life? Not really, but I couldn't think about that right now. I needed to focus on helping Chris. I could figure everything else out later.

Calmer now, I closed my eyes and concentrated on listening to the thoughts swirling around in my brain. Picking and choosing which ones might mean something, and pushing out the others. I heard plenty about the case, along with others who were hungry, tired, and more than ready to go home.

Nothing threatening Chris. From what I could pick up though, it sounded like he was winning. Was anyone mad about that? I kept my mind open, and the constant barrage brought the beginning of a headache. Then I heard it. A woman's familiar voice thinking, *why isn't he losing? I thought for sure my note would work.* It was Kate!

I scanned the crowd, looking for a woman with red hair. Nothing matched. Maybe she was wearing a hat? Or her hair was pinned back. She had to be somewhere nearby.

Suddenly, the judge slammed down his gavel, adjourning court for the day. Everyone stood as the judge left, cutting off my view. I heard something about tonight, but lost it in the bustle of people leaving.

I rushed out the door and followed the crowd to the elevators. Most of them continued on to the stairs, and I hurried in that direction, figuring that if I couldn't hear her in the crowd, I could beat the elevators and pick her up as she got out. I got as close to the middle of the crowd as I could, but couldn't pick up her thoughts.

I continued out through the main doors and lingered nearby, listening to everyone who was leaving. Focusing outward, I heard her. She was off to the side, and halfway across the square. This time she was wondering why Chris hadn't taken the bait. It wouldn't have been that hard to lose the case. Was Chris in Manetto's pocket? She never thought that would happen. Regardless of her feelings, she'd have to let her partner take care of him. Better do it tonight.

I spotted her about fifty feet ahead of me. She removed a hat, shaking out her fiery red hair. It fell down her back in all its glory. I clenched my teeth. Seeing her shot a wave of hot anger through me. As she neared the street, a black car pulled up, and she quickly opened the door to get in. Turning her head, she shot a glance in my direction. Finding my gaze pinned on her, she slowly smiled, stopping me in my tracks. *Gotcha.* Her thought blazed through my mind like a siren. Then she was gone.

Chapter 11

My hands started to shake, and I couldn't seem to catch my breath. Gotcha? Had she been playing me this whole time? Did this mean she knew about me? I thought back to the shoot-out in Uncle Joey's office the last time I'd seen Kate, and tried to remember exactly what I'd said.

Had I actually told her I could read minds? Oh no! I had. I remembered it was the only way I could think to distract her or Walter from shooting me. But I never thought she'd believed it. Maybe she hadn't. Until now. I'd just confirmed it, and she gloatingly let me know with that one word.

I staggered, turning back to the courthouse, hardly seeing what was in front of me. Were any of her threats against Chris real? Or just meant to draw me out? I couldn't risk Chris' safety, no matter what. So that brought me to the big question. Why had she done it? What did she have to gain? Did she even care about the case? Was it all an act to find out the truth about me?

With these thoughts swirling through my mind, I entered the courtroom, hardly remembering how I got there. Chris and David stood at the table, talking in quiet tones, the only people left in the room. Chris glanced at me, his words coming to an abrupt halt, and his eyes widening with concern.

"Shelby... what's wrong?" He hurried toward me. "You look like you've seen a ghost. What's happened?"

"I... um... it's Kate," I sputtered. "I saw her leaving. She's the one who's been sending you those threats."

Chris frowned. That didn't surprise him, since it was something we'd already suspected. So why was I so upset? I should be happy to know who it was. What was wrong with me?

"Here." David handed me a bottle of water. "Drink this. It will help." He'd seen people in shock before, and I looked just like them. What was going on? What had me so rattled?

I took the water and noticed my hand was still shaking. The first swallow seemed to settle me down, so I drank a little more until I felt better. Wiping my mouth with the back of my hand, I handed the bottle back to David. "Thanks," I said. "That helped."

"Keep it," he said. He was thinking about the threats and figured that if I'd seen Kate here, it was a pretty safe bet that she was behind everything. "I wish we knew what her plans were."

"Tonight," I said. "I think she's planning something for tonight." David's brows rose questioningly. "I... um... heard her talking on her cell phone to her partner. She said something about making her move tonight."

"Oh," David said. "Okay. That's good to know."

"What else," Chris said. He glanced at me shrewdly. "Did she spot you? Is that what has you so upset?"

"Yes," I said, latching onto his explanation. "I guess I blew it." I'd never told Chris the whole story about what happened that day with Kate. He didn't know I'd told Kate I could read minds. "Do you think the fact that I heard her will make a difference in what she has planned for tonight?"

"I don't know, but probably not." Chris didn't think anything would change, since he figured I had listened to her mind, not a phone call like I'd told them. He glanced at David. "What do you think?"

"It doesn't matter," David said. "We'll be prepared, either way." He took this threat seriously, since it was his job to keep Chris safe. At all costs, he had to make sure Chris arrived at the trial in one piece tomorrow. Even if that meant having a team watch him through the night. Nothing was going to happen to Chris on his watch.

"Good." I relaxed, reassured that even if Kate didn't mean it, Chris would be safe.

Now that I knew he was going to be all right, it was time to figure out my next move. I had to tell Uncle Joey what was going on. He was the only one who could protect me from Kate. If she knew about me, then I probably wasn't safe. She could use me, and I had no doubt it would be a hundred times worse than anything Uncle Joey ever did.

I also knew that as much as I hated it, I couldn't tell Chris that Kate knew my secret. It would just make him worry, and I had to think about his safety. "I have to make a phone call. I'll be right back."

Chris didn't like that I was leaving, but I hurried out of the room before he could stop me. The hallway was empty, so I quickly called Uncle Joey's number. He answered after the second ring.

"It's Kate," I blurted. "I saw her here at the trial."

"What?" Uncle Joey said. "Are you sure?"

"Yes," I answered. "But there's more. I think this whole thing has been a set up. The threats against Chris, everything."

"Why would she do that?" he asked.

"She was trying to find out if my secret is true." I tried to keep my voice steady, but it was hard. "Don't you remember? At the shoot-out in your office, I told Kate and Walter what I could do. They didn't believe me at the time, but I think Kate's been thinking about it ever since. Today proves it."

"But how did she find out? Wait... maybe you'd better come over here and explain." After a short silence, he continued. "How long ago did she figure this out?"

"About ten minutes. Why?"

"And she left? You saw her leave?" he asked.

"Yes. In a black car... with a smug smile on her face," I added.

"And you're still at the courthouse with Chris and David?"

"Well, yeah," I said. "I'm out in the hall where they can't hear me, but I'm still here."

"Okay, good. Stay there. In fact, go back into the courtroom with them. Give the phone to David, and I'll tell him what to do."

"Do you think she'll come after me here?" I asked.

"I would," he said. "And knowing her, she's got something planned. She's probably waiting for you outside. At least you're relatively safe in the courthouse. Security isn't the best, but at least they don't allow guns."

"Except for the security guards," I said. "One's coming toward me right now, and I don't like the way he's looking at me." Without taking time to listen to his thoughts, I hurried the few steps back to the courtroom and shoved open the doors.

Chris and David both jerked in surprise. "There's a security guard out there," I said. "I think he's coming after me."

Chris' brows furrowed. What the hell? What did a security guard want with me? Why was I so rattled? David took up a protective stance in front of us. Manetto had told him to trust me at the beginning of this job, so he didn't question what I said was going on.

A squawking noise came from the phone, reminding me that Uncle Joey was still on the line. I thrust it at David. "He wants to talk to you," I said.

He took the phone. "This is David." As he listened, his eyes narrowed. "Yes sir." He disconnected, and handed the phone back to me. Before I could question him, the door opened.

The security guard poked his head in, giving us a friendly wave. "Sorry folks. It's after five, and I need to lock up."

"Sure," Chris said. "We were just leaving."

"Appreciate it." As the security guard held the door open for us, I scanned his mind. He was thinking that I was acting weird, like I had something to hide, and he'd better keep an eye on me.

I sagged in relief. He wasn't a bad guy. He was just doing his job. As we walked toward him, David was getting ready to hit him in the head and take his gun. Alarmed, I grabbed David's arm. "Stop!"

All three men froze, glancing at me like I was nuts. I smiled and gave a little laugh. "I think I left my phone back there." I smiled at David, and motioned with my head toward the security guard, hoping he'd get my message. "He's good. He'll wait." I moved my gaze to the security guard. "Right?"

"Sure," the guard agreed. "Not a problem." He was thinking something was wrong with me. As I turned up the aisle to get my phone, I heard him whispering to Chris and David. "Is she okay?"

"It's been a long day," Chris replied. "Sometimes being in court stresses a lot of people out. But she'll be fine. We'll take care of her." He knew I had the phone in my hand. What was going on?

"Okay. Good," the guard answered.

By now, David was convinced the guard was for real, and relaxed his stance. How did I know the guard was okay? I must have picked up on something... like he didn't have shifty eyes. And the thing with the phone was brilliant. Oh, well. It didn't matter. He was just glad he hadn't knocked the guy out.

I pretended to look for my phone on one of the benches, then with a flourish, I held it up. "Here it is! I found it!" I smiled with giddy pleasure, and hurried back to join them. "Thanks for waiting. You know how awful it is to lose your phone. I'd have to go without it for a whole night. And then hope someone would turn it in, and then have to come back tomorrow to get it. I can't imagine how awful that would be."

"Yeah," the guard said, thinking I was way too attached to my phone. "I'm glad you found it."

At least he was being sympathetic. Chris was a little embarrassed by my act, and he hoped David didn't think I was... a silly woman? I raised my brows, a little hurt. David thought I was brilliant. Why couldn't Chris be more like that?

We exited the room, and the guard locked the doors behind us. "Have a good night," he said, grateful to leave us behind. He continued down the hall, and we turned in the other direction toward the elevators.

Chris was dying to ask me what the hell was going on, but gritted his teeth instead, knowing he couldn't say anything in front of David. I wanted to tell him to quit swearing so much and chill out a little. But of course, I couldn't say that either. Which was probably a good thing.

Leaving the elevator, we walked through the lobby toward the outside doors. Telling us to wait, David left my side and stopped at the security desk. After exchanging a few words and showing him a card, the guy at the desk jumped up and unlocked a door behind him. A moment later, he returned carrying a gun in a waist holster. David thanked him and clipped the gun to his belt before coming back to join us.

"How did you do that?" Chris asked.

"Special permit," David said. He didn't explain further, even though he knew we were both wondering how he got it. "It's nice to have some protection for the walk back, don't you think?"

"Yes," I said fervently. "It's great."

David smiled, glad it helped me feel better. He took Manetto's orders to protect me seriously, and kept his attention on our surroundings for any kind of threat. He was good, and I did feel safer with him by my side.

We made it to Chris' office without incident, and David left to make a phone call, which I knew was to Uncle Joey. Chris shut his office door and rounded on me. "What's going on? Why did you freak out back there?"

Since I didn't want to tell him about Kate knowing my secret, I had to improvise. "I called Uncle Joey about Kate, and he thought we might be in danger. While I was talking to him, the security guy came down the hall, and I thought maybe since he had a gun, he was working for Kate. I know it sounds crazy now, but it could have been true."

Chris frowned, thinking my logic was more on the paranoid side, but then again, reading minds made my life complicated. He sure wouldn't like it.

"David thought he was a threat," I said defensively. "David was going to hit him, and once I realized the guard wasn't a bad guy, I had to make up that part about my phone to stop him."

"Yeah, okay." Chris shook his head. He could see why I had to stop David from hitting the poor guy. All of a sudden, the whole situation made him chuckle. Watching me march up the aisle to look for the phone when it was in my hand, and then act like I'd just found it... yeah, that was pretty funny. He knew I'd just heard that, so he changed the subject.

"So... why are you so afraid of Kate?" he asked.

"I'm not afraid of her," I said. "I just don't like her. For good reason too, I might add. Plus, I thought she was gone, and now she's back."

Chris furrowed his brows, thinking he'd missed something. "We know Kate's the one behind all of this," he reasoned. "But why? Is it because... of revenge against Manetto? This case really isn't about Manetto, but if Adam Webb was convicted of paying someone off, it could lead back to him. But that would be a whole different trial, and it's kind of a stretch."

"Yeah, I know," I sighed. "But that must have something to do with it. Remember, she was also thinking about a partner. So we know she's not working alone. There must be more to it."

Yeah, and I knew what it was... my secret. Guilt washed over me. I wanted to tell Chris, but I was afraid he'd think I'd been stupid to tell Kate in the first place. Plus, he'd be mad that I didn't tell him about it before. Maybe I could say that I told him, and he just doesn't remember. That could work. Only, it was a little too late for that. I should just tell him and get it over with.

I took a breath, but right before I could speak, my phone rang. "It's Uncle Joey," I told Chris. "I'd better answer." Chris sent me a pained look and sat down at his desk.

"Hello?" I said.

"Can you come to my office?" Uncle Joey asked. "I need to know what's going on. Everything. Now."

"I think so," I said. "I just need to finish talking to Chris, and I'll be right over."

"Good," he said, and disconnected.

"I need to go and explain things to Uncle Joey," I said. "But David will be here, so you should be okay. Are you staying long?"

Chris pursed his lips, not liking how I jumped when Manetto called. It also bothered him that Manetto had interrupted our conversation. He had a feeling I was about to tell him something important. "I think I've got everything prepared for tomorrow, but I need to go over it a few times." Checking his watch, he added. "Probably a couple of hours. I should be home around eight."

"Will you call me before you leave?" I asked. "I'm still a little worried about tonight and Kate's 'plans.'"

"Yeah, sure. Don't worry about me. I'll be fine." He couldn't believe Kate would still come after him. No, there was something else going on. But what? "When you figure out what it is, will you tell me?"

"You can count on it," I said. For the first time, I realized Chris wasn't upset with me for reading his mind. In fact, he talked to me like I already had. This was amazing!

"Good." He pulled me into his arms and hugged me tight. "Get David to walk you to your car. All right?"

"Sure," I agreed. "See you in a bit."

We kissed, and he watched me leave. He thought I was probably hiding something from him. Well, not exactly hiding, but there was something I hadn't told him. He was sure of it. Why wouldn't I tell him... the door clicked shut, blocking his thoughts, and I stopped in my tracks. He knew I'd heard him just now. If I didn't go back in, and tell him he was wrong, he'd know he was right. Damn!

I pushed the door back open, finding him in the same spot. His eyes softened, and his lips lifted in a quick smile. "Okay, here's the thing," I began. "Kate knows my secret. I think that's what she's been going for all along. She caught me following her, and with an evil grin, she said "gotcha" in her mind. So now I'm on my way to talk to Uncle Joey. Hopefully, he'll take care of it. I'll let you know what he says when you get home tonight."

I backed out and quickly shut the door before he could respond. Okay, maybe I'm a coward, but at least I told him. I hurried down the hall before he could stop me. David was waiting by the entrance and offered to walk me to my car. I agreed, and in no time, I was on the road to Thrasher Development.

I pulled into the parking garage for the second time today. Hadn't I just left? I dragged myself out of the car and shuffled to the elevators. All at once, I was hungry and tired. It was all getting to me, and I just wanted to go home and sleep.

I entered Thrasher Development and made my way to Uncle Joey's office. The door was open, and I could hear him talking to someone. I rounded the doorway to find Uncle Joey on the phone. He motioned me inside, but instead of sitting in front of his desk, I took the couch. I sank into cushioned softness, surprised to find it a lot more comfy than it looked. In fact, it was so soft, a person could fall sleep on this couch. It would only take a minute to lay back her head and close her eyes, and she'd be out.

"Shelby."

"Huh? What?" I quickly sat up. Had I fallen asleep?

"You need to wake up."

"Oh, sorry. I didn't mean to fall asleep."

"That's okay," Uncle Joey said. "I'm off the phone, so tell me what happened with Kate, and why you think she knows you can read minds."

"Oh yeah." It all came flooding back. I told him everything that happened, how I'd followed her and basically gotten caught. "Until then, I forgot I'd told her about my secret."

"Damn!" Uncle Joey said. "I guess you're right. This whole thing was a ruse to find out the truth about you." He was thinking this was bad. But something seemed off.

"What should we do?" I asked.

"We have to stop her," he said. "She's got to be coming after me. Probably tied up in all that gang stuff somehow. Doug Carter must be her partner. It was probably him in the hall, listening to us. Remember?"

"Oh yeah," I agreed. "I'll bet you're right. Even back then she was trying to find out if my secret was true."

"I just wish I knew how she planned to do it." Sadness engulfed him. He could hardly believe that she wanted him dead. In fact, he didn't believe it. Something must have happened to her in Seattle. Sure, he wanted his money back, but he let her go in the first place didn't he? He should have sent Chris and me to Seattle earlier. If he could have checked up on her sooner, maybe this wouldn't have happened. Was she in some kind of trouble? After everything they'd been through together, he didn't know if he could give the order to end her life.

"Are you sure you can't just expel her or something?" I asked.

"No Shelby, that's not how it works in this business. I don't want her to die, but I have to get used to the idea, so if it comes to that, I'll be ready." He watched my face turn into a frown. "I don't think she's a killer, but that doesn't mean she'd stand in the way of someone else doing the job for her." He was thinking he was probably a target, as well as others close to him. He glanced at me. "You though... she'll probably want alive."

"Okay. I get it," I said harshly. "When do you think she'll make her move?"

"Soon. I just got off the phone with Ramos. One of his friends works at the club, and he found out something big is happening tonight. His source said Lanny's really nervous."

"Do you think it's Kate?"

"If it was Kate, Lanny wouldn't be nervous. No, it's something bigger than that."

"What then?" I asked.

"That's what I'm going to find out tonight." He noticed the bleak expression on my face. "Don't worry. I have lots of resources. It'll be a piece of cake."

I smirked, knowing a lot of his bluster was how he intimidated people. Although, I had to admit, it sure worked on me. "That's good. What should I do?"

"Don't get caught," he said. As the blood drained from my face, he rushed to smooth it over. "Don't worry, I've got you covered. David's already got people watching your house. Nothing's going to happen to you. I think they'll come for me first. They figure once I'm out of the way, getting to you will be a different story. But that's not going to happen. I won't let it."

"Do you want me to help you tonight?" I asked.

"No. I want everything to look normal so they won't suspect I'm on to them. That includes you. Now that Kate has shown her hand, she's waiting for me to make the next move. Probably setting up a trap of some sort. No, I want you to go home and do normal stuff. I'll call with a plan in the morning."

"All right." I shrugged my shoulders to release the tension. Uncle Joey may think Kate wouldn't come after me, but what if taking me was the trap she was planning on using? Of course, that didn't mean Uncle Joey would fall for it. If they wanted to get rid of Uncle Joey, they'd have to get rid of them all. That meant the leaders of his entire organization.

I remembered reading about the 'Valentine's Day Massacre' in history. Where rival mobs killed each other off. Was something like that about to happen?

It was going to be a long night.

Chapter 12

I got up to leave, but Uncle Joey stopped me. "Wait, Ricky's going with you. I may not think Kate will come after you tonight, but I'm not about to take any chances."

"He's coming home with me?" I asked, surprised.

"Yes. He'll ride home with you to make sure you get there safely, but someone will follow behind to pick him up. David's got people taking over after that, and I don't know what he has planned. But he'll make sure you and your family are safe tonight."

"That's great," I said, surprised at how relieved that made me feel.

Uncle Joey nodded, his thoughts turning to the problem at hand. He was thinking that he had a pretty good idea where Kate might be hiding. Glancing at me, he quickly cut off his thoughts. "Um... Ricky should be waiting. You can go now."

"Oh, yeah... right," I said. "See you later. Let me know if anything changes or if you need me." I backed out the door, and closed it firmly. It was hard to believe I'd just volunteered to help him. It was a far cry from how I normally felt.

I was glad I'd heard him thinking about where Kate was, though. It gave me more confidence in his abilities. Maybe he'd get her before she got him. Wouldn't that be something?

Ricky was sitting at Jackie's desk and stood as I approached. "You ready to go?"

"Yup," I answered.

He was thinking that Manetto must really care about me. That was nice. He hoped I wouldn't put up too much of a fuss to let him drive my car home. If anyone tried to run us off the road, he could handle it, and he wasn't sure I could.

We reached the parking lot, and I dangled the keys in front of him. "Would you like to drive?" It was worth it to see the astonished look on his face. "It's a great car, just like Uncle Joey's."

"Sure! Thanks." He smiled his delight, thinking that was a lot easier than he'd imagined. It made him want to do something nice for me, so he opened the car door like a true gentleman. I smiled my thanks and slid inside.

The drive home under Ricky's watchful eye was uneventful. As we pulled into my driveway, I opened the garage door and Ricky drove the car inside. "Have you still got your stun flashlight?" he asked.

"Yes. In fact, it's here in the glove box. Thanks for reminding me." I took it out and slipped it into my purse.

"Good," Ricky said. He was wishing I had a gun. That would be much better. He got out of the car and handed me my keys. "Jimmy will be here in a minute. I'll just wait out here for him."

"You can come in if you'd like," I said.

"Oh, thanks, but no. I'll just wait here." Going inside with me made him uncomfortable. Even though I was a lot older, he still found me attractive. Someone like my husband, or even Jimmy, might get the wrong idea.

Really? How much older did he think I was? I couldn't be that much older than him; maybe five or six years at the most. Of course, I couldn't be too upset, since he thought I was attractive too. I was saved from more embarrassing thoughts when Jimmy pulled into the driveway.

"There he is," Ricky said. He turned to me. "I spotted a couple of our guys watching your house. David's got a good team, so you should be fine. I'm supposed to call him when I leave to let him know you're here safely. As soon as I leave, close your garage and lock the doors."

"Okay, thanks," I said.

I went inside, closing and locking the doors. I checked to make sure my kids were home, and found Josh playing a video game, and Savannah in her room. It was after six-thirty, and I needed to make dinner. It was tempting to call for a pizza, but I didn't want anyone I couldn't recognize coming to my door.

I had plenty of eggs and found some sausage links in the freezer. In no time, we were eating breakfast for dinner, and my stomach was finally satisfied. My kids only complained a little when I told them they had to stay home tonight. I debated on telling them that Chris had received some threats, but I didn't want to scare them. I'd only tell them if David stayed in the house with us. I hoped he wouldn't. That would be awkward.

Shortly after eight, Chris walked through the door, locking it behind him. I'd never been so glad to see him. "Are the kids home?" he asked.

"Yes, we're all here," I answered.

"Good. I'll sure be glad when this is over."

"Me too." We hugged, and he pulled me onto the living room sofa. "So Kate knows your secret. How did that happen?"

"At the shoot-out." I explained what happened, and how telling her was my only choice.

"Why didn't you tell me?" he asked.

"I don't know," I said. "It was never the right time, and then I forgot. I didn't think Kate believed me. And come to think of it, she didn't, until today." I told him what Uncle Joey was doing about it, and that something big was happening at the club tonight.

Then I spilled my guts about my visit with Dimples to the FBI. "After Razor left, an undercover agent came in to hear my premonitions. I forgot all about it until I went to the club with Uncle Joey and saw him there."

"The undercover agent?" Chris asked.

"Yes. Razor was there, too. He was one of the fighters."

"So what were your prem... I mean what did you tell them?" Chris was getting a little agitated with me, but trying to be patient.

I explained about the truce between the gangs, and how that meant someone new was in town. "Basically the same things we found out at the club, minus that they were coming after Uncle Joey next. The undercover agent was really impressed, and thought he could find out more at the club. I didn't know what he was talking about until I went there with Uncle Joey and heard him."

"Heard him?" Chris asked.

"Yeah. He spotted me and was thinking I looked familiar, kind of like me, only I was wearing my black wig and glasses, so it was all right."

Chris was stunned. What wig? What glasses? Was this something else I hadn't told him? Holy hell! How much more was there?

"Honey!" I said. "Calm down. It's just a wig and glasses. Not a big deal. And I think that's the only thing left that I haven't told you about."

"You think?" he asked.

"Yeah," I answered. "Geeze, you don't have to be sarcastic about it." I thought maybe making him feel guilty would help ease the tension. Especially since I was pretty sure there were other things I hadn't told him. Like my motorcycle ride with Ramos. Should I tell him about that too? Nope. Not a chance.

"Ricky brought me home tonight," I added. "He drove my car, and Jimmy picked him up. Uncle Joey wanted to make sure I got home okay."

Chris took a deep breath and sighed. "It's okay. You don't have to tell me every little thing. But the FBI? You should have told me about that."

"But I wasn't ever planning on going back there," I said. "It gave me the creeps. I thought it was over."

"Okay. It's okay. Forget it. Let's get back to the undercover agent. Did you pick up anything else from him?"

"No. I was trying to stay out of his way. But at least we know the FBI is involved."

"Yes, that's a good thing," he said. "I think. Unless you were to get caught, but you're not even there so it doesn't matter." He was thinking I could be there in the future. That might be bad.

"Uncle Joey said he'd call in the morning, and let me know what they found out tonight. He's also looking for Kate. Maybe by tomorrow, this will be over. I know he doesn't want me involved. That's good. Right?" I asked.

"He knows Kate well," Chris said, ignoring my question. "What does he think she wants anyway?"

"He thinks she wants to take over his organization."

"But what does she want with you?" he asked.

"Same thing as Uncle Joey," I said. "Use me for herself."

"Then who is the big threat at the club, if it isn't her?"

"I don't know," I huffed. "Her partner?"

"Doug? The security guy?"

"Yes," I said.

"Do you really think it's him?"

"No. It has to be someone else." I knew this was true because of the drug dealer we'd questioned, but I wasn't going to tell Chris that because then I'd have to tell him about the motorcycle ride, and I'd upset him enough already.

"I think you're right," Chris agreed.

"So all we can do now is wait," I said. "Is David around here somewhere?"

"I don't know," Chris answered. "But he said he's watching the house."

"I think it might be a good idea to leave some lights on tonight. People don't break into houses that have lights on. At least that's what I've heard."

Chris smiled. "That's sounds good. We can leave one on in the kitchen and the bathroom... the upstairs hallway, and the porch." He was thinking about his gun and glad he had that too.

"I've got my stun flashlight as well," I added.

"Then we should be set." He hated that we were worried about someone breaking into our own house. We were supposed to be safe here. He hadn't thought it would actually happen, but now he was beginning to hate Kate almost as much as I did. He visualized her breaking into our house and threatening us with a loaded gun, and how satisfying it would be to shoot her.

I glanced at him with raised brows, and he reddened. "It's okay," I reassured him. "I think things like that all the time. If you want to know the truth, lots of people do."

"But I didn't think it with words," he said. "You pick up images too? I didn't realize."

"If it's in your thoughts, I can read them. Images, feelings, words, it's all part of what I can do."

"Does Manetto know that?" he asked.

"Well... no. I've never explained it before. I've only told him I can pick up thoughts, but I wasn't specific about how I did it."

"That's interesting," Chris said. His stomach growled, reminding him he'd missed dinner. "I'm starving. Do you have any dinner left?"

The rest of the evening flew by, and soon I was lying in bed, trying to sleep. Chris had placed his gun on the nightstand, and I was actually okay with that. But I found it hard to relax. Even with the lights on, the smallest sound brought me fully awake. I couldn't help it.

Around four in the morning, I finally drifted off. Unfortunately, I slept so soundly that I missed my alarm, and Chris had to wake me up. David was at the door, ready to take him to court. I got out of bed to say goodbye, and promised I'd see him there.

It was a rush to get the kids off to school, especially since it was my turn to drive the carpool. I got back and, after showering, pulled on dressy dark jeans and my new black blouse since I hadn't officially worn it yet. To finish off my make-up, I applied my deep red lipstick, liking the contrast with my blond hair and black blouse. Plus, I needed that feeling of power it gave me. Now I was ready to go.

I placed my small purse into a larger black bag, and slipped my stun flashlight inside. I found Chris' gun in the safe where he normally kept it and slid it inside the bag as well, making sure the safety was on. I wasn't real comfortable taking a gun, but on the other hand, what if I needed it? But could I actually use it? To shoot a real person? It was probably better to just stick with my stun flashlight. I put the gun back, and hoped I'd made the right choice.

My stomach did a little flip-flop. It was eight twenty-seven, and I still hadn't heard from Uncle Joey. Was something wrong? I called him, and my breath hitched when it went to voice mail. I left a short message to call me, and tried Ramos. As the beep sounded for his voice mail, my heart sped up. I left another message and punched in the number for Thrasher Development. It went straight to voice mail too. A sick feeling came over me. Had something bad happened last night? Were they all dead?

My phone rang, and I let out a relieved breath. One of them was calling me back. Only... the caller ID said it was Dimples. Was he calling to tell me the bad news?

"Hello?" I answered.

"Hey Shelby," Dimples said. "I found something I thought you'd be interested in."

"What's that?"

"You're still working on that stolen bank money case, right?"

"Oh, yeah... I am." I'd almost forgotten about that with everything else going on.

"Well, I was looking through a backlog of unclaimed property and found some crates of underwear listed. I don't know if they're what you were looking for, but I thought I'd let you know."

"That's great! Can I take a look at them?"

"Well, that's the thing," he said. "They're up for auction tomorrow, so they're not here. But you can come to the auction if you want. You can even bid on them, although my girlfriend might not like it."

"Your girlfriend?" My heart sank. "Is this the same girl you were telling me about?"

"Yeah, the one I met at the coffee shop a few months ago. We're dating pretty steady now. In fact, that was the first time I've called her my girlfriend." He chuckled. "It's a little weird. I mean she's a beautiful woman; who would have thought she'd go for me?"

"Don't be ridiculous, lots of girls would go for you. You're a great guy." It was true, and I hoped saying that would help soften the blow. I hated to burst his bubble. In fact, this was going to be awful. "Why wouldn't she like it if I bid on the underwear?"

"She owns a lingerie shop, so she'll be bidding on them. Actually, she's the reason I checked. She was asking about auctions and said there was no way the police would ever have lingerie to auction, since that was the only thing she'd ever be interested in bidding on. We were both surprised to find not one, but two crates of lingerie up for auction." When I didn't say anything he asked. "Are you still there?"

"Yes, sorry." I had to ask, even though I already knew the answer. "Um... is her shop called Betty's Bra Bar by chance?"

"Yes it is!" he exclaimed. "How did you know?"

"Darn! I hate to tell you this, but with my investigation of the stolen money, I've been watching her shop." I gentled my voice. "She knew Keith Bishop, the bank robber. He sent lingerie to her a couple of times from his aunt's shop, Novelty Creations. He was working there before he got arrested." I let that sink in before continuing. "I think she might have something to do with the stolen money. But I don't know for sure."

"Huh," he said.

"Listen," I rushed into the silence. "I could be wrong. Maybe she doesn't have anything to do with it."

"No, no, it's all right." He found his voice. "It kind of makes sense to me now. Her bumping into me and all." He sounded so sad it broke my heart.

"What do you want to do about it?" I asked.

"Hmm... I think we should see this through. I was planning on going to the auction with her, and I can still do that. Maybe you could come and see if you get any premonitions from her. You'll know if she's part of it or not, right?"

"Yes. I should pick up something. Do you think it would be all right if I told Keith's cousin about the auction too? She's the owner of Novelty Creations now. If she's in on it, I'll know that too." I had to give him an out, and this seemed the best way to do it.

"That's a good idea," he said, more like his old self. "Especially if you think she might know something about it. Between the two of them, maybe you'll pick up where the money is."

"Exactly," I agreed. "You never know. It might help me solve the case."

"That's right," he said. "And just to be on the safe side, I'll go over the crates ahead of time. Just to make sure the money's not hidden inside and we missed it."

"Great idea," I said. "If you find it, could you please give me a call so I can let the bank know?"

"Of course," he agreed. "But don't count on it being there. The police department may have problems, but we're not that incompetent."

"I'm sure that's true." I quickly wrote down the time and address for the auction. Before disconnecting, a thought popped into my head. "Hey, do you remember the FBI guy we talked to? About the gangs?"

"Oh yeah, Henry."

"That's right. I might have something for him about the gangs. Do you think I should talk to him?" I asked.

"Are you sure you want to get involved with that?"

"I don't know," I answered. Involving Dimples and the FBI might be stupid or brilliant, depending on what happened. Should I tell him? I took a deep breath and went for it. "I keep getting premonitions about that kid. I think he's in trouble. The name Lanny, or Larry keeps coming up in my mind. And it's like the kid's fighting, and then there are lots of guns involved. I know it sounds weird, but it might be worth checking out."

I hoped that was vague enough to pique his interest, and not get me in trouble at the same time.

"Let me talk to Henry," Dimples said. "I've heard of a guy with that name. He owns a club. In fact, I think it's a fight club. So you might have something there. I'll get back to you on it."

"Great! Thanks so much. Call me if you hear anything, all right?"

"Sure," he hesitated. "Is there something you need to tell me?"

Maybe I'd been a little too specific. Too bad I couldn't read his mind over the phone. "I'm just nervous about it. Sometimes, that's how my premonitions work. Once I know everything's okay, I'm sure I'll feel better."

"Oh, okay," he said. "I'll let you know what happens."

"Thanks." We disconnected, and I hoped I'd done the right thing. At least I had a solid lead on the stolen money. But if the money was in the shipment, how did the police miss it? Betty must think that's where it was, and she'd gone to a whole lot of trouble to get close to Dimples to find out. Her using Dimples that way really made me mad. I was glad he'd called about the auction tomorrow. I'd know if it was her, and probably what she did in that shop as well. I just hoped that by then I would still be alive to find out.

My phone rang. This time it was Uncle Joey, and I heaved a sigh of relief. "Did you find out anything?" I asked.

"Not yet," he replied. "Ramos went to the meeting last night and he hasn't returned. I'll let you know as soon as I hear from him."

"Is he okay?" I asked.

"I don't know, but it's Ramos. He should be fine."

"Let me know when you hear from him," I said.

"I will," he answered. "In the meantime, I need you to be careful. Why don't you go to the trial where David can watch out for you? I'll see about Ramos."

"Okay." We disconnected, and my stomach clenched. I hoped Ramos was all right, but I couldn't shake the bad feeling his absence caused.

I backed out of my driveway, my senses alert for anything out of the ordinary. I couldn't spot anyone following me and soon pulled into Chris' parking garage. I left my big bag with the stun flashlight in the car, knowing I could never get it through security, and slung my little purse over my shoulder.

I hurried to the courthouse, through security, and up to the third floor courtroom. More people were crowded into the room today, but I found a place to the back on the right side and sat down.

From everyone's thoughts, I gathered that Chris was wrapping up his defense, and maybe even today the jury would be sent out to deliberate. I couldn't help admiring my husband. He looked so handsome and confident. Everything he said and did was impressive.

Lots of people were thinking the same thing, and my heart swelled with pride. One thought stood out over the others, sending a spike of alarm into my chest. It's one thing for me to think my husband is hot, but it's a different matter for someone else, especially when that someone sounded an awful lot like Kate. How dare she? What was she doing here?

This time, I kept my cool. I wasn't going to let her catch me again. Keeping my back ramrod straight, I glanced over my shoulder. She was sitting one row behind me in the center section. She'd been waiting for me to find her. As our gazes met, she winked.

I turned my head away, but not before I caught her amused smile. Yuck. Did she really think that would faze me? Probably. Jerk. I caught a glimmer of amusement from the man sitting beside her and glanced at him. It wasn't her partner, Doug Carter. Nor was it anyone I'd ever seen before. He had close-cropped, dark hair, a hard-edged face with deep-set eyes, and a hawk nose. His mind was like a cavernous black hole, full of dark things like greed, hate, and envy.

The power of those feelings shook my senses, and I recoiled from them like I would a poisonous snake. Bile rose to my throat in revulsion, and I instantly threw up my shields. Who was this guy? Was he Kate's partner?

My phone vibrated in my pocket, signaling a text message. I glanced at the message, anxiously chewing my bottom lip. Before I could read it, I heard the words in my mind, *Run Shelby! Get out!* I was sure it came from Kate. But why would she be telling me that?

Confused, I checked the text message. It was from Ramos, and it said, "Get out of there. Now." What? He was telling me the same thing? How did he even know where I was? With my heart pounding, I decided to follow Ramos' advice, and left the courtroom in a rush, hurrying down the hall to the staircase.

Footsteps pounded behind me, and I doubled my speed. Kate and her partner weren't supposed to be following so quickly. How did they get out so fast? I glanced back to find two men in suits rushing down the stairs. One of them was wondering where I was going in such a hurry. The other guy was thinking about his client, and hoping she'd wait until he got to the office. I slowed down, relieved they weren't after me.

After they passed me, I continued through the lobby and pushed through the double doors leading outside. I spotted Ramos standing beside Uncle Joey's black car, and started toward him, dizzy with relief.

All at once, something sharp jabbed me in the ribs, followed by a harsh whisper in my ear. "Keep walking. Don't make any sudden moves, or I'll put a bullet in you." It was Doug Carter. He clamped his hand on my shoulder and roughly jerked me against him.

He was thinking I'd messed everything up by leaving the courtroom so fast. He pulled me toward the parking garage and down the steps to the bottom level. I knew I had to make my move soon. If I got in a car with him, I might as well be dead, so what was the difference?

I listened to his mind again, but his thoughts kept repeating, *don't think about it, don't think, don't think, she'll hear it, she'll hear, she'll hear.*

Good grief! How many people had Kate told? At least he was lousy at covering his thoughts. Beneath his mantra, I picked up his intention of throwing me in the trunk. But that's as far as I got before I heard my name. *Shelby! Drop!*

I let my legs go limp and sagged to the ground, catching Doug by surprise. As I slipped from his grip, a bullet hit him in the shoulder, and he lost his hold on me. He spun around and took aim, firing several shots muffled by the silencer on his gun. I covered my head and cowered until the whizzing of muffled bullets stopped.

Dropping my arms, I found Doug lying in a pool of blood, his eyes glassy in death.

"Shelby? Are you all right?" Ramos hurried to my side.

"Yes," I answered, my voice shaking.

"Come on, let's get out of here." A car came to a stop beside us, and he helped me stand. He opened the back door, and I caught a glimpse of Uncle Joey at the wheel. He had a baseball cap on his head and wore dark aviator sunglasses. Ramos pushed me inside and jumped in behind me. As he pulled the door shut, the car took off.

"That was close," Uncle Joey said. He circled the car to the main floor exit and gave the attendant his ticket. She opened the gate, and we were free.

"What's going on?" I asked.

"Let's go back to my office, and I'll explain everything," Uncle Joey said. He was thanking his lucky stars they'd got to me in time. With this victory, he could put his plans into action, as long as I went along with it. There was some risk involved, but it was the only way out of this mess.

"What mess?" I asked.

Uncle Joey sighed. He'd forgotten I was listening to him.

"Never mind," I said. "I'll wait. We're almost there anyway."

Uncle Joey glanced in the rearview mirror and smiled at me. Ramos was thinking I didn't have to worry so much on his account. That mind-reading thing I did probably saved my life. It was pretty cool too. He could imagine whole conversations where he didn't have to say a word. How sweet would that be?

We pulled into the parking garage to find Ricky waiting for us at the elevators. "All clear?" Uncle Joey asked.

"Yes sir," Ricky answered. He pulled out a radio and talked to someone on the other end. "They're waiting for you upstairs."

"Good," Uncle Joey said.

We entered the elevators, and Ramos positioned himself between the doors and us. Since he couldn't secure the entire building, he wasn't taking any chances of someone getting to me by stopping the elevator on one of the other floors.

Picking up on his apprehension, I could barely breathe as we passed each floor, finally relaxing when we stopped on twenty-six. The doors opened. Vic and Jimmy were standing guard. They nodded at Ramos, and followed us into Thrasher Development.

There was no sign of Jackie, and I picked up that Uncle Joey had packed her up to a safe location with his son, Miguel. Wow, if he was worried about them, this was super serious. My motherly instincts flipped into overdrive, and panic clawed up my spine. As soon as we entered Uncle Joey's office, I blurted, "Are my kids okay? And Chris? What's going on?"

Ramos closed the door, and Uncle Joey sat down behind his desk before answering. "They're fine," he assured me. "Once I explain what's going on, you'll know what I mean."

The panic slowed, and I sat heavily in the vacant chair in front of his desk. Doug's death was catching up to me, and my legs couldn't hold me any longer. "Doug knew about me. He kept thinking that he shouldn't be thinking anything. I wonder how many other people Kate told. This is terrible! I knew something was wrong with Doug when he worked here. He was guarding his thoughts then. I should have picked up on that."

"You had no idea," Uncle Joey said. "This is all Kate's doing."

"What did you find out?" I asked.

"Apparently while Kate was in Seattle, she made friends with Eddie Sullivan, Seattle's crime boss. He's the force behind everything that's been going on here. The drugs, money, guns, everything can be traced back to him. Last night, Eddie set up a meeting with Lanny to negotiate an agreement. I'm sure Lanny thought he could keep his lucrative business going in return for favors like he does with me, but Eddie didn't see it that way.

"Eddie wanted his business, but he was willing to let Lanny manage it for him, as long as he got most of the profits. Lanny wouldn't hear of it, and threatened Eddie to leave or be killed by his men. That was when Eddie had three of Lanny's security men brought in. All of them were dead, killed by Eddie's new gang members.

"Of course, Lanny caved. But it didn't matter. Eddie shot him right there in front of everyone. He was sending a message, you see. Then he took over the business. That's where he's setting up shop right now. He's declared war on me, and he's got the gangs on his side. Or so he thinks."

"Not the South End, right?" I asked.

"No," Uncle Joey said. "They've gone underground. Along with others who've seen what Eddie's up to."

"Why is he coming after you? Is he really doing all of this for Kate? So she can get revenge by taking over your organization?"

"That's part of it, but not all." Uncle Joey grimaced, before looking me straight in the eyes. "No. It's you that he wants, Shelby. He's doing all of this for you."

Chapter 13

"**M**e?" I squeaked. Then it hit me. "Kate told him about me." I felt the blood drain from my face as the implications set in.

"Yes," Uncle Joey agreed. "You were relatively safe until yesterday, when she proved it to him. That's when Eddie decided to make his move. She must have made a deal with him. Take me out and set her up in my place. In return he would get you."

"And she would get my husband." The familiar stirrings of hate ran through my blood, replacing the chill that had been there a moment before. "Well, she can't have him."

Uncle Joey smiled. "It might have worked if they'd been able to grab you. Lucky for us, that didn't happen. Now all I have to do is find an incentive for Eddie to leave my city." He was thinking about a favor he needed to call in.

My phone rang, making me jump, and I fumbled to see who it was. "It's Chris," I told Uncle Joey. "I'd better answer." He nodded and I pushed talk. "Hey Chris."

"Shelby! I saw you leave in a hurry. Are you all right?"

"Yes. I'm with Uncle Joey and Ramos." I could tell him about Doug Carter and my near-abduction later. "What's going on?"

"Plenty," he said, his voice filled with anger. "We're having a quick recess, and I just got a note from Kate. She claims she has proof of Adam Webb's guilt, and will turn it over to the prosecution unless Manetto agrees to meet with her."

"Proof? Where would she get something like that?" I asked.

"Kate was actually working on this case with Gary," Chris said. "She must have made a copy of all her case files before she left. Or at least the files related to Manetto. She was his main contact in the firm you know."

"That's right," I groaned. "Just a minute. Let me tell Uncle Joey."

I repeated Chris' message, and Uncle Joey's eyes narrowed into tiny slits. He was wondering what Kate was up to. It didn't make sense. There was no way... "Tell him to let her know there's no need for that. I'll meet with her and Eddie, but no one else."

I relayed the message to Chris. "Who's Eddie?" he asked.

"The guy with her," I explained. "That's her partner. And Chris, stay away from him, he's bad."

He sighed. "Got it. I'll call you back."

I turned to Uncle Joey. "What are you doing? It's got to be a trap."

"I'm sure it is," Uncle Joey said. He glanced at Ramos. "Why don't you take Shelby to your apartment and get her a drink or something. I've got some phone calls to make." Dismissing me, he picked up his phone and scanned through an old address file on his desk.

"Come on," Ramos said. He glanced at me with a sympathetic smile, holding the door open. "Don't worry," he said, as we passed into the hallway. "Manetto will take care of this."

I couldn't muster the strength to answer and followed mutely behind Ramos. I sure hoped Uncle Joey knew what he was doing. He seemed to be feeling sorry for Kate, and I didn't like that. She wasn't a nice person. But why had she told me to run? It didn't make sense, unless she thought Doug would have a better chance to catch me. But it seemed like he was thinking I'd come out earlier than he'd expected. Of course, with Ramos and Uncle Joey there, he had to get me first.

This Eddie person was bad. I felt sorry for Lanny, getting shot like that. Then I remembered Doug. He was dead too. How many more people would die before this was over?

Ramos ushered me into his apartment and grabbed a Diet Coke from his refrigerator. Without asking, he filled a glass with ice and poured the drink. How did he know I liked it best that way? I took it and followed him into the living room.

He was thinking about the meeting last night, and how his friend, Bennie, who was a part-time security guard there, had let him in to spy on the meeting. They'd hidden from view and watched the whole thing. There was nothing they could do to save Lanny or the other guards, and it had taken them most of the night before they could slip away without being seen. Which turned out to be a good thing since he'd overheard Eddie telling Doug to grab me during the first recess at the courthouse.

By the time he'd slipped out, Doug had already left for the courthouse. It was a close call, but they'd gotten me away from him. Now was the time to take advantage of the situation, but they needed to act fast. It was good to know Bennie wasn't the only one willing to help them avenge

Lanny's death. With Manetto working quickly to find others, they could win this fight.

Ramos thought about me and realized I'd just heard what he'd been thinking. He didn't mind too much. I needed some encouragement, and he was happy to provide it. Especially when he didn't even have to say a word.

I chuckled. Ramos was one of a kind. "You know the first time I met you, I was surprised you liked country music. I'll bet not too many people know that about you."

He grimaced. "You're right. It doesn't fit my image. I should be more like the heavy metal type, right? Just don't tell anyone."

"Your secret's safe with me."

"I'll bet you know a lot of secrets," he said. "Most you probably shouldn't." He was thinking about Uncle Joey.

"A few," I agreed. "Although knowing what people think has been tough, and mostly downright awful."

"When did it start?" he asked, curious.

I told him the story of getting shot in the head at the grocery store. How I knew Kate was after my husband clear back then. I also mentioned how hard it was for Chris at first, but now he seemed to handle it better. I explained how Kate found out, and how all this time I forgot she knew. "That sure back-fired," I said.

"Yeah, but you had to do something," he said. "Or they might have killed you."

I shook my head, wishing I had been more careful. How many more people knew my secret because of her? "The worst time though, was with the Mexicans." I laughed. "They thought in Spanish, so that didn't help me at all."

"I'll bet," he chuckled. "Good thing you got away from them."

"Yeah, well... that's your fault." Besides today, Ramos had saved me plenty of times. I wanted to tell him thanks, or maybe smack him in the arm, but he was uncomfortable enough right now.

"What about your help with the police?" he asked, filling in the awkward silence. "Do they know?"

"Nope. They think I'm a psychic, and that I have premonitions."

"Ah," he grinned. "That explains a lot."

I told him about saving the little girl's life at the apartment complex, and how scared I was. "But it sure felt good to save her. It was a close call though." I'd never forget her struggle for breath with the plastic wrapped around her head. Just thinking about it sent chills up my spine.

My cell phone rang. It was Chris. If anything, the chills got worse.

"Kate wasn't happy," Chris began. "But she agreed to hold off on her evidence. I just wish you were here to tell me if she was lying or not. I told her to talk to Manetto herself, and leave me out of it. I hope that was okay. Court is reconvening now, so I have to go. Did they... are you sure you're all right? That Eddie guy is one cold dude."

"Yes. I'm safe. I'll fill you in on all the details later. Now you need to concentrate on the trial. David's still with you, right?" I asked.

"Yes, don't worry about me. I'll call as soon as I can."

We disconnected and I let out a sigh. "She's agreed to meet. I guess she'll call Uncle Joey herself."

"Good," Ramos said. "We'd better go back and let Mr. Manetto know."

"I wonder what he has planned," I said.

Ramos smiled and said, "Something good."

He was wondering what had happened to Kate. It was hard to believe she could turn so hard on Manetto. She always was the selfish type, but Manetto had taken her under his wing. She should be more loyal than that. Sure, she had gotten involved with Walter, and run off with Hodges, but Manetto had let her go. Now she was with Eddie Sullivan. That had him worried. He was a ruthless killer, but that also made him a lot of enemies. Nice that Manetto knew a few of them.

"Good to know," I said. Reminding him that I could hear everything he was thinking. When he didn't seem angry about it, I had to ask, "Why doesn't what I do seem to bother you?"

He shrugged. "I don't let things bother me."

"Right," I said. It was mostly true. That's how he became Uncle Joey's right-hand man. On the other hand, I knew he had a soft spot for me, and that was more likely the real reason.

Ramos knocked on Uncle Joey's door, and we entered.

Uncle Joey ended the call he was on and glanced up at us. "That was Kate," he said. "She wanted to set up the meeting at Lanny's in one hour. Just me and Shelby with Kate and Eddie."

"You're not going to agree, are you?" I asked, alarmed.

"I already did," he said. "It's better to do it now, before Eddie has all his men in place. What do you think, Ramos?"

"I can call Bennie and make sure Lanny's other guards are with us."

"Do it," Uncle Joey said.

Ramos left the room and I frowned. "What does she want? What if it's a trap?"

"I'll deal with it," Uncle Joey said. He glanced at me and sighed. "I'm sorry you have to come. Kate's promised to leave Chris and your kids alone if you're there."

"Damn her," I swore under my breath.

"Don't worry," Uncle Joey said. "I've got your family under my protection. Nothing will happen to them. But I still need you there."

"You're forgetting that they know I can read their minds."

"No, I'm not," he said. "Kate might be pretty sure you can hear them, but they don't know the whole truth. You might make all the difference in the outcome, and I'm not above using your ability for that. As long as you're willing."

"Of course," I answered. "But how will we communicate? I can't just tell you what they're thinking."

"Why not?"

"They'll hear," I said. He raised his brows like I was forgetting something. "Oh, I guess they already know."

"Exactly," he agreed. "It could work against them. I want to know exactly what Kate is thinking, and I'll bet Eddie does too."

"Yeah, until he has a sharp-shooter take you out. Then I'll be stuck with him forever."

"That's not going to happen," he said. "I have a plan."

One hour later, we pulled into the club's parking lot in a stolen car. Part of Uncle Joey's plan was to leave no trace that we'd been here, and Ricky had provided us with this car. It was wiped clean, and we wore gloves to keep it that way. Another vehicle was waiting with Ricky nearby for a fast get-away.

Riding in a stolen car was bad enough, but arriving here, my heart started to race, and I thought I might faint. Could I do this? Was I ready to face Kate, and the black-hearted Eddie Sullivan?

Not really, but I didn't have much choice. Uncle Joey was counting on me, and so were a lot of other people. I got out of the car on shaking legs, and forced myself to walk toward the doors. It felt like I was walking toward a firing squad, and it took all my courage to put one foot in front of the other. I sure hoped Uncle Joey's plan worked.

His friends from the South End had agreed to keep the other gangs away. He called in a lot of favors, and several other friends had agreed to take up position around the club as an extra layer of defense. They were out there somewhere, watching us right now.

The club had a deserted air about it, giving a false sense of security. Eddie had agreed to meet with us alone. But on his turf, I doubted he'd stick to it. He probably had people watching us too, and chills ran down my spine.

Ramos should be inside by now. He came ahead with Bennie. Apparently there was a secret way in. If Eddie had some of his men hidden, Ramos should find and disarm them before they could shoot us. At least that was the plan.

Uncle Joey glanced at me. He was thinking I looked terrible, like I was about to puke or something. I needed to straighten my spine, throw my shoulders back, and hold my head up. Negotiating called for looking tough and smart, not like a whipped puppy. Where was that sassiness he admired in me?

"Okay, I got it," I whispered, straightening my back. There was a compliment in there somewhere, right?

Uncle Joey pulled open the door, and it squeaked loudly in the silence. That was nothing compared to the bang as it slammed shut behind us. "Really?" I frowned at Uncle Joey, but he just shrugged.

Dim light came from a few windows, and it got dimmer as we approached the arena. At the top of the stairs, we could see two spotlights shining on the ring below, keeping the rest of the arena in darkness. Kate stood in one corner of the ring with Eddie pacing beside her. I took a deep breath, pausing to get my bearings before starting down the stairs.

Uncle Joey went first, and I followed behind, worried about how Ramos was supposed to find Eddie's men in the dark. Of course, Uncle Joey was thinking it was good it was dark, since that would help Ramos do his job. Hmm... maybe he was right, and I should think more like him.

Hearing our footsteps, Kate glanced up at us, relief showing on her face for a split second, before she covered it with a sneer. From here, I couldn't get a good reading on her thoughts, but I could sense her sweating with nervous energy and fear. In contrast, Eddie seemed to have nerves of steel. Sweet anticipation rolled off him in waves. We had come. Now was the moment of truth.

What did he mean by that? My shoulders slumped and I stopped in my tracks. Uncle Joey noticed I wasn't following and glanced back at me. "Come on," he said. "Shoulders back. We've got a job to do. Don't dawdle."

Dawdle? Was that even a word? I hurried to catch up with him, realizing at the last moment that I couldn't hear his thoughts. Was he blocking them? My stomach clenched. Why would he do that right now? I needed to know what he was thinking to do my job, but I couldn't tell him that now, or Kate and Eddie would hear.

We reached the bottom of the arena, and Uncle Joey climbed up the rickety stairs to the ring. I followed more slowly. He held up the ropes for me and I entered, trying to get my terrified expression under control. I tried for sassy, but I couldn't get my lips to work right, so I just gave up. Besides, my heart was beating so hard, I was sure Eddie or Kate could hear it anyway.

"Uncle Joey," Kate cordially greeted him. "Please have a seat."

She brought two chairs from the corner and set them about ten feet apart in the center of the ring, motioning him into one, and Eddie into the other. As they took their places, I stood behind Uncle Joey and scanned Eddie's mind.

He was thinking his reputation must have preceded him, since this was almost too easy. Although, now that he could see Manetto's eyes, he was disappointed to find no fear in them.

Eddie glanced at me, and I tried to imitate Uncle Joey's steely-eyed composure. Eddie's lips twitched in amusement. He thought I might have pulled it off, if I hadn't taken that small step back.

"What are you doing here Eddie?" Uncle Joey began. "This is my town, and you're not welcome here."

Oh great! Way to get us killed.

If anything Eddie's smile got bigger. "I'm just here to help Kate get back what is rightfully hers... and make a few lucrative investments. Like this place. I wouldn't have known about it without Kate."

I glanced at Kate. She stood behind Eddie the same way that I was standing behind Uncle Joey. Only now that Eddie couldn't see her face, she licked her lips, visibly shaken, and trying to hold it together. What was going on with her?

"And why would you do that for Kate?" Uncle Joey asked.

Eddie thought he might as well tell Manetto the truth. "She told me a fantastic story about a woman who could read minds. That would be a profitable asset in my line of work, so I figured I'd come help Kate out. I'm even willing to negotiate for Shelby's services."

"Kate?" Uncle Joey said. "Is this true?"

"Yes," she said, raising her chin in defiance. "I don't want to take your place right now. I just want to take over when you retire. Like we were planning before the whole Walter thing."

"What makes you think I'd negotiate?" Uncle Joey frowned, his eyes filled with sadness and disappointment. "Kate, you know me better than that. Why would you put me in this position?" He glanced around the arena, motioning toward the room above, where Lanny entertained his important guests. "Remember how you used to come here with me? We had some fun times watching the fights and placing bets. Now poor Lanny's dead. He was good to you. How could you betray him?"

Stricken to the core, Kate's composure fell and tears filled her eyes. She was thinking she hadn't meant for any of this to happen, and I almost felt sorry for her.

When Kate didn't answer, Eddie broke the silence, upset that Uncle Joey was making it so personal. "Kate has some files that I believe belong to you. As long as she keeps her position in your organization, you will be safe. Push her out, or kill her, and the files go straight to the police."

Eddie was thinking that he had the place surrounded, and Manetto had better surrender, or he was a dead man. All it took was one signal from him and he was dead. I could prevent that if I went with him peacefully. It was me he wanted. Because of Kate, he knew all about my family and how to get to them. If I didn't want to see Manetto die, or my family get hurt, I'd do the right thing, and go with him now. It was over. Manetto couldn't protect me anymore.

He glanced at me expectantly, his eyes lighting up with anticipation. He didn't think with words, but his eagerness came through loud and clear. He wanted me to tell Uncle Joey exactly what he was thinking. But underneath it, I sensed his acute desire to kill Uncle Joey and Kate, no matter what I said or did.

At the same moment, Kate was practically screaming in her mind, *don't say it, don't say what Eddie's thinking, it's a trap, please don't say it!*

Was she serious? How could I trust Kate after everything she'd done? Her thinking that could be the trap. But Kate must have told Eddie I could read his mind. He wanted me to give myself away, and give up at the same time. Doing what he wanted couldn't be good, especially if he was lying. Maybe it was a trap.

Uncle Joey was thinking the files didn't exist. He knew Kate didn't have any files like that. The fact that she was threatening him with 'fake files' was what made him think she was in trouble in the first place. Now he knew it was true, and he had to help her.

What? The files were fake? How did Uncle Joey know for sure? And he thought Kate was in trouble? He was going to help her? What made him think she wouldn't double-cross him? He glanced at me and motioned with a nod to Kate, so I listened in.

She was desperate for Uncle Joey's help. She'd gotten in too deep with Eddie, and this was her only way out. He'd killed Hodges, and would have killed her if she hadn't made this deal with him. Uncle Joey had to help her. He was the only one who could get her out of this mess. She'd do whatever he wanted. Disappear from his life forever, pay him back for the money and jewels she stole, anything, if he just did this for her. Otherwise she was as good as dead.

Damn! It was true.

"Well Shelby? What do you say?" Uncle Joey asked. "Is Eddie telling the truth, or is he lying?"

I opened my mind outward, hoping to hear if Ramos had found Eddie's men. If we were surrounded like Eddie was thinking, did we stand a chance of getting out alive? Or was it all just a big bluff? I listened as hard as I could, but nothing reached me. Then I heard Ramos. *Shelby! I need more time. A little more time. Stall him.*

Hell and damnation!

"Um..." I said, going with my gut instincts. "First of all, Eddie is bluffing. He really wants to help Kate because... he's secretly in love with her." I swallowed, and tried to keep a straight face. This was a whopper. "Kate has no idea he feels this way."

I glanced at Kate, including Eddie with a sympathetic smile, and shrugged my shoulders. "So now Kate, I guess you know the truth. Don't go through with this diabolical plan. You've hurt Uncle Joey enough. Take this chance at true love. It might be the only chance you get. Eddie really does love you with all his heart. He's not so bad. In fact, if you only knew what he's already done for you – he took a huge risk coming here, and putting his life on the line with Uncle Joey. He knows Uncle Joey's reputation, but he was willing to do it all for you. He's thinking right now that he could be killed at any moment, but he's okay with that..."

"Shut up!" Eddie shouted. He jumped to his feet, sending his chair crashing behind him. "You're messing with me. But it won't work. I've got my men pointing guns at you. Now tell Manetto and Kate the truth! Tell them what I'm really thinking."

"The real truth? Or the lie?" I asked, stalling for time.

Eddie's brows creased in confusion. "What?"

I was saved from answering by Ramos' voice in my mind. *Got them. There were three. You're good to go.* Relieved, I turned to Uncle Joey and nodded, my signal that Ramos was in position.

"It's over Eddie," Uncle Joey said, a hint of steel in his voice. He stood tall, facing Eddie squarely. "Here's what's going to happen. You will take your men, your drugs, your guns, and your stinking self, and get the hell out of my town!"

Eddie jerked back like he'd been slapped. He hadn't expected Manetto to talk to him like that. Not when he was surrounded. Rage burned his blood, but he held back the seething storm and smiled.

"I don't think you understand the situation," he said. "I'm taking Shelby. She's what I came for, and I'm not leaving without her. Make a move, and my men will kill you." He was thinking they were going to kill him anyway, but not until he had me in his clutches.

"You're a fool!" I said to Eddie, trying to distract him. "No one can read minds. That's impossible. I'm not going anywhere with you, and you can't make me. I'd rather die first!"

Eddie's face turned red. "That can be arranged!" He raised his arm, and in one motion, a small gun slid from his sleeve into his hand. He aimed it directly at me and opened his mouth to shout an order for his men to shoot us, but suddenly jerked back instead.

A knife protruded from his chest, and blood blossomed in the center of his white shirt. He clutched at the knife, his eyes wide with disbelief, and sank to his knees. He fell further onto his side, and tried to raise the gun to shoot, but Uncle Joey was there, stepping on his hand. "They don't call me Joey 'The Knife' for nothing," he growled.

I realized my mouth was hanging open, and I quickly snapped it shut. It had all happened so fast that I could hardly believe what I'd just witnessed. Where had that knife come from? It was stuck in Eddie's chest clear to the hilt.

A moment later, Eddie's fingers relaxed, and his head fell back. He was dead. Uncle Joey knelt down and pulled out his knife. He wiped it on Eddie's jacket before folding the blade and slipping it into his pocket.

Ramos rushed down the stairs behind us, his friend Bennie coming from the other side. They were dressed in black with guns and all kinds of gear strapped around them. "We've got to go," he shouted. "Ricky just called. The feds are here. They just pulled into the parking lot."

"The feds?" Uncle Joey almost lost his composure at that. "All right. Lead the way."

We scrambled down the steps, and Ramos motioned us to follow Bennie down a long ramp under the arena leading into the fighter's dressing rooms. After passing through the lockers and showers, Bennie unlocked a door at the back of the room. He flipped a switch, and several lights flicked on, showing a long narrow hall that reminded me of a tunnel.

He motioned us all through, then shut and locked the door. We hustled to the other end, finally coming to another door. Bennie unlocked it for us, and we hurried out into a stairwell. "Go on up," he said, flipping off the lights and bolting the door shut. "The stairs lead up into the building across the street from the club. We'll be safe there."

At the top of the stairs, the door opened into a hallway that led to a kitchen on one side and a living room on the other. It was simply furnished with a couch, lazy-boy recliner, and a flat-screen TV set against the back wall. The small kitchen had a stainless steel sink and matching appliances, with a small table and chairs in the corner. Another set of stairs led up to what I assumed were bedrooms. This was someone's house.

Bennie confirmed it. "This is Lanny's place. Er... was." His face flushed with anger and sorrow. He shook it off, and turned to look out the window. He cracked the blinds open, and we all crowded around him to see what was happening at the club. Several agents with bulletproof vests and guns entered the building. Others gathered around the stolen car.

Uncle Joey was thanking his lucky stars the car we left couldn't be traced back to him. We'd barely made it out of there in time as it was. He wondered who had tipped off the feds? Was it Kate? He glanced at her, but decided not to pursue it, taking pity on her disheveled and frantic state. Thank goodness he didn't glance in my direction.

She caught him looking, and turned to him with tears in her eyes. "You saved me. Thank you so much. I don't think I could have gotten away without you. I'm so sorry for all the trouble I've caused. I'll pay back all the money I took, as well as the jewels. I'll do whatever you want to make up for it. I promise."

She threw her arms around him, and wept into his jacket. Uncle Joey patted her back. "It's over now. I'm sure we can work things out." After a moment, he pushed her from him. "We should probably leave while the feds are busy over there."

"Oh, yeah. Good idea." Kate pulled herself together, wiping her eyes with her sleeve. She glanced at me and quickly looked away, guilt at how she'd treated me flooding through her. She was thinking that I probably hated her, and it made her uncomfortable.

She glanced at me with widened eyes, realizing I'd heard that. I pursed my lips, and raised my brow in silent acknowledgement. She jerked her gaze away, and I sighed. I wasn't quite ready to be nice to her, let alone forgive her. Plus, I hated the fact that she knew my secret.

However, on the bright side, at least she'd know she couldn't pull one over on me. It gave me the upper hand, and something settled inside. Maybe I could deal with her after all. As long as she stayed away from Chris.

"This way," Ramos said. He stood beside a door in the kitchen that opened into the alleyway between the buildings. We scurried down a couple of stairs, along the brick wall, and came out on the other side of the block where Ricky waited with the car.

Uncle Joey slid into the front seat with Ricky, leaving me to ride in the back with Kate. Ramos and Bennie jumped into their car and drove off in the opposite direction.

Kate squeezed into the corner, keeping her distance from me, and worked hard at not thinking anything important. It would have been funny if she hadn't kept thinking about the way Eddie died. I quickly put up my shields and tried to ignore her.

We made it to Thrasher Development without getting pulled over, and I sighed with relief. Was it over? I still had a hard time believing how this had all turned out. Eddie was dead, but the rest of us had made it out alive, thanks to Joey 'The Knife' Manetto. That was some throw for an old guy.

I was a little worried about the FBI showing up. Could they trace the killing back to Uncle Joey? I probably shouldn't have told Dimples anything, but how did I know it was going to turn out like this? I just had to make sure Uncle Joey never found out it was me who'd told them.

I got out, ready to go home, and realized my car was still in Chris' parking garage. Would Uncle Joey let me leave now? "We're done here, right?" I asked Uncle Joey. "I mean, no one else is trying to kidnap me, or kill us. So is it okay if I go home?"

Uncle Joey glanced at Kate. He was thinking it had been a close call, and he wasn't sure he trusted her. "Sure, you can go. But let's have a little chat with Kate first." He wanted to know the truth about Kate and Eddie, and knew he'd get it if I were there.

"Okay, sure," I agreed. Uncle Joey wasn't taking any chances, and I couldn't help but admire him. Especially since I didn't trust her either. Did she have something else up her sleeve? I wouldn't put it past her.

We rode the elevator in silence. Kate stood as far from me as she could, making sure Uncle Joey and Ricky separated us, as if that would make it harder for me to hear her thoughts. She understood what Uncle Joey meant by having this chat, and part of her was terrified. She didn't know me all that well, but after the things she'd done to me, she worried that I'd make up something bad about her. Just for spite. And she'd end up getting killed.

I was starting to get angry. Maybe I'd wished she were dead, but not because of anything I did or said. As soon as the three of us entered Uncle Joey's office, I rounded on her. "I'm not spiteful Kate," I said. "Besides, I'm sure the truth is probably worse than anything I could make up. Don't forget I saved your life back there. Eddie was planning on killing you all along. You're lucky to be alive."

"Well, so are you," she shot back. "Uncle Joey's the reason I survived, not you. You think I didn't know he was going to kill me? Why do you think I did what I did? I'm just glad you didn't ruin everything. But saying he was secretly in love with me was a huge mistake. He knew you were making that up. It just reinforced to him that you could read his mind. You were playing him, and his pride wouldn't let him take it. You might as well have told us what he was really thinking!"

"I said all that because I was buying time for Ramos to take out Eddie's men. It worked didn't it? So don't tell me it was a mistake!" How could she say that to me? I was angrier now than I'd ever been.

"That's enough," Uncle Joey said. "Sit down Kate. You too, Shelby." He waited until we sat before he continued.

"You have a lot of explaining to do Kate. But first we need to get our stories straight for the police. I have no doubt they'll be coming to talk to us."

A knock sounded at the door, and Ramos poked his head in. "I'm here if you need me." He'd heard our loud voices and thought he'd better check on us.

"Good. Come in," Uncle Joey said, wanting reinforcements just in case Kate and I came to blows. "We're just discussing what to tell the police. I want you to fix the video feed in the office to show us coming back about a half hour earlier than we did. We can tell them that we met Kate at her place, and then came back here." He turned to Kate. "Will that work? You still have your condo?"

"That will work," Kate answered. "I've been back there a few times this week, so that's a legitimate scenario."

"What if they ask what we were doing there?" I asked. "What should I say?"

"If they ask, tell them we were there for business reasons," Uncle Joey said. "That's all you need to say."

Kate smirked, thinking that was a stupid question. I glanced at her, ready to tell her off, but Uncle Joey did it for me. "Kate! Wipe that smirk off your face, and be nice."

Kate jerked, surprised to have been caught for something she didn't even say. She lowered her eyes and wondered how anyone could stand being around me, knowing I could hear every little thought. How awful. She felt sorry for... oops. She stopped, catching herself before saying my husband's name.

That did it. Time to tell Uncle Joey the truth. "Kate got involved with Eddie and did something that made him mad, so he killed Hodges," I began. "She made a bargain with him, which included getting back at you, and getting rid of me. But it backfired when she found out he was just using her to take control of your organization. Kind of like how she was using him. But his main goal was to find out if I could really read minds." I glanced at Kate. "How am I doing so far?"

She lowered her head in defeat, upset with me because she would have made it sound like it was all Eddie's fault. Now Uncle Joey knew the truth, and it made her look even worse than she wanted.

"That's when she realized she had to make up the part about the files so you'd know she was in trouble. She sent threats to Chris about the trial to catch me reading her mind, thus proving to Eddie that I was for real. I think that about covers it." I glanced at Uncle Joey. "Just so you know. If she stays, I'm gone."

Uncle Joey raised his brows in surprise. I really wanted him to kill her?

"No," I said quickly. "Not that. I just can't work here if she's here." I didn't add that he'd be a fool to let her stay, mostly because I figured he already knew that.

"Thank you, Shelby," Uncle Joey said. "She won't be staying. If you don't mind, I'd like to discuss this with her in private."

"Sure." I jumped up, more than ready to leave.

Ramos opened the door for me and followed me out. As we walked down the hall he said, "I'd hate to be in her shoes right now."

"Yeah, but I don't feel sorry for her. She deserves whatever he dishes out."

Ramos wasn't surprised I felt that way. He didn't like Kate much either. "Manetto will figure it out. He's good at that. I'm just glad everyone got out of there alive."

"Me too," I agreed.

"When you started talking about how much Eddie loved Kate, I nearly lost it," he chuckled. "Lucky for us, Eddie's men were so riveted by your story that it was easy to take them out. But it was a close call for you. If Manetto hadn't thrown his knife... let's just say, I didn't have a clean shot at Eddie."

Chills ran up my back. "Good to know... I think."

"Well... I'd better take care of that video feed," Ramos said. He was thinking he probably shouldn't have told me that, but it just slipped out.

"It's okay," I said. "I've been shot at before, right?"

"True," he agreed. "But maybe you should try not to get shot at so much." He was thinking it was okay to care about me just a little, as long as it didn't interfere with his job.

"Yeah," I smiled. "I'll work on that."

Ricky was sitting at Jackie's desk, and hung up the phone. "You leaving?" he asked.

"Yes," I answered. "But I need a favor. My car is parked at my husband's office. Can you give me a lift?"

"Sure," he agreed.

As we neared Chris' office, I realized that he was probably still in court, so I had Ricky drop me off at the courthouse. It seemed like days had gone by since I'd last stepped inside, rather than a few hours.

I entered the courtroom, surprised to find it crowded, and sat in the back. The judge asked the jury if they'd reached a verdict, and I realized I'd missed the deliberations and everything. Wow, they must not have deliberated long. That was a good sign.

The jury foreman handed the verdict to the judge who opened it and read, "Not guilty." Adam Webb lowered his head, and closed his eyes as if praying. After a moment, he smiled and shook Chris' and then David's hands. The rest of the proceedings went quickly, and soon I was standing beside Chris, a big smile on my face.

"You're all right." He hugged me tight, letting his worries and fears for my safety melt away. "I was so worried."

"Everything's good," I said.

"You sure you're all right?" he asked.

"Yes. I'm fine," I reassured him. He was wondering if Kate had survived, or if she was lying dead somewhere. "She's fine too," I said, not quite so happy he was thinking about her. "I'll tell you all about it at home." I turned to leave.

"Wait, don't go yet," he said. "Let me gather my things. Since you're parked at my office, we can walk back together."

"Okay," I agreed.

Chapter 14

David walked with us to Chris' office, still in protection mode until Uncle Joey told him otherwise. It was kind of annoying, as well as a relief, since I could put off telling Chris everything that happened until we got home. I knew he would not like hearing how I'd almost been killed, and the anticipation of telling him about it tied my stomach in knots. He walked me straight to my car.

"Are you going to be long?" I asked Chris.

"Just about half an hour more, I think."

"Good." I nodded toward David who was talking on the phone. "It looks like he's letting Uncle Joey know the good news."

"So what happened?" Chris asked, unable to stand the suspense. "Did anyone die?"

"Yeah, one of them was Eddie." I answered. Chris took a sharp breath. "But it was him or me, so be glad it was him."

Chris closed his eyes. "I was afraid you'd say that." He let out a big sigh and pulled me into his arms. "I'm probably not going to like this story am I?"

"I think you'll like it just fine," I said, wanting to be positive. "As long as you keep an open mind. Besides, it all turned out right in the end. What's not to like about that?"

He chuckled and kissed my forehead. "That's true. So, how many lies did you have to tell to get out of this one?"

I laughed. "A big one. In fact, it was a doozy."

"Can't wait to hear it." He pulled away. "I better go, but I'll see you soon."

He watched me drive out of the parking lot, and I smiled, knowing he would always be there for me. Even when crazy things happened. I realized something had changed between us in the last few days.

Then it hit me. Lately, he hadn't been annoyed or angry with me for reading his mind. It was like he'd finally accepted my ability. My smile widened. This was huge. If I didn't have to worry about that, it wouldn't be so hard to tell him things.

He also seemed more accepting of my work. Like he finally realized this is what I do and who I am now. For the first time since it happened, it was okay that I could read minds. A huge weight lifted from my shoulders. Having Chris on my side made all the difference, and I actually looked forward to telling him what had happened.

I pulled into the driveway and hurried inside, ready to have a normal evening. I'd neglected my kids for the last couple of days and felt a pang of remorse. Maybe we could all go out to dinner to celebrate Chris' win.

Tomorrow was Saturday, and I could catch up on all the housework I'd missed. That reminded me of the police auction and the crates of underwear. This might be the last piece of the puzzle in solving the case, and I needed to be sure I was there.

I called Novelty Creations and let Emily know about it. "Could you tell your Uncle too?" I asked. "I never did get to talk to him, and this would be a good time to meet."

"Sure," Emily agreed. "He's off his regular job on Saturdays, so he should be able to come."

"Great." I gave her the address and time of the auction and disconnected. Tomorrow I'd know if the money was hidden in the crates and if Betty was Keith's unknown partner like I suspected.

Chris got home, and we finally had a chance to talk. I took him out to the deck and we sat together on the cushioned swing. "It all started this morning at the courthouse," I began. "I wasn't there long when I heard Kate thinking about you."

"Me? What was she thinking?" He had an idea I didn't like it, so he really wanted to know.

I frowned. "You're right. I didn't like it, and I'm sure you can figure out why." He was thinking it was probably because Kate thought he looked hot and admired his courtroom persona.

"Courtroom persona?" I raised my brows.

"Yeah. I'll bet you were thinking the same thing, right?"

I pursed my lips. "Do you want to hear the story or not?"

He grinned, enjoying teasing me. "Of course. Go on."

"I think she did it to catch my attention, which she did. That's when I saw Eddie Sullivan sitting next to her. Talk about creepy." I shivered. "Right after that, I got a text from Ramos to leave, so I did. But it was really weird, because Kate was telling me the same thing in her mind."

Chris wrinkled his brow. "Then what made you go?"

"I trusted Ramos. So I left. I got outside, and Doug grabbed me. He had a gun and pulled me into the parking garage. Luckily, Ramos stopped him, and I ended up at

Thrasher Development with him and Uncle Joey. That's where I was when you called with Kate's threat."

"So where's Doug now?" Chris asked.

"Probably at the morgue. Ramos had to shoot him."

"Oh." Chris took a deep breath. "Go on." He didn't like that I could have been killed again. Plus, now he owed Ramos for saving me, which he liked even less.

I explained about Kate's bargain with Eddie, and how she set up the meeting with Uncle Joey.

"What? You went there? To the club?" Chris asked, surprised. "Wasn't it a trap?"

"It all worked out, if you'd just let me finish." I was losing my patience.

"Yeah, okay." He tried to relax and sat back in his seat. "Go ahead."

"It turned out that it was a trap," I said, and Chris smirked. "We went mostly because Uncle Joey knew Kate was in trouble, and he wanted to help her."

"What? That's kind of hard to believe after everything she's done." Chris said.

"I know. But you have to remember, she's like a daughter to him. I guess he still has a soft spot for her. Anyway, he knew the files she was threatening him with didn't exist. I listened to Kate and found out it was true. She was desperate for Uncle Joey to save her from Eddie, and kept thinking I shouldn't say what Eddie was thinking, because it was a trap. Eddie wanted me to tell Uncle Joey what he was thinking. Only what Eddie was thinking wasn't exactly true, but he didn't think I'd pick up on that."

"So what did you say?" Chris asked, slightly confused.

"I made up a story. I went on and on, telling them that Eddie was doing it all for Kate because he was in love with her."

Chris let out a surprised laugh. "I bet that made him mad."

"Yeah, that's for sure," I agreed. "But it gave Ramos enough time to find Eddie's men that were hiding in the arena and take them out before they could shoot us. With them out of the picture, Eddie's threats were empty. I let Uncle Joey know that Ramos was successful, and Uncle Joey told Eddie off. You should have seen him! He said 'take your drugs, your guns, your men, and get the hell out of my town.' It was awesome."

Chris frowned, and our gazes met. "But how did you know Ramos was... wait... he knows?"

Oops. "Yeah," I confessed, but quickly continued before he got upset. "But I didn't tell him. He kind of figured it out. He was there a lot when Uncle Joey asked me questions, and I knew stuff that I'd only know if I could read minds. He just figured it out." I knew I was repeating myself, but what could I say? It was the truth. "I know he won't tell anyone. If that's what you're worried about."

Chris sighed, not happy to have one more person know. "I guess it was inevitable. Just be more careful, okay? I mean... look what happened with Kate. You can't let people know."

"I know," I said. "Believe me, if there's one thing I understand, it's that."

"Um... good. I'm sure you do. I don't mean to sound upset, it's just... you know, a big deal." He glanced at me with a quick smile to take away the sting of his words. "So what did Eddie do after Manetto told him off?"

"He tried to shoot me," I said bluntly. "But lucky for me, Uncle Joey threw his knife and hit him square in the chest." What a throw, I could still hardly believe it. I couldn't help adding; "I guess they don't call him Joey 'The Knife' for nothing."

Chris sat back, amazed I'd made it out of there alive. He was thinking, *'Joey The Knife,'* and it all made sense. "So he killed Eddie."

"Yeah. Right after that, we had to leave in a hurry because the feds showed up." I explained how we got out, and the story Uncle Joey wanted me to tell if the police asked me any questions. "I got a phone call from Dimples before I left this morning, and I told him I had a premonition about the club. He said he'd tell the FBI, so I'm probably the reason they showed up."

"Better not let Manetto know that," Chris said.

"I know," I agreed. "Dimples also told me about his girlfriend." I went on to explain who she was, and about the auction of underwear tomorrow. "I'm planning to go, and with any luck at all, I might solve the case."

"That's great," he said. "But I can't see how the money could be in the crates of underwear. The police would have found it. Still, this Betty person must think that's where it is, or she wouldn't want them. Doesn't make a lot of sense, does it?"

"No, but if she's thinking about the money, at least I'll know she's Keith's partner. But if the money's not there, I don't know how we'll prove it. I'll just have to see what happens tomorrow. I'd sure like to find that money though."

"You will," Chris said. "I mean, you can read minds, how hard can it be?"

"Damn straight," I said, pleased he was being so supportive.

"So what happens with Kate?"

"Good question," I said. "Uncle Joey told me she wouldn't be staying, so he must have some place to send her. Good thing, because I would be happy if I never saw her again."

The next morning, I eagerly drove to the old city hall where the auction was being held. All the auction items were available to preview between eight-thirty and nine-thirty, with the auction starting at nine-thirty. Since I hadn't heard from Dimples, I knew the money wasn't inside the crates. But Betty didn't know that, and I hoped to hear her reasons for bidding on them were because she was Keith's partner.

I pulled into the parking lot, surprised to find it nearly full. I'd never been to a police auction before, but with all the people here, it looked pretty crowded. There must be some really good deals. Good thing I brought my money in case I found a great deal on something I needed.

Inside the hall, the items were displayed on tables at the back of the room. The other end of the hall held a podium and several rows of chairs where the bidding took place. Each item had an assigned number, and everyone moved between them, jotting down the items they were interested in bidding on. Most items were done by silent auction with people writing their bids on sheets of paper. Only thirty were scheduled for the actual auction.

It was hard not to join the line and inspect everything I could buy, but I needed to focus on the underwear first. I caught sight of Dimples and Betty on the other side of the room and hurried over. My heart raced with anticipation. In a moment I'd know the real reason why Betty was here.

"Hey," I said to Dimples. "Imagine finding you here."

"Hi Shelby," Dimples said. He was glad I'd made it, and was thinking he'd never had a chance to tackle looking inside the crates. Since Betty was determined to buy them, he was sure he'd get the chance at her place. If she wouldn't let him help her with the crates, he'd know she was using him. After everything she'd meant to him, he was determined to find out if she was involved in the bank robbery.

We exchanged pleasantries, and he introduced me to Betty who was thinking she'd seen me before.

"Hi," Betty said, wrinkling her brow. "Don't I know you from someplace?"

"You look familiar to me too," I said, playing along. "Oh, I know! You own that bra shop, Betty's Bra Bar. I was just there a few days ago."

"That's right," she said. "So... do you work with Drew?"

"Drew? Who's... oh! You mean Dimp... I mean Detective Harris. Yes. I work with him. Sorry for the confusion, I just never knew his first name till now. I always call him Dimples. Kind of a nick-name, you know?"

"Oh, yeah," she said. "He does have great dimples!" She was thinking he probably hated it. At least she would.

I glanced at Dimples. Did he hate it? He smiled good-naturedly. He was thinking that he didn't mind if I called him that, but he sure didn't want Betty to start. Or anyone else for that matter. Of course, she might not be in his life much longer if she was really a crook. He sure hoped she wasn't.

I concentrated on Betty, but didn't get much. "So what brings you here?" I asked.

"Drew told me about some crates of underwear they're auctioning off, and I thought I could bid on them for my business."

"That's nice," I said. "Where are they?"

"Over there, number twenty-seven." She was hoping no one else would bid on them, but it didn't matter, since she was prepared to outbid anyone here. She had to get those crates. That's the only place it could be. "Are you interested in bidding on them too?"

"Me? Oh, no," I said. "I'm just surprised they're selling them all together. I'd bid on them if I didn't have to buy the whole crate. Most people probably would. I wonder why they're doing it that way."

"That's just how they'll start out," Dimples explained. "But I might have had something to do with that. When Betty told me she wanted to bid on both crates, I relayed that to the people in charge, and they were more than happy to sell them all together."

"Got it," I said, then turned to Betty. "Good thing you've got friends in the police department, huh?"

"Yes," Betty agreed, smiling. She didn't like that I insinuated she was using Drew for her own purposes. It was true, but she didn't want him to know that. She tugged on his arm to get his attention and gave him an intimate smile. "Shall we find a seat?" She hoped I'd take the hint and leave them alone.

"Hey, save me a place, will you?" I asked. She wasn't going to get rid of me that easily, especially since it looked like she was Keith's long-lost partner, and it was going to break Dimples' heart. "I'm going to look around some more, but I'll come find you."

"Sure," Dimples said, thinking he'd go along with whatever I wanted. He trusted me, and now that he could look at Betty a little more objectively, his instincts were kicking in, telling him that something wasn't quite right. Like she was probably using him.

I gave him a big smile, glad to know he could see through her. I hurried over to the table with number twenty-seven on it, only to find a few pieces of underwear on display. I glanced behind the table and sighed with relief to see the crates stacked next to the wall. I studied the crates, trying to figure out where Keith had hoped to hide the money. It didn't look promising, but if the money was hidden inside, maybe there was a false bottom or something.

"Shelby?"

I turned to find Emily from Novelty Creations. "Hi. Good... you made it." I noticed an older gentleman with glasses and salt-and-pepper hair standing behind her. "You must be Dean," I said. "I'm Shelby Nichols, the consultant the bank hired to find the stolen money."

"Nice to meet you," Dean said. "Emily told me about you. Sorry I never called you back."

"That's okay," I answered. "I'm glad you could come today. Does that look like your inventory?"

He glanced at the crates. "I don't think so. Emily told me you thought they were ours, but there's nothing in the ledgers to say we're missing any crates, so how could they be?"

He was lying. He knew they were his.

"Our shipments usually come in boxes," Emily added. "Not crates like that." She examined the underwear on the table. "But this is the same brand we sell." She shrugged. "What do you think?" she said to her uncle. "Should we bid on them?"

"Why not?" he glanced at me. "Are you going to bid?" He thought maybe I was, since I probably figured the stolen money might be in the crates.

"No," I said. "But there is someone else here that is." I turned to Emily. "You remember Betty's Bra Bar?" Emily nodded, and I continued. "The owner's here to bid on them."

"Really?" Emily said.

Dean straightened, his attention focused sharply on me. "Who's this?"

"Betty," I said. "She's right over there, on the end of the third row." I pointed in her direction, but all we could see from here was the back of her head.

Waves of excitement rolled from Dean. He was thinking this might be it. He never imagined Keith's partner was a woman. All this time, and he could never figure out who it was. He shook his head. It had finally paid off to leave the crates with the police. Now he'd know who'd turned Keith to a life of crime. At least he'd outsmarted her. Was she ever in for a surprise. "Let's find a seat."

"Okay," Emily said, confused at her Uncle's behavior. "See you after," she said to me.

I watched them walk away, shocked at my discovery. Keith's father knew where the money was, and now, so did I. He wanted to be there when Betty opened the crates, but that probably wouldn't happen. If she thought the money was in them, she'd wait until she was alone to open them. How was I going to get her to admit to any of it? I had to come up with something, or Dimples might get killed, and Dean might do something stupid.

The bidding began, and I tried to tune it out, wracking my brain to come up with a reason to look in the crates with Dimples there. Then it hit me. Why not use my job as the investigator for the bank? Once she had the crates, I could mention it to her and ask to look inside. She couldn't refuse without looking suspicious. It could work.

"Interesting company you're keeping."

I jumped, surprised and dismayed to find Rob Felt standing behind me. "What are you doing here?" I thought I'd seen the last of him.

He snickered. "Following you, of course. It looks like you have a pretty good lead here. I mean... look at those crates of underwear." He'd seen me talking to Emily and her uncle. "Is that where Keith hid the money?"

"If it was, why would I be standing here?"

"Because you don't know for sure. Maybe you want to see who bids on them, and then you'll know who Keith's partner is. Not that I care. I just want the finder's fee." He was thinking he'd make sure he got a look inside the crates. Long before whoever bought them could leave. This might be his only chance. He inched in that direction.

"Don't you even think about it," I said, grabbing his arm. "You can look inside the crates when the bidding is over, and not one second before."

He jerked his arm away and frowned. "Fine. I'll wait. But I'm not going anywhere until I see what's inside them."

"Just stay out of my way, and let me handle this. You could ruin everything, and I'm not going to let that happen."

"As long as I get to see inside, I'll keep my distance, but if you push me out, you'll be sorry."

"Not as sorry as you," I said, fingering my stun flashlight in my purse. I wanted to stun him right then and there, but the auctioneer holding up number twenty-seven caught my attention.

"Hey," Felt said in a hushed whisper. "Isn't that Betty, from Betty's Bra Bar?" He was thinking how he'd checked up on a couple of her clients, and had finally identified them a few hours ago. They both had bounties on their heads. He was planning to take them into custody and collect, but he had to wait for the right moment. If Betty was bidding on the crates, that might explain her involvement with those men. Maybe they were part of her crew.

At her uncle's prodding, Emily placed a higher bid than Betty, and the bidding wars began. "Is that the girl from Novelty Creations?" Felt asked. "If they're bidding against each other, does that mean they both know the money's in the crates?"

"I don't know," I answered, wishing he'd shut up. The bid amount rose until Dean shook his head, and Emily ceased bidding, leaving Betty with the final bid. The gavel slammed down, and the word 'sold' echoed through the auditorium.

A collective sigh came from the crowd, and Betty smiled in relief. A few minutes later, the auction was over, and Betty gathered her ticket to pay for the underwear. She disappeared down the hall to the cash register.

Dimples joined me beside the crates, glancing questioningly at Felt. He recognized him a second later, and swore under his breath. He was wondering what Felt was doing here. If Felt messed up this investigation, Dimples would do what he could to get his license revoked. He then imagined smacking Felt around a few times, and I had to smile, knowing exactly how he felt.

As we waited for Betty, I noticed Dean and Emily standing nearby. Dean was hoping to get a chance to confront Betty about what she'd done to his son. He wanted to tell her how she'd ruined Keith's life, and that Keith had been a good person until he'd met her. He wanted her to admit that she'd had him killed, even if he had to threaten her with his gun. His son never would have done what he did if it hadn't been for her. If Dean didn't do anything, she'd probably go free, and he couldn't live with that.

Yikes! Dean had a gun? He could end up in jail if he hurt Betty. He wasn't thinking straight, and I had to stop him. The only way to do that was to out Betty myself. But how? I wasn't sure asking her to let me look at the contents of the crates would make her admit to anything.

The minutes stretched out, and most of the people who'd bought items were long gone. What was taking her so long? Dimples glanced in my direction. "I'd better go see where she went," he said. He turned to leave but stopped when the double-doors at the back of the hall opened. I caught sight of a van backing into the space and realized it was a loading dock. Two men climbed the stairs through the doors and headed toward the crates.

They looked slightly familiar, but I couldn't place them. Felt tensed, thinking these were the guys with the bounties on their heads. With Dimples here for backup, now might be the perfect time for him to nab them and collect the money. As they knelt to pick up the crates, Dimples stopped them.

"You can't take those," Dimples said. "They belong to Betty."

"It's all right," Betty said, coming in from the double-doors. She leaned against the loading dock. "They're with me. They do all the heavy lifting for me, so I called them to bring the van."

They picked up the crates, but Felt stepped in their way. "That's far enough," he said, pulling a gun. "These two are wanted felons with bounties on their heads, and it's time to collect." He moved to slap handcuffs on the wrist of the man nearest him. Before he could blink, the man neatly backhanded Felt across the face without losing his hold on the crates. Felt staggered back, trying to gain his balance, and brought his gun up.

"Stop!" yelled Betty. "Don't shoot anyone!" She jumped in front of the crates. "At least wait until they get the crates loaded. After that, you can take them in." She couldn't let anything stop her now. Once the men had the crates in the van, they could drive away before Felt could stop them.

Dimples had seen enough. If he let them get the crates into the van, he might never see them again. "Hold it right there!" he said, pulling out his gun. "Let's slow down a minute and figure this out. Betty, move away from the crates. I don't want you to get hurt."

With two guns trained on them, the men stopped, and Betty's brows drew together. He couldn't do this to her. She edged away from the crates, but closer to the van, in case she had to make a quick getaway.

"Put the crates down, and lift your hands up," Dimples commanded. "Felt... now would be a good time to use those handcuffs."

Felt holstered his gun, and pulled their arms behind their backs to cuff them. That accomplished, he took his gun back out and made them sit on the floor with their backs against the wall.

"Let's see what's in here, shall we?" Dimples said. He put his gun away, and pulled off the lid. He started throwing underwear every which way until it piled up on the ground.

"Wait. What are you doing?" Betty hurried toward the crate. "You'll get everything dirty."

As he emptied the crate, I decided to block Betty's escape by moving to the double-doors. I knew she was ready to run, but couldn't resist the pull of finding the money. Now at least if she bolted, she'd have to get past me.

Dimples knocked on the wood at the bottom. "Sounds funny," he said. "Could there be a false bottom in here?" He pulled the crate apart, and the flimsy wood gave way, revealing an inner compartment. "Would you look at that?"

Betty ran to his side, and her breath caught. "It's empty! Where..." She glanced at Dimples, realizing she'd nearly given herself away.

"Let's check the other one," he said.

As Dimples pulled the other crate apart, Betty stood back, her face going pale. Finding the same false bottom in it, he motioned her over. "Come take a look."

She hurried over and glanced inside. "Nothing's there," she said. Shrugging her shoulders, she tried to act like she didn't care. "That's strange. I wonder what could have been in them?"

"Do you?" Dean asked, stalking toward her. "I think you know exactly what was supposed to be in there. The money. That's where Keith put it. He was going to ship it to you, but something stopped him. Maybe he found out that you were using him all along, and he needed some leverage in case you tried to take it all for yourself."

"I don't know what you're talking about," Betty said, backing away.

"Oh, I think you do," Dean continued. "You let him take the fall for the death of that hostage, even though it was you who shot her. While he was in prison you looked everywhere for the money, but he'd hidden it too well, and you couldn't find it. When his trial began, he'd had enough. He was ready to tell everyone about you. But you had him killed before he could. You finally tracked down the crates to the police department, but you couldn't get near them until now. But it was all for nothing. You still don't have the money."

"You don't know anything," she said.

"But I do," he answered, his voice low and husky. "I know where the money is."

She saw the truth in his eyes and snapped, going for the gun concealed in her jacket. She pressed it tight against Dean's neck, and jerked his arm behind his back. "Good. Then you'll take me to it," she ordered. She wrenched his arm hard, and he stiffened in pain. Then pulled him toward the double-doors.

Dimples made a move toward her. "Stay back," she yelled. "Or I'll shoot him."

She didn't know I was behind her, and I had my stun flashlight ready. As soon as she started moving toward me, I shoved it under her arm and pushed the button. She jerked a few times before her limbs gave way, and she slid to the ground in a wilted heap. Kind of like she was melting.

Dimples rushed to her side and, with immense satisfaction, cuffed her. Looking me in the eye, he smiled. "Nice work." He was thinking I was the best damn partner he'd ever had. I anticipated her move and was ready. Of course, on second thought, that might have something to do with my premonitions. But still, he was impressed.

Sirens sounded in the distance. "Someone must have called the police," Dimples said.

"That would be Emily." I nodded toward her. She was hugging Dean and wiping her eyes. Dean's involvement had been a shock. She could hardly believe he knew where the money was.

Felt couldn't either. "Where's the money?" he demanded, rushing to Dean's side. The men he'd been guarding forgotten. Seeing their chance, they struggled to their feet.

"Felt!" I yelled. "They're getting away!" He hesitated for a second, but his good sense won out, and he went after them.

"I'd better rescue Dean before Felt corners him again," I told Dimples.

"Good idea," he agreed. "Just make sure he doesn't go anywhere." He was thinking that if Dean knew where the money was, it was time he told them. Too bad he might have to be arrested for obstruction of justice, but he'd do what he could to get him off. In light of revealing Keith's partner, it was a good bet they'd let him go.

"You did it," I said to Dean. "I wasn't sure she was going to crack, but you got to her. You should be a cop or something. That was brilliant."

He pursed his lips. "I did it for Keith. Plus it helped that she was greedy." It was satisfying to see her snap, but it shook him up. And now he had other things to worry about. Like the money. A part of him wanted to return it, but another part didn't. In some ways, he'd like to just leave it where it was until it rotted. Look at what it had done to his son. It just left a bad taste in his mouth, but he supposed he'd better do the right thing.

"Yeah, telling Betty you knew where the money was..." I said. "Even though you were probably bluffing. I mean, if you knew where it was, you would have told the police a long time ago. Otherwise, they'd have to arrest you."

"You think so?" he asked.

"Yes. But I think I know what Keith did with it." I emphasized Keith's name so he'd know I was putting it all on Keith, even though it was Dean who'd hidden the money.

"You do? Where?" he asked. I told him, and he relaxed. "How did you figure it out?"

"I've been investigating this for the bank, and after putting all the facts together, I think that's the only place it could be."

"Well," he said, rubbing his chin. "You have my permission to look."

"Thanks," I said. "I'll call the bank today, and let them know." He nodded, and I added, "Do you mind keeping this between you and me? I don't want to get anyone's hopes up in case it's not there."

"Sure," he agreed. "I was bluffing anyway, so it's not like I know where it is." His conscience satisfied, he was happy to let me handle it.

The police arrived and talked to each of us about what happened. Betty was officially arrested and carted off to jail. Felt had to go to the police station in order to get his bounty on the men, but that didn't stop him from harassing Dean. After telling him a third time that he was bluffing, I told Felt to leave Dean alone.

"Did you ever find out what Betty was doing in her shop?" I asked him, hoping to take his mind off the money.

"Not for sure," he said. "But I think she was producing forged birth certificates and social security numbers, stuff like that."

"Wow," I said. "I never would have figured that out."

"Yeah, the guys that went there were looking for new identities. They were all crooks with records."

"I wonder why she would rob a bank if she was making money doing that?" I asked.

"Who knows," he said. "Maybe some of the people she helped were bank robbers. They could have been part of the crew that pulled off that robbery."

"Knowing how Betty operates, they're probably all dead now."

He chuckled. "That, or she'll give up the names for a lighter sentence. Anyway, if I want those bounties, I'd better go."

I made it home an hour later. Chris was still coaching Josh's soccer game, and Savannah had gone to a friend's house. Now was a good time to call Blaine Smith. I pushed in his cell number and waited with anticipation to tell him the good news.

"Are you sure?" he asked, his tone excited.

"Yes," I said. "And he gave his permission."

"Okay. I'll call them right now and meet you there in half an hour."

I left early, arriving at least ten minutes before Blaine. I found the director and told him who I was. He already had a crew at the site, and I wandered in that direction. I'd always liked it here. It seemed so peaceful.

I arrived at the site just as Blaine drove up. He had two security men with him, carrying guns and bags for the money. He wasn't taking any chances. He greeted me, and we watched the small backhoe dig up the earth surrounding Dottie Weir's grave.

Several minutes later, they pulled her casket to the surface. I'd never seen a body that had been that long in the grave, and I was a little spooked. The director opened it up, and there she was, lying on a bed of cash. Dottie even had a smile on her face, like she enjoyed it.

"I don't know how you figured it out," Blaine said. "But thank you." He was troubled that he'd gypped me out of the finder's fee. "I'll be sure to include a bonus for your hard work."

"Thanks, that would be great," I said. After what I'd been through, I was okay with a bonus. "If you don't need me, I'm going to go home now. You'll let the police know, right?"

"Yes," he agreed. "Once the money's safely in the bank, I'll let them know and call a press conference."

"Good deal." I drove home with a happy heart, knowing I'd solved my first case. Shelby Nichols Consulting Agency was now a bona fide success. Who knew? It was bound to be good for business, and maybe I'd even get my name in the paper.

I got home, excited to find Chris and tell him the whole story.

"How'd it go this morning?" Chris asked.

I told him everything, including that I'd already been to the cemetery with Blaine Smith to dig up Dottie's grave. "She was lying on top of all that money," I said. "So I guess even though my clue from Keith about the money being in a box or something didn't turn out because his father found it and hid it inside his sister's casket, it was still the right clue because "underwear" sounds a lot like "under Weir." Get it?" I laughed at my silly joke and punched Chris in the arm.

He just shook his head. "That is pretty crazy." He was thinking that I should have asked for the finder's fee, instead of getting paid hourly. But now that I had some experience, I'd know better.

"How much do you think I should charge an hour?" I asked. "I guess fifty dollars is kind of low, compared to other private investigators."

"Yes," he agreed. "I'll bet they charge between three hundred and five hundred an hour, and they don't have a super-power like you."

I laughed. "Oh, so it's a super-power now?"

"I think it fits in that category. Better that than calling it a curse, don't you think?"

I had to agree with him, although sometimes it did feel like a curse. Like with Uncle Joey, and how Kate had told my secret to a man like Eddie Sullivan. Every time I thought about it I got the shivers.

The next morning, my picture was on the front page. There I was, standing beside Blaine Smith at the cemetery with the heading, "Bank Recovers Stolen Money in Cemetery." How did that happen? The director, or one of the workers must have taken the picture with their cell phone.

The article included a mug shot of Betty as the alleged robber. It went on to say that they'd interviewed Detective Harris, the arresting officer at the scene, for more details. He mentioned me as the private investigator working on the case, and it was my expertise that led them to Betty. They also spoke to the bank manager, Blaine Smith, who praised my abilities to crack the case and find the stolen money.

I scanned the rest of the paper and found a small article on two unsolved murders that happened at a private club. They were reported as gang related, and asked for anyone with information to please come forward. With no arrests or apparent leads, I hoped they didn't think about asking me for help, since I couldn't exactly tell them the truth.

Not long after the paper came out, my cell phone was flooded with calls. I'd turned my phone off since it was Sunday, and when I turned it on later, I was shocked to find my voice mail full. A few were from reporters wanting an exclusive interview for their magazines or papers. Several others were from people wanting to hire me. Only two were from people I knew. One was from Dimples, and the other from Uncle Joey.

Dimples said he was grateful for my help, not surprised I'd found the money, and that he'd called the FBI about my premonition. He hoped I didn't mind that he told them it was a tip and kept my name out of it. My relief was so profound; I would have kissed him if he'd been here... on the cheek, of course.

Uncle Joey said he'd seen the paper and wasn't happy about my success, worried that my secret wouldn't be safe. I thought it was probably more that he wanted me all to himself. He asked that I call him first thing Monday morning, and if I was busy, to remember he was my first and most important client.

I waited until nine on Monday morning to call him back.

"Shelby! Thanks for calling." He sounded lots more cheerful than I thought he would, so I relaxed a bit.

"Sure," I answered. "How's it going?"

"Good," he said. "Congratulations on solving the bank case. You had a busy weekend."

"That's for sure. Good thing I'm leaving on vacation next week."

"You are?" He sounded disappointed.

"Yes," I said enthusiastically. "We're taking the kids to Orlando to see Disneyworld and Universal Studios. It should be a lot of fun, and I'm really looking forward to it."

"Well, you certainly deserve a break."

"So, how did things go with Kate?" I asked. "Did you figure out what to do with her?"

"Yes. That was one of the reasons I called. I wanted to let you know that I've sent her back to Seattle. Now that Eddie's gone, things have changed, and I arranged for her to get her business back. She'll get a new start and her foot in the door to manage things up there."

"Wow. That was nice of you, and probably more than she deserved."

"I think everyone would agree with you on that," he said. "But I know Kate needs a challenge, and this will keep her busy and occupied."

"What about my secret? Will she keep her mouth shut?" I asked.

"I have a guarantee that she will... under penalty of death," he added. "So your secret is safe for the time being."

"Whew, that's good. I don't need any more crazed, insane people after me."

He chuckled. "No, you have plenty of those already."

Was he making a joke about himself, or just being sarcastic? "Ha, ha," I said. "Well, if you don't need anything else, I'll talk to you later."

"Actually there is something else," he said. "Since you're going to Orlando, you can do me a favor while you're there."

"What's that?" I asked, cautiously.

"Don't worry. It's simple. Just deliver a letter for me."

"Why can't you just mail it?"

"It needs your special touch," he said. "So I'll know how he takes it. It means you'll have to stay while he reads it, but I'll tell him to give you his answer before you leave. All right?"

If there was any way I could turn him down, I would, but I knew that was not going to happen. "Sure." I sighed.

"Excellent," he said. "Stop by the office after Wednesday, and I'll have it ready for you."

We disconnected, and I was a little angry that I couldn't even go on vacation without Uncle Joey involved. But maybe delivering a letter wasn't so bad. It was better than getting shot at, or kidnapped, and easier than looking for lost treasure.

Just thinking about that made me wish I could tell my Grandpa all about it. I'm sure he'd be proud, and telling everyone he knew that I was his granddaughter. He'd tell me he was proud that I'd used my 'super-power' to help people. Maybe he was looking down on me from heaven right now, with a big smile on his face.

I realized I had a lot going for me. I had solved my first major case. I had plenty of business for my agency. And I was still alive. Best of all, I was going on vacation with my family. Being with them for fifteen straight days would be fun. I'd just have to work on my shields. Then maybe I could handle it.

I only knew one thing for sure. No matter what happened, it was bound to be an adventure.

Thank you for reading **Lie or Die: A Shelby Nichols Adventure**. Ready for the next book in the series? **Secrets that Kill: A Shelby Nichols Adventure** is now available in print, ebook and on audible. Get your copy today!

If you enjoyed this book, please consider leaving a review on Amazon. It's a great way to thank an author and keep her writing!

NEWSLETTER SIGNUP For news, updates, and special offers, please sign up for my newsletter on my website at www.colleenhelme.com. To thank you for subscribing you will receive a FREE ebook.

ABOUT THE AUTHOR

USA TODAY AND WALL STREET JOURNAL BESTSELLING AUTHOR

As the author of the Shelby Nichols Adventure Series, Colleen is often asked if Shelby Nichols is her alter-ego. "Definitely," she says. "Shelby is the epitome of everything I wish I dared to be." Known for her laugh since she was a kid, Colleen has always tried to find the humor in every situation and continues to enjoy writing about Shelby's adventures. "I love getting Shelby into trouble...I just don't always know how to get her out of it!" Besides writing, she loves a good book, biking, hiking, and playing board and card games with family and friends. She loves to connect with readers and admits that fans of the series keep her writing.

Connect with Colleen at www.colleenhelme.com

Made in the USA
Monee, IL
15 November 2020